THE JOHN HARVARD LIBRARY

Bernard Bailyn
Editor-in-Chief

THE JOHN HARVARD LIBRARY

Ten Nights in a Bar-Room, And What I Saw There

By

TIMOTHY SHAY ARTHUR

Edited by Donald A. Koch

THE BELKNAP PRESS OF
HARVARD UNIVERSITY PRESS

Cambridge, Massachusetts

1 9 6 4

Originally published in 1854

813.54

Ar 7t

Distributed in Great Britain
by Oxford University Press, London

67712
October, 1969

INTRODUCTION

1: *The Life and Work of T. S. Arthur*

In his delightful study entitled *Queer Books*, Edmund Pearson devotes a full chapter to the peculiar nineteenth-century literary genre known as "temperance novels." With tongue in cheek Pearson comments on the moral nature and "extraordinary innocence" of these novels and then tells of his first encounter—through a play version—with the classic example, Timothy Shay Arthur's *Ten Nights in a Bar-Room, And What I Saw There* (1854):

The dreadful power of strong drink was never so thoroughly impressed upon me as when I sat, one afternoon, probably in the early '90's, and waited for the successive risings of the curtain, with its picture of the Bay of Naples, which separated us from the stage, in the Newburyport City Hall. As the grog shop was revealed in all its horrors we felt that dramatic realism was in our midst. When the drink-crazed father hurled the rum bottle into the *left wing*, the little daughter obediently trotted on from the *right*, exclaiming:

"Oh, Papa, you have killed me!"

Then she fell dead in the centre of the stage, and we suspected, as I have often suspected since, that the Demon Rum does not always get fair treatment from his foes. We felt sure that not even a drunkard could pitch such a curve as that.[1]

This anecdote doubtless has its familiar counterparts in the memories of many of those born early enough in this century to witness some of the last performances of *Ten Nights in a Bar-Room* by the old traveling repertory companies. My own first acquaintance with Arthur's grim saga of the "Sickle and Sheaf" was through a play version and differs from the experience of Pearson only in a few slight details. The time was the early 1920's, the place a little mining town in central Pennsylvania, and the setting the Lodge Hall of the local chapter of the Loyal Order of Moose, with *its* canvas curtain depicting the Apotheosis of Homer rather than the Bay of Naples. But the effect of the play was identical: the awful power of strong drink! the lurid realism!—and the uneasy feeling that perhaps the moral lesson was a bit overdone.

For over a century American audiences in countless cities and hamlets have alternately grieved and rejoiced over the demise of little Mary Morgan and the redemption of her errant father. The novel in its play form has run the gamut from stark tragedy to burlesque comedy, but the old temperance message is still intact and the spirit of humanitarian concern that Arthur first captured in his book has hallowed it. The literary faults of the novel have long ceased to be

[1] *Queer Books* (Garden City, N.Y., 1928), pp. 5–6.

a measure of its importance—if, indeed, they ever were—and the general public no longer distinguishes the novel from William Pratt's dramatized version of it. The story as originally told by Arthur has passed over into our national mythology. *Ten Nights in a Bar-Room* is as firmly lodged in American folklore as Weems's *Life of Washington* and Mrs. Stowe's *Uncle Tom's Cabin.*

Posterity has not kept faith with Timothy Shay Arthur as it has with his novel. While *Ten Nights in a Bar-Room* gradually gathered its patina of legend, the author faded into an obscure corner of American cultural history. He is remembered, mainly on the strength of this one book, as a temperance tractarian, one of the early "prophets of prohibition" who preached total abstinence and urged the suppression of liquor by law during the colorful nineteenth-century Temperance Crusade. This single image of Arthur as a cold-water zealot does not do him justice. In an ebullient time of causes he spoke out against smoking, gambling, business speculation, materialism, mesmerism, and credit buying. He defended dancing, card-playing, women suffrage, and socialism. He was the first after Gilbert Imlay to discuss divorce and marital maladjustment openly in his fiction, and he pioneered in the use of "business" [2] as a theme, an-

---

[2] See Warren G. French, "Timothy Shay Arthur: Pioneer Business Novelist," *American Quarterly,* vol. 10, no. 1 (Spring 1958), pp. 55–65.

ticipating the economic novel of the later nineteenth century. The only major social concern of his day that seems to have escaped his pen was slavery, perhaps because as a writer who lived for a time in a southern city he felt obliged to avoid it.

Arthur was recognized by his contemporaries as a temperance reformer, but they also knew him as a capable editor, a successful publisher, and a prolific author. During his busy lifetime he published over two hundred novels and collections of tales.[3] Six percent of all the native fiction published in the United States during the 1840's came from his pen, and by 1860 his books were said to have sold over a million copies.[4] Next to Samuel Goodrich ("Peter Parley") and Joseph Holt Ingraham, author of *Lafitte, Pirate of the Gulf*, and scores of other ten-penny dreadfuls,

[3] There is no complete bibliography of Arthur's published works. The *Library of Congress Catalog of Printed Cards* lists only 84 titles. Lyle Wright's *American Fiction* records 206 works and editions up to 1875, but Arthur continued to publish until his death in 1885. The task of assembling a comprehensive list is complicated by the fact that Arthur sometimes published anonymously, as well as under such pseudonyms as "Uncle Herbert," "Aunt Mary," and "Mrs. Mary Elmwood." His practice of frequently reissuing a collection of previously published pieces under the title of a newly added tale makes it difficult to distinguish a new work from an edition, especially since many of his volumes are lost, existing only as items in catalogs. The British Museum's *Catalogue of Printed Books 1881–1905* and the *General Catalogue of Printed Books 1931–1954* lists titles not found in American bibliographies. These are probably titles of pirated English editions of Arthur's books.

[4] James D. Hart, *The Popular Book, A History of America's Literary Taste* (New York, 1950), p. 109.

Arthur was perhaps the most voluminous and widely read of all the ante-bellum "popular" writers. It was not uncommon for first editions of Arthur's books to run to 25,000 copies, and press notices from widely scattered places in the United States prior to 1850 seem to indicate that his reputation was well established even before he wrote *Ten Nights in a Bar-Room*.

In the late forties a reviewer for *Graham's Magazine* in Philadelphia enthusiastically reported that "in the princely mansions of the Atlantic merchants, and in the rude log-cabins of the backwoodsmen, the name of Arthur is equally known and cherished as the friend of virtue." About the same time, the Circleville, Ohio, *Watchman* declared, "T. S. Arthur is one of the best literary writers of the age." In 1850 the Gallatin, Mississippi, *Argus,* after praising Arthur's *Sketches of Life and Character* (1850), added, "the name of the author is sufficient guaranty to the reading public of its surpassing merit." And the New York *Sun* commenting on the same volume said "Arthur's tales . . . bear strong attraction for the generality of readers . . . he is eminently successful." After *Ten Nights in a Bar-Room* was published in 1854, the New Haven *Palladium* pulled out all stops:

It is sufficient recommendation of this little volume to say that it is from the graphic pen of T. S. Arthur, whose work will be read and reread long after he has passed

away. He is as true to nature, as far as he attempts to
explore it, as Shakespeare himself, and all his works, consequently, have an immense popularity. The best of all
is that his writings tend to make men better as well as
wiser.[5]

The *Palladium's* prophecy that Arthur's work would
endure failed except for a single book, but its warm
praise for the author accurately reflects the attitude
of his contemporary following.

Arthur's audience was the generation of American
readers reared on Godey's *Lady's Book* and the
McGuffey Readers--the pious, optimistic, unsophis-
ticated men and women who confidently expected
to achieve perfection for themselves and their in-
stitutions within their own lifetime. They were the
semiliterate, semieducated shopkeepers, artisans,
housewives, chambermaids--the middle and lower-
middle masses of Americans who were emerging as
a dominant part of our national culture. They were
accomplished in their politics but uncertain in their
intellectual and artistic goals. Such an audience demanded little in the way of quality and form in its
literature. It appreciated brevity, sensation, variety,
and the familiar; whatever reflected its own mores,
customs, and idiom, it took fondly to its bosom. It

[5] From a catalog of press notices appended to T. S. Arthur,
Golden Grains from Life's Harvest Field (Philadelphia, 1850),
pp. 1–3.

was indiscriminate and often neglectful in its choice of writers, responding enthusiastically to a Byron, a Scott, or a Dickens, but indifferently to a Poe, a Hawthorne, or a Melville. Without apology or self-consciousness, it proclaimed its Fanny Ferns, its Mrs. Southworths, and its T. S. Arthurs. Perhaps most characteristic of all was its devotion to that class of writers known as "magazinists."

In 1831 the brilliant young French analyst, Alexis de Tocqueville, while traveling in this country observed that in America, "the only authors . . . are the journalists . . . They speak the language of their countrymen and make themselves heard by them." [6] His observation was indeed an accurate appraisal of the literary scene in the adolescent age of American letters. Our writers, great and small alike, first sought fame and fortune through the pages of periodicals. Our best frequently failed where our poorest prospered. Those who truly spoke "the language of their countrymen" were heard, and Timothy Shay Arthur was among the foremost. Arthur began his career in 1833 when the opportunity came to edit a small magazine, and until the end of his life he never thought of himself as anything other than a journalist. "I continued to write as I had begun," he explained in a brief sketch of himself published in the late

[6] Alexis de Tocqueville, *Democracy in America*, trans. Henry Reeve, ed. Henry Steele Commager (London, 1952), p. 329.

fifties, "prompted by an impulse that I felt little inclination to resist . . . The necessity to write as a
means of livelihood, and to write a great deal, has
brought me so frequently before the public, that I
have almost ceased to think about the matter as anything more than an ordinary occurrence." [7] Most of
Arthur's work first appeared in the magazines; *Ten
Nights in a Bar-Room* is one of the few exceptions.
His great temperance novel was published at precisely the right moment in history and it treated the
right theme in exactly the right way to set it apart
from all his other work. Posterity views it as a kind
of phenomenon without really inquiring very far into
the life of the author. But Arthur's other work holds
an abundance of fresh evidence that tells us much
about the temperament and climate of his age; his
personal history deserves a longer look than it has
hitherto been given.

2

Arthur was born on June 6, 1809, near Newburgh[8]
in Orange County, New York. He was the second of
four sons of William and Anna Shay Arthur. There

[7] From a "Brief Autobiography" printed with T. S. Arthur,
Lights and Shadows of Real Life (Philadelphia, 1859), p. 8.

[8] A "Portrait" in the November 1844 issue of Godey's *Lady's
Book* gives Arthur's birthplace as "near New Windsor" in Orange
County. Newburgh and New Windsor are adjacent communities;
Arthur preferred to name Newburgh. In addition to the Godey's
"Portrait," the main biographical sources are Arthur's "Brief Auto-

was probably a fifth child, a daughter named for the mother, but the earliest records are vague and notably devoid of specific details. His parents were devoutly religious people whose English-Irish antecedents settled on the terraces above the Hudson about the time Josua Kocherthal led his band of fifty-three followers from the Rhenish Palatinate to the heights along the river. Arthur's forebears were undistinguished, except for his maternal grandfather, Timothy Shay, who served as an officer in the Revolutionary Army under General Washington, and who after the war declined "high public office" proffered by the admiring townspeople of his native North Salem. Both Arthur's mother and his grandfather were described as "shy and retiring." The grandson seems to have inherited the family modesty as well as his grandfather's name. He was unusually reserved both as a child and as an adult. Beyond a few brief statements, he could never be persuaded to disclose the details of his life.

Arthur spent his childhood in the vicinity of old Fort Montgomery on the Hudson, where his earliest memories recalled the beautiful scenery, the quiet but happy companionship with his brothers, and some less happy hours of recurrent illness from an

biography," an anonymous pamphlet titled *T. S. Arthur, His Life and Works by One Who Knows Him* (Philadelphia, 1873) in the holdings of the New York Public Library, and a sketch by Allen Nevins in the *Dictionary of American Biography*.

unnamed ailment that plagued him from birth. The disease affected his vision so that he was unable to attend school until his ninth year. He remembered the patient care of his mother and the "Bible stories" with which she used to amuse and instruct him. His father, too, was remembered as a man who sought "to inspire his children with a regard for religious truth, and both by precept and example, to lead them into the practice of such things as were honest and of good report." [9] Doubtless this strongly religious home training influenced the pious character that later distinguished Arthur's writings. Certainly it inclined him toward the Swedenborgian faith that he adopted as a young man, and whose "good works" principle he used as the core of all his fiction. The editor of Godey's *Lady's Book* declared in 1844, "Mr. Arthur . . . owes little or nothing to the school—everything to the fireside discipline . . . the earnest training of pious parents gave his mind an impress of firmness, conscientiousness and perseverance in the path of duty, which has rendered him a benefactor to his race." [10]

In 1817 William Arthur moved his family to Baltimore, Maryland, as much in search of a healthier climate for his sickly son as of better employment

[9] "Brief Autobiography," p. 5.
[10] "Godey's Portrait Gallery. No. I: T. S. Arthur," Godey's *Lady's Book*, November 1844, p. 193.

opportunities for himself. Apparently the change proved fruitful on both counts. In the fall of that year young Timothy was enrolled in a small private school along with two of his brothers. He was now well into his ninth year and the late start in formal schooling gave rise to unpleasant experiences that he recalled bitterly years later. They began in the first days when his teacher gave him a slate and soapstone, and without further explanation, told him to find the sum of an addition problem. The word "addition" held no meaning whatever for the uninstructed youngster, but keenly aware that he was expected to "add" the figures on the slate before him, he tried to fathom the meaning but could only stare at the slate and do nothing. When the teacher stopped beside Arthur's bench later to examine his progress, he found only the empty slate. He interpreted Arthur's ignorance as an act of stubbornness, and with the brutality characteristic of early schoolmasters, hauled the frightened boy out of his seat and caned him before the eyes of his classmates. In the weeks that followed, the scene was repeated many times until at last Arthur was "utterly discouraged." It was several months before he understood the principle of addition, and then he moved on to the mysteries of subtraction, multiplication, and division with scarcely better success. In time he mastered "half the common rules" of arithmetic, learned to write, and studied

English grammar but without reward: "grammar was to my mind completely unintelligible." [11] For four years more Arthur continued in this manner, gaining little more than the reputation of "dullard."

At the end of the fifth year Arthur's teacher despaired of any further attempt to educate the boy and recommended to the father that his son be apprenticed to a tradesman. The elder Arthur agreed, and at thirteen, Timothy found himself in what was probably the shop of a tailor. Reminiscing nearly thirty years afterward, he ruefully commented on this period of formal education:

With such a mind, and such a teacher, it is no wonder that I made but little progress during the few years that I went to school. I needed a careful, judicious, and patient teacher, who understood the character of my mind, and was able to come down to it with instruction in the simplest and clearest forms; thus helping me to think for myself and to see for myself. Instead of this, I was scolded and whipped because I could not understand things that were never explained.[12]

Arthur graciously withheld the name of his teacher, but the association with him remained painfully vivid.

The precise nature of Arthur's trade is unknown. Both watchmaking and tailoring have been conjectured, but there seems to be more evidence to support

[11] "Brief Autobiography," p. 6.
[12] "Brief Autobiography, p. 6.

tailoring. Among Arthur's writings there are several works which deal with tailoring and which were obviously written with a knowledge of the craft. These include *The Seamstress; A Tale of the Times* (1843), *The Tailor's Apprentice: A Story of Cruelty and Oppression* (1843), *Trials of a Needle-Woman* (1853), and *Lizzie Glenn: or; The Trials of a Seamstress* (1859). Whatever the trade, the closeness of the work further aggravated Arthur's eye ailment, so that by the time he finished his apprenticeship he was unable to engage in it.

Two years after he entered the tradesman's shop Arthur began a program of self-education. Despite his difficulties in the private school he regretted the lost opportunity for an education. But at fifteen he was hardly his own best teacher and his program suffered for lack of direction. "There was no one to select books for me, nor to direct my mind in its search for knowledge," he explained in his autobiography, nevertheless "day after day I worked and thought, and night after night I read and studied . . . and thus time went on until I had attained the age of manhood." [13] One sees in Arthur during this period the embodiment of Hogarth's "Industrious Apprentice." For a brief time he attended a "mechanic's school" trying to master a little higher mathematics, but the venture proved to be as much a failure as his

[13] "Brief Autobiography," p. 6.

regular schooling. Finally at twenty-one, educated to
no particular profession and deprived of his trade by
threat of blindness, he decided to enter business. For
three years he worked as a clerk in a Baltimore
countinghouse; then in 1833, lured by higher salary,
he accepted employment with the Susquehanna
Bridge and Banking Company as one of its branch
agents. The Susquehanna Company was an invest-
ment concern like scores of similar companies that
mushroomed on speculation in the thirties. It originated in Baltimore but had holdings in several other
cities. In the summer of 1833 Arthur went to Louis-
ville, Kentucky, as its western representative. He
worked only a few weeks when he received word that
the company had failed. Disillusioned after two un-
rewarding attempts at business, Arthur returned to
Baltimore in the late fall determined to try his hand
at writing, an occupation that had appealed to his
fancy while he was still an apprentice.

3

The change from business to writing was not as
startling nor as hazardous as it might seem. Author-
ship was undertaken quite cavalierly by many young
men at this time and with perfect confidence. As de
Tocqueville had noted, the authors were journalists.
There was an enormous market for periodical literature and the public was easy to please. American

readers had few aristocratic tastes; they liked simple literary fare and a quick turnover in their reading matter; and they especially enjoyed the diversity of magazine reading because it gave them the feeling of being informed and "kept up to date." In general, magazines were compartmentalized; there was a place for nearly anything a writer might produce— poetry, essays, fiction, editorials.

There was also a sociological circumstance of still greater import that made magazines a ready vehicle for any young hopeful. In the absence of well-developed public school facilities in the thirties, magazines were an important source of instruction for the masses. As late as the fifties, Dr. Philip Schaff, a visiting German theologian who shrewdly observed American society while he held a professorate at Mercersburg Academy, could look back at this era and declare, "the American received his education . . . from the enormous mass of periodical and other literature that circulates through the land . . . Such reading tends, unquestionably, to diffuse a kind of culture among all classes of people; but it equally tends to superficiality . . . and dissipates the mind almost as much as novel reading, in the place of which, to a great extent, it there comes." [14] The condition

[14] Philip Schaff, *America. A Sketch of Its Political, Social, and Religious Character,* ed. Perry Miller (Cambridge, Mass., 1961), pp. 64–65.

noted by Schaff explains at least in part why any fresh talent, any peddler of new ideas, or any career-hunting beginner could readily find his way into print, and why the American public was so keenly attracted to magazines.

Like his humble countrymen, Arthur was also attracted to the magazines. While still employed by the countinghouse, he began to entertain the idea of contributing to the literary papers in Baltimore. An anonymous friend told how Arthur would snatch moments from his duties to practice writing poetry:

He used to sit at his work all day long revolving a couplet or a stanza in his mind; and when he got it to suit him, he would watch for an opportunity when no one was observing him, and with an old stump of a pencil which he kept in his pocket, (would) scratch off the lines on a scrap of paper and slip it out of sight.[15]

The effort never resulted in the publication of more than a handful of poems,[16] though it led to the career marking him one of the most prolific prose writers in the nineteenth century.

After returning jobless to Baltimore in 1833 Arthur accepted the invitation of a young journalist named John McJilton to coedit a weekly literary magazine

[15] T. S. Arthur, His Life and Work by One Who Knows Him (Philadelphia, 1873), p. 10.

[16] For examples of Arthur's poetry see the 1844–1846 issues of Arthur's Magazine (successor to Miss Leslie's Magazine).

which they called the *Baltimore Athenaeum and Young Men's Paper*. McJilton had already earned a local reputation for a series of interesting sketches which he signed "Giles McQuiggen." With one of the editors thus known to the public the magazine got off to a good start. For the next three years they issued their magazine every Saturday from their editorial offices at the corner of Baltimore and Sharp streets. It rarely ran to more than eight pages, but it contained just the right mixture of fiction, poetry, humorous sketches, and articles on hunting, angling, the military, and fashions to please the casual reader. Early in 1836 McJilton withdrew from the partnership to follow other pursuits and Arthur assumed full editorial charge. In the January 23rd issue of the magazine there appeared the following excerpt from a letter by McJilton:

Engagements have increased upon me, and I am now compelled to withdraw myself from your assistance, and, in so doing, permit me to say, that, to yourself is due much the greater share of credit for the high esteem in which the "Baltimore Athenaeum and Young Men's Paper" is held; the only gratifying feeling I have, in giving up my portion of the control of its columns, is, that I leave it in your hands.[17]

Arthur continued to publish the magazine by himself

[17] *Baltimore Athenaeum and Young Men's Paper*, 2 (January 23, 1836), 81.

for the next nine months, without any decline in the contents. After three years of experience, he had mastered the facile style and timely article that readers expected in their periodicals. At the end of September Arthur stopped publication of the *Athenaeum*. Its three-year life was a testimonial of success for both the *Athenaeum* and its editor. For most magazines in the 1830's, survival beyond the first year was the exception rather than the rule. Of seventy-two new periodicals announced for publication in Baltimore between 1815 and 1835, forty-seven disappeared before or by the end of the first year.[18]

A week after Arthur stopped issuing the *Athenaeum,* the reason became apparent. On October 8, 1836, a new weekly called the *Baltimore Literary Monument* was offered for sale in the "city of monuments," and its editors were identified as John McJilton and T. S. Arthur. When McJilton left the *Athenaeum,* it was for the purpose of starting a more sophisticated literary paper with a Baltimore friend David Creamer. The venture fell through and McJilton asked Arthur to join him in launching the *Monument.* Arthur did, but apparently on his own terms, for he was listed in the first issue as both co-editor and publisher. The *Monument* thrived during the next three years, acquiring by 1839 a reputation

[18] John C. French, "Poe's Literary Baltimore," *Maryland Historical Magazine,* vol. 32, no. 2 (June 1937), p. 104.

as, "next to the *Emerald,* the best literary periodical of the 'Monumental City' . . ." [19] The *Baltimore Minerva and Emerald* and *Niles' Weekly Register* were the two leading periodicals, but the *Register* was more a general than a literary magazine. The *Monument* drew better known contributors than the *Athenaeum*—Park Benjamin, Maria Sedgwick, Mrs. Anna Dorsey, Mrs. Lydia Jane Pierson, and J. H. Hewitt, the Baltimore poet who nearly bested Edgar Allan Poe in the prize article contest conducted by the *Baltimore Saturday Visiter.* In addition to selections by "popular" writers, Arthur included some of William Gilmore Simms's historical romances, pirated extracts from Byron and Wordsworth, and he serialized Lockhart's *Life of Scott.* All in all the *Monument* was a solid success and established Arthur as one of the rising young editor-publishers.

Baltimore was a flourishing literary center in the thirties. In considerable numbers men of artistic talent and genius gravitated to the Chesapeake city in the years of economic prosperity following the War of 1812. Among the better known literati who lived there were writers like John P. Kennedy, author of *Swallow Barn* and *Horseshoe Robinson,* and William Wirt, creator of the *Letters of a British Spy.* When Arthur commenced to edit and write in 1833, there

[19] Frank Luther Mott, *A History of American Magazines, 1741–1850* (New York, 1930), p. 381.

were two distinct literary groups in Baltimore. The first of these were the older writers of substantial reputation, men such as Kennedy, Wirt, and the lawyer-novelist John Neal. They formed the "Tusculum Club" named for the home of William Gwynn where they regularly met.[20] They were the idols and models of the second group made up of young writers just beginning to gain recognition in Baltimore. Among these, besides Arthur and McJilton, were the two promising editors with literary ambitions Nathan Brooks and Rufus Dawes, an erstwhile scholar William Carpenter, the poet Hewitt, the brilliant historian and cofounder of the Maryland Historical Society Brantz Mayer, and a starveling, debt-ridden poet recently arrived in Baltimore named Edgar Allan Poe. There were, of course, many other young writers drawn to the city by the journalistic *Zeitgeist* and the possibilities of earning a place in the world of newspaper, magazine, and book publishing, but these were the most prominent.

The younger group were more typically journalists than litterateurs. For mutual benefit and companionship they gathered into little coteries, usually associated with one or another of the local periodicals. There were at least six such groups in the city in the thirties: the *Amethyst* group, the *Rainbow* group, the

[20] Hervey Allen, *Israfel. The Life and Times of Edgar Allan Poe* (New York, 1934), p. 285.

Red Book group, the *Emerald* group, the *Baltimore Saturday Visiter* group, and one that took its name from the tavern where they met, the Seven Stars group. Arthur moved in the *Amethyst* and *Visiter* circles by virtue of contributing to the former and later owning the latter. But his most interesting association was with the Seven Stars.

How Arthur came to mingle with the "galaxy of wits that sparkled at the Seven Stars (tavern)" [21] is not clear. Perhaps McJilton who knew one of the group intimately introduced Arthur to his friend and the others. The tavern's name was an easy cognomen for the coterie, since, after Arthur and McJilton joined them, they numbered seven. In addition to Arthur and McJilton the others were Edgar Allan Poe, Brantz Mayer, a poet who styled himself "the bard of Milford" John Lofland, Edgar's cousin William Poe, and a seventh companion identified only as a relative of William Poe. [22] Between 1833 and 1835 the group met more or less regularly in the back room of the ramshackle tavern on Water Street near Marsh Market Space in the warehouse district of Baltimore. The Seven Stars Tavern had the distinction of being the first meeting place in America of the Odd Fellows Lodge. Perverse fortune could not have gathered a

[21] Mary Phillips, *Edgar Allan Poe: The Man* (Chicago, 1926), I, 459.
[22] *Edgar Allan Poe,* p. 460.

more incongruous set of "odd fellows" than these seven who assembled periodically in the same decrepit structure for their evenings of literary discussion.

Arthur and McJilton were quiet young men of virtuous habits and commonplace talents, both engaged in writing as a business. Poe was an anguished genius seeking escape from a plebian "world of sweets and sours" and content only to "dwell where Israfel hath dwelt." Brantz Mayer was the cold, unimpassioned scholar, prizing solid historical fact above all else in literature. And John Lofland the bard of Milford was a magnificent fraud whose vestigial verses arose from the bottle and the opium pipe. As for William Poe and his "relative," they seem to have completed the complement as spectators *ad captandum* on certain memorable occasions like the following:

One evening when a table in the back room of The Seven Stars was thus well surrounded and liquid inspiration set the tongue of every man extolling his own talents, Poe said he could write more verses in a given time than any man present. The Bard (Lofland) said he would try his skill with Poe if he could let the wager be the cost of an evening for the whole party at The Stars. The offer was accepted, and the trial fixed for the next afternoon. The Bard won in quantity if not in quality, writing several more verses than Poe. The wager was paid, the party greeting the dawn the following day with diluted songs and recitations.[23]

It was a queer company, drawn together out of the common struggle to earn a livelihood in the capricious world of letters, rather than out of genuine friendship. It is highly unlikely that Arthur and McJilton ever engaged in the excesses of such evenings—still, they did share the amenities of companionship with the other "stars."

The association between Arthur and Poe during the latter's brief interval in Baltimore led to two occasions a few years later when Arthur proved to be of service to Poe. In 1838 Arthur and another Baltimorean, William Carpenter, undertook the publication of an anthology of works by local writers. Although Poe had left the city by this time, Arthur deliberately made room in *The Baltimore Book* for Poe's tale "Siope—A Fable." The small fee Arthur could pay the needy poet was doubtless welcome, but there is no record that Poe ever acknowledged the kindness. *The Baltimore Book* is noteworthy today mainly because Poe's story was first published in it, but in 1838 the writings of Poe were far less attractive to readers of the annual than those of T. C. Atkinson, Nathan Brooks, Mrs. Anna Dorsey, J. H. Hewitt, and others who were included in it. Arthur printed three selections of his

[23] *Edgar Allan Poe*, p. 461.

own—"Confessions of a Platonic Lover," "The Spirit of Poesy," and "The Only Daughter"; and one by McJilton, so the "seven stars" were well represented. A few years later in 1846 Arthur again came to Poe's assistance when he published "The Sphynx" in his newly established *Arthur's Magazine*. He paid Poe handsomely for the tale, but the generous act seems to have called forth more resentment than gratitude from Poe. Shortly after the story appeared, Poe wrote to Philip P. Cooke, a Baltimore acquaintance: "'Arthur's Magazine' gave me, not long ago, $10 a page for a paper 'The Sphynx'—but the pay is no pay for the degradation." [24]

The letter to Cooke was not the first indication of how Poe regarded his old "friend" of the Seven Stars days. In 1841, replying to a letter from his benefactor Dr. Joseph Snodgrass, Poe acidly commented:

You say some of your monumental (Baltimore) writers 'feel small'—but is not that, for them, a natural feeling? I never had much opinion of Arthur. What little merit he has is negative. McJilton I like much better. He has written one or two *very* good things. As a man, also, I like him better.[25]

It seems abundantly clear that the idle hours spent in the back room of the Baltimore tavern meant noth-

[24] *The Letters of Edgar Allan Poe*, ed. J. W. Ostrom (Cambridge, Mass., 1948), II, 314.
[25] *The Letters of Edgar Allan Poe*, I, 175.

ing more to Poe than an opportunity to use Arthur when the occasions presented themselves. If Arthur felt Poe's disdain, it did not deter him from offering Poe financial aid when the poet sorely needed it. Poe made one final pronouncement about Arthur some years later when he wrote in his "A Chapter on Autography":

Mr. Arthur is not without rich talent for description of scenes in low life, but is uneducated, and too fond of mere vulgarities to please a refined taste. He has published 'The Subordinate' and 'Insubordination,' two tales distinguished by the peculiarities above mentioned. He has also written much for our weekly papers, and the 'Lady's Book.' His hand is a commonplace clerk's hand, such as we might expect him to write. The signature is much better than the general manuscript.[26]

The obvious contempt Poe held for Arthur was not entirely that which genius holds for mediocrity. The sting of envy may also have been present in Poe's comments. When the separate lives and fortunes of the two men are compared, a number of small ironies emerge.

The two writers were born in the same year, 1809 —Poe in staid Boston; Arthur in Newburgh, a place associated more with a lobster dish that features

---

[26] Edgar Allan Poe, *Eureka and Miscellanies,* in *The Works of Edgar Allan Poe,* eds. E. C. Stedman and G. E. Woodberry (Chicago, 1896), IX, 239–240.

Madeira than with the champion of teetotalism. While both men were alive, Arthur's reputation as a writer eclipsed that of Poe both in Baltimore and in Philadelphia where at one time they both lived. Poe's lifelong ambition was to own and publish his own magazine—one he never realized; Arthur realized the same ambition not once but several times. It was Poe who anxiously awaited word whether or not his "M.S. Found in a Bottle" had won the fifty-dollar prize offered in a contest by the *Baltimore Saturday Visiter*, and Arthur who later had the satisfaction of owning the same periodical. It was Arthur's mundane fiction that was welcomed in the coveted pages of Godey's *Lady's Book*, while Poe's prose was grudgingly admitted, usually in the back pages. And finally it was liquor, in a sense, that gave Arthur his greatest fame, and Poe his greatest notoriety. The judgment of a contemporary who knew both men summarizes rather well the assessment of their generation:

There was no sympathy between the two men, in thought, work, or life. Poe's ambition was that his literary work should be of the highest artistic finish and beauty, but he had no ambition as to his own life. Mr. Arthur, in his pen work, had no ambition to dazzle before a select few, but, with an abiding desire to aid in making happier and better the many, he wrote for the masses, less artistically than Poe, but not less purely, and never in a slovenly way. In the higher work . . . the fine development of personal character and its exemplification in daily life, Arthur was the artist and Poe a sloven and debauchee.[27]

When Poe died in 1849 his work was all but forgotten, while Arthur's work continued to gather wider and wider acclaim. But the tastes, like the values, of one age seldom survive into the next. A century after they flourished, their reputations are exactly reversed.

The same year that Arthur began the *Monument* with McJilton, he married Eliza Alden, daughter of a prominent New England family who had settled in Baltimore. From 1836 until 1841 Arthur expanded his editorial work, acquiring the *Baltimore Saturday Visiter* from the owner Charles F. Cloud in 1837 and conducting two periodicals until he suspended the *Monument* in October 1839. The *Visiter* was moribund when Arthur obtained it. A scandal arising from a lawsuit that occurred when Cloud fired his editor in order to make a place for his brother-in-law William Ponder caused the circulation to dwindle. Arthur bought the periodical hoping to halt its decline, but he failed and after an interval sold it to Poe's friend Dr. J. E. Snodgrass. During this period two sons were born to Timothy and Eliza, and in 1840 Eliza was expecting their third child. The increased responsibilities of a growing family prompted Arthur to try to

[27] D. L. Milliken, "Methods of T. S. Arthur," *The Writer* (1887), I, 142.

publish some of his writings in periodicals other than his own.

While struggling to revive the *Visiter,* Arthur sent a story titled "The Soft Answer" to Godey's *Lady's Book* in Philadelphia. For several months he heard nothing concerning the story, then one day he received a check for fifteen dollars and a note from Louis Godey apologizing for the long delay. The note explained that Arthur's manuscript had become "lost" in a pile of old manuscripts, and by chance, was discovered by Mrs. Lydia Sigourney, one of Godey's editors. She was enthusiastic about the story and informed Godey that this was exactly the type of wholesome tale she wished to print in the *Lady's Book.* Godey read the story and agreed, whereupon the check and the note were dispatched. The note contained one further important item; it asked for more tales of the same nature from Arthur. He responded immediately and during the next ten years the *Lady's Book* printed over sixty of his tales and sketches. The appearance of his work in this popular women's magazine opened the door to other well-known magazines and helped give him a national reputation by the mid-forties.

By January 1840 Arthur had disposed of both the *Visiter* and the *Monument* and had accepted employment from the publisher-politician General Duff Green as editor of the *Baltimore Merchant.* The fol-

lowing April he covered the activities of the newly
formed Washington Temperance Society, attracting
considerable attention by his articles and earning his
earliest recognition as a temperance writer. But Baltimore by then was waning as a literary center. Editors
like Louis Godey and George Graham were enticing
authors to Philadelphia by offering higher pay for
magazine contributions, and professional writers began to turn to the seaboard metropolitan areas. With
the financial needs of his family increasing Arthur
found it necessary to write more and more for the
periodicals. After the *Lady's Book* accepted several of
his tales in the fall of 1840 and winter of 1841, Arthur
decided to follow his market, and in April 1841 moved
his family to the Quaker City.

4

The 1840's were Arthur's greatest years of literary
production. The flood of novels and tales he produced
taxed his strength, but it brought him to the attention
of every major publisher and editor along the Atlantic
seaboard. Scarcely a publishing house of any consequence failed to number him among its authors during the next two decades. Soon after taking up
residence at No. 5 Franklin Place in Philadelphia, the
site of Ben Franklin's former home, Arthur set to
work on six temperance tales which Louis Godey
published separately and then as a collection in 1842

under the title *Six Nights with the Washingtonians*. The book was a reworking of his earlier articles on the Washington Temperance Society, and its reception firmly established Arthur's literary career. Other tales appeared almost immediately in the *Saturday Evening Post, Peterson's Magazine,* the *Union Magazine,* and the *Delaware Gazette.* And every issue of Godey's *Lady's Book* that appeared between 1842 and 1850 contained at least one tale or sketch by Arthur. Addressed to a female audience, the tales were invariably woven from ordinary household problems and incidents that were already familiar to the overburdened American housewife. The average wife and mother saw herself as the heroine in the tiny domestic dilemmas Arthur presented, and she welcomed the advice he always included as the point of his tale. These points or "lessons" were usually implicit in the titles: "Tired of Housekeeping," "Let Her Pout It Out," "A Peevish Day, and Its Consequences," "Engaged at Sixteen." The abundance of Arthur's sketches insured adequate coverage of almost any facet of domestic life about which a reader might seek advice or from which he might take comfort that others had the same problems.

From the early forties until late in the seventies Arthur poured out a steady stream of didactic books and articles that never went beyond the range of common taste and interest. In his longer works he applied the domestic novel formula as expertly as Susan Warner, Mrs. E. D. E. N. Southworth, or Maria Cummins. Such novels as *The Martyr Wife* (1844), *The Heiress* (1845), and *Mary Moreton; or, The Broken Promise* (1852) illustrate to perfection the religious sentiment, the romantic love, and the thesis that submission to suffering is the only true way to happiness, which characterize the work of the domestic sentimentalists. Temperance always remained a favorite theme with Arthur, but he wrote no more than a dozen books in which it was used as the main subject. More often he spun his narrative homilies around less striking considerations such as the value of good manners, or the ways to domestic felicity, or the equality of the sexes. He treated the topics of mesmerism and spiritualism on two occasions: in *Agnes; or, The Possessed. A Revelation of Mesmerism* (1848) and in *The Angel and the Demon: A Tale of Modern Spiritualism* (1858). In these he fascinated his readers with vivid scenes depicting hypnotists and occultists at work and warned that "everywhere professors of, and experimenters in, this new science have sprung up." [28] He appealed to the reader's reason by pointing out that "the Lord gave man a rational

---

[28] From a later edition of T. S. Arthur, *Agnes; or, The Possessed. A Revelation of Mesmerism* (Philadelphia, 1855), p. 9.

mind and free will, and never inteferes with them
. . ." [29] and concluded by asserting that "it cannot be
according to the order of God's laws, that one of his
creatures should be thus enslaved by another." [30]

Underlying the moral concern and the inspirational
uplift present in all of Arthur's fiction is something
deeper than the prevailing religiosity of his times. He
firmly believed in the concepts and principles of
Emanuel Swedenborg. The pious lessons in his writings were in actuality expressions of the doctrine of
correspondence and the prophetic optimism found in
Swedenborgian teachings. Arthur formally adopted
Swedenborgianism as his religious faith soon after he
moved to Philadelphia. Early *Records* still preserved
in the files of the Church of the New Jerusalem at
22nd and Chestnut Streets show that he joined that
church on January 30, 1842. Two months later on
March 27, 1842 his three small children were baptized
in the faith, and when the next two children Henry
and Charles were born, they were similarly baptized.
The *Records* contain no mention of the last two of
Arthur's children, a son and a daughter, but it may be
presumed that they were also taken into the church.

For forty-three years Arthur remained an active
Swedenborgian, rising steadily to a position of responsibility in the Church of the New Jerusalem. He

[29] *Agnes,* p. 33.
[30] *Agnes,* p. 82.

was one of twenty selectmen who founded on June 5, 1855, the First New Jerusalem Society of Philadelphia, an organization that currently numbers four hundred members. The selectmen created the society to perpetuate four basic tenets which they set forth in Article V of its constitution:

1. That there is one God, in whom is a divine trinity, not of persons but of principles; and that one and sole God is the Lord Jesus Christ.
2. That the Sacred Scriptures contain the Word of the Lord, which has a celestial and spiritual as well as a natural sense.
3. That salvation consists in a life according to the Ten Commandments, which are to be obeyed as of ourselves, yet in the humble and sincere acknowledgement that the power to obey them is given to us by the Lord alone.
4. That Emanuel Swedenborg is the servant and messenger of the Lord, by who He has been pleased to reveal the spiritual sense of His Holy Word.[31]

Along with Arthur's signature as endorsers of this credo were those of such prominent Philadelphia business and professional men as John Frost, Richard Gardiner, William Aitken, Josiah Cobb, Codt'n Chesebrough, and Joseph Siddall.

It was probably through John Frost that Arthur

[31] *Hand-Book of the First New Jerusalem Society of Philadelphia* (Philadelphia, 1948), pp. 13–14.

came to know George Graham, editor and publisher of *Graham's Magazine*. Frost wrote wildlife sketches for *Graham's*, and shortly after Arthur became associated with Frost in the Swedenborgian movement, his tales began to appear in *Graham's Magazine*. In addition to a number of brief sketches Arthur published a novel, *The Young Artist*, in several issues of *Graham's* beginning in January 1850. *Graham's Magazine* and Godey's *Lady's Book* had the largest circulation of all the Philadelphia magazines, and the appearance of his work in these two periodicals gave Arthur a local prominence almost immediately. Through Godey's editors, Mrs. Sigourney and Mrs. Sarah Hale, Arthur was introduced to Eliza Leslie, sister of the portrait painter Charles R. Leslie. Miss Leslie was well known for her stories for children and especially for a series of highly popular cookbooks. In January 1843 she engaged Arthur to edit her latest project, *Miss Leslie's Magazine*. During the first year Miss Leslie did most of the editorial work herself and Arthur was listed as the publisher, but in December she sold out to Arthur and he changed the title of the periodical to *The Ladies' Magazine of Literature, Fashion and the Fine Arts*. After another year Arthur shortened the title to *Arthur's Magazine*, under which caption it continued until July 1846, then Arthur sold it to Louis Godey who merged it with his *Lady's Book*.

Between 1845 and 1850 Arthur apparently expanded his publishing activities considerably. He entered into a partnership with one major Philadelphia firm and seems to have had an association with several others. A legal release drawn up on May 10, 1850, indicates that he was in business with E. Ferrett and Company.[32] Arthur's books during the twenty-year period from 1840 to 1860 bear the imprints of some thirty different publishers; the entry notices (copyrights) show that he had joint publishing arrangements with a number of these.

In October 1850 Arthur began what proved to be the most successful of all his magazine projects, a weekly which he called *Arthur's Home Gazette.*[33] Next to *Ten Nights in a Bar-Room* it was his greatest single achievement. The subtitle of the magazine announced to its subscribers that it was "a journal of pure literature for home reading." The contents were designed to interest women and children, but the magazine attracted a sizable number of male readers among the circulation of ten thousand that it gathered during its first two years. In 1852 Arthur reprinted

[32] The waiver signatures included those of Louis Godey, King and Baird, and Abraham Hart of Carey and Hart. The original waiver and several other pieces of Arthur's business correspondence are among the holdings of the Pennsylvania Historical Society in Philadelphia.

[33] *Arthur's Home Gazette* through its successor *Arthur's Home Magazine* was one of the longest lived periodicals of the nineteenth century. For a descriptive sketch see Mott, *History of American Magazines,* II, 416–418.

the weekly issues with a few alterations in a monthly number for subscribers who preferred to receive the magazine once a month. Both periodicals seemed to flourish although there was strong competition from *Peterson's Magazine* and the *Lady's Book,* the two other leading women's magazines in Philadelphia. For two years Arthur continued both the weekly *Home Gazette* and the monthly counterpart which he identified as *Arthur's Home Magazine,* then in 1854 he stopped issuing the weekly and devoted all his efforts to the *Home Magazine.*

The following year Arthur hired an associate editor, Miss Virginia Frances Townsend, who was only twenty years old but who had a remarkable aptitude for the kind of editorial work necessary to make the *Home Magazine* successful. Together they built the circulation of the magazine to thirty thousand subscribers by 1860. Arthur and Miss Townsend wrote most of the serials and short stories that appeared in their magazine, but works by such well-known authors as Lucy Larcom, Alice Cary, and Ella Wheeler were also included. Miss Townsend took charge of the purely "feminine" contents of the magazine such as the fashion plates, patterns, and pieces of music that occurred in each number. She also persuaded Arthur to establish "departments" devoted to cookery, health, children's interests, and book reviews.

Miss Townsend remained with Arthur as his co-

editor from 1855 to 1872, keeping the magazine alive
almost singlehandedly during the sixties when he suffered a breakdown from overwork and emotional
depression. The furious pace of his writing had taken
its toll. Recurrent spells of severe illness confined him
to his bed for long periods of time. His eye condition
also gradually grew worse, making it necessary to
dictate his writings to amanuenses. On the eve of the
war the death of his mother, followed in rapid succession by the loss of his oldest daughter from tuber-
culosis and his youngest son from a fever, added to
his depression. The deaths of his children together
with concern for the safety of his two oldest sons—
James, who had entered federal service as an engineer
in the navy, and William, who was a captain of light
artillery in the Union Army—brought Arthur to a low
ebb in 1861. For a time Eliza and his friends despaired for his life, but through Eliza's tender care
he was finally nursed back to health.

By 1867 Arthur had so far recovered that he could
once more actively engage in his journalistic ventures.
In January of that year he started a magazine for children called *The Children's Hour*. It was filled with
pleasant moral tales and attractive illustrations, and
at the end of its first year it had a circulation equal
to that of *St. Nicholas*, the best-known juvenile periodical of the era. In 1869 Arthur began an eclectic
magazine, *Once a Month*, which contained selections

from popular foreign publications but enough of its own to give it a character. It was designed to compete with *The Atlantic Magazine* and the *Living Age*. It failed to gather sufficient subscribers and Arthur abandoned it in favor of *The Workingman* after one year. *The Workingman* was intended "to furnish good reading for mechanics and their families," and to offset "the ill-offices of the many sensational family papers available to the public." [34] But it, too, failed to gather readers and in 1872 Arthur disposed of both *The Children's Hour* and *The Workingman* keeping only his greatest enterprise, the *Home Magazine*.

From 1872 until his death in 1885 Arthur devoted his attention to his remaining periodical, taking his two older sons into partnership and eventually turning the magazine over to them along with his publishing business. He continued to write books and articles on behalf of temperance and to perform numerous services for civic and philanthropic agencies. In 1876 he accepted the chairmanship of the executive committee for the Centennial Exhibition in Philadelphia, and in the late seventies he helped found the Franklin Home for Inebriates, serving as its chief director until he died. During his last years he kept up an active correspondence with all manner of people who made requests for causes and favors. He

[34] *T. S. Arthur, His Life and Works,* p. 19.

complied with generosity whenever it was possible, often exerting himself to oblige total strangers.

Early in February 1885 Arthur could no longer go to his publishing offices at 227 South Sixth Street. Complications resulting from a combination of old age (he was just a few weeks short of seventy-six years old), anemia, and a kidney disorder forced him to remain at home. Sensing that his end was near, the kindly old man who had "brought happiness to millions" through his moral writings maintained a cheerful aspect for the benefit of his family as he gave instructions for the disposal of his property. In his last hours he confided to a friend, "I have never written a line except with the earnest desire to do good, and never a line I would wish expunged." [35] On March 6, 1885, Arthur died. He was buried in the cemetery of the Church of the New Jerusalem in a service attended by many of Philadelphia's most illustrious citizens. [36]

II: *Arthur and the Temperance Movement*

Timothy Shay Arthur is traditionally associated with the great nineteenth-century Temperance Crusade. His antiliquor writings have become his

[35] "T. S. Arthur" (obituary), *The Philadelphia Inquirer* (March 7, 1885), sec. 2.

[36] "T. S. Arthur" (obituary).

hallmark and *Ten Nights in a Bar-Room* is his acknowledged magnum opus. All of his major temperance works and most of his minor pieces were
occasioned by some crisis or development arising
within the crusade; consequently they reflect the history as well as the character of the movement. He
drew his subject matter respectively from the Washingtonian Revival, the antisaloon movement, the
battle over legal coercion, and the Women's Christian
Temperance Crusade. His books were crowded with
all the lurid propaganda vocabulary and devices that
give temperance literature its peculiar stamp. But he
was not a "professional" liquor reformer after the
fashion of a Lyman Beecher or a John Gough or a
Neal Dow, or, for that matter, the pledge-signing,
placard-carrying, mildly hysterical average citizen
who caught the fever of reform. As far as the records
show, he never took part in a mass meeting or a
torchlight parade, nor gave a temperance lecture. As
a young man he joined a temperance society in
Baltimore (the myth exists that it was the same one
Poe allegedly joined), but there is no evidence that
he ever attended or participated in meetings. His interest in liquor reform remained constant over a forty-
year period, but his hope for a better America ranged
so widely that for one of his books, *The Good Time
Coming* (1855), the charge of socialism was leveled
against him. If his antiliquor writings seem to dom-

inate his other work, it should be remembered that he was a journalist who earned his living by capitalizing themes of current public interest. And temperance was one of the most absorbing of all the humanitarian reforms that preoccupied nineteenth-century American society.

2

Social concern over the problem of drinking turned into a vigorous movement to control and regulate the use of intoxicants during the three decades prior to the Civil War, but the problem itself had its origin in the hard-drinking habits of our seventeenth-century English forebears. When the earliest New England settlers explored their New World environment, they discovered that an abundance of wild fruit, berries, and cereals grew on the hillsides and in the meadows. It was counted a sin by the colonial puritans not to make use of God's plenty, and the readiest way of utilizing such provender was to turn it into wines, cordials, and beer. Drinking among the puritans, including the clergy, was commonplace, and that it was early a problem is amply illustrated in the literature of the colonies. In 1673 Increase Mather speaking to his congregation warned that,

Drink is in itself a good creature of God, and to be received with thankfulness, but the abuse of drink is from

Satan; the wine is from God, but the Drunkard is from the Devil.[37]

Other seventeenth-century records of the Bay Colony show liquid refreshment to be as familiar as prayer: "no cellar but contained cider—ten to forty barrels to last out the season"; and that "cider and beer were the universal drinks, served to all with every meal, while cider-brandy and rum, distilled at Boston and Newport, made headier beverages." [38] It was not a recent custom that the nineteenth-century temperance reformers elected to fight, but a social practice as old as the country itself.

If the puritans had their problems, the trouble saw little abatement in the eighteenth century. The brewers, distillers, and vintners found beverage making a profitable business and encouraged the widespread use of stimulants. Distilling and exporting rum was a significant part of the New England economy, and little effort was made to regulate consumption by law. The church failed to resist seriously—and often condoned—the custom of social drinking, as is evident in the frequent reports of gala ordinations such as those of the Reverend Edwin Jackson in Pennsylvania and the Reverend Leonard Bacon in New Haven,

[37] From a sermon by Increase Mather titled "Wo to Drunkards." See Perry Miller and Thomas H. Johnson, *The Puritans* (New York, 1938), p. 2.

[38] *The Puritans*, p. 383.

when the former was installed in 1729 with the aid of six and a half barrels of cider, twenty-eight gallons of wine, two gallons of brandy, and four of rum, and the latter in 1829 by "an impressive service after which free drinks were furnished (by the church) at a near-by bar to all who chose to order them." [39] The average man in the eighteenth century and early nineteenth century needed no special occasion such as an ordination to indulge his thirst. Any wedding, christening, funeral, house-raising, harvesting, or quilting party served his purpose—served so well, indeed, that the estimated annual consumption of ardent spirits in the United States per capita in 1792 was two and a half gallons, in 1810 four and a half gallons, and in 1823 seven and a half gallons.[40] In 1812 Parson Weems printed a tavern bill in his *The Drunkard's Looking Glass* that he declared was typical of those of most travelers he met in the course of his book-peddling tours. It showed that the traveler in question had three mintslings before breakfast, nine tumblers of grog and three glasses of wine and bitters before dinner, two ticklers of French brandy after dinner, and wine with his supper.

A few voices were raised in protest against excessive drinking before 1800, but most of them were

[39] Alice Felt Tyler, *Freedom's Ferment* (Minneapolis, 1944), p. 312.
[40] *Freedom's Ferment*, p. 312.

cries in the wilderness. Anthony Benezet worked with some success among the Pennsylvania Quakers and Timothy Dwight urged his Yale students to sobriety, but the first really effective agitator for temperance was Dr. Benjamin Rush, eminent Philadelphia physician and man of distinguished public service. As a former physician-general to the Continental Army and as a private practitioner, Rush had gathered data which convinced him that drinking hard liquor produced harmful effects on both the mind and the body. In 1784 he published his views in a pamphlet, *An Inquiry into the Effects of Spiritous Liquors on the Human Body and Mind,* which became one of the most influential of the early protest documents. It went through eight editions by 1815, and by 1850 various temperance organizations had distributed over a hundred and seventy thousand copies. The pamphlet described the effects of stimulants on both the inexperienced and the habitual drinker, recommended substitutes for ardent spirits, and analyzed the reasons for excessive drinking. Its scientific basis provided the framework for numerous quasi-medical "reports" that swelled the mass of temperance literature in the thirties and forties.

The attention his *Inquiry* received prompted Rush to pursue the temperance cause. He persuaded a friend in New England, Jeremy Belknap, to promote the message contained in the *Inquiry,* and another,

Dr. David Ramsay, to do the same in South Carolina. He corresponded with officials of the Methodist Church and appeared before the Presbyterian General Assembly to enlist their aid. In 1808 a copy of Rush's pamphlet fell into the hands of Dr. William Clark of Moreau, New York. As a physician he recognized the truth of Rush's observations and joined with the town's Congregational minister, Lebbeus Armstrong, to form what is generally accepted as the first organized temperance society, the Moreau Society. Out of Rush's plea to the churches came an ally in the person of Lyman Beecher, who read the *Inquiry* and being already a staunch advocate of temperance proceeded to issue a work that became a famous anti-liquor manifesto, his *Six Sermons*. By the time of Rush's death in 1813 the great Temperance Crusade was already on its way.

3

The most vigorous and concerted action against intemperance occurred between 1825 and 1860, when the reform movement swept over the nation like a great wave, attracting more than a million organized followers in its wake. The formation of the American Society for the Promotion of Temperance in 1826, under the guidance of Dr. Justin Edwards of Andover, was the beginning of a rapid growth of similar organizations in the next few years. By 1829 there were

1000 such groups with a membership of 100,000, and by 1833 there were 4000 with over 500,000 active members.[41] A good many, but by no means all, of these societies evolved from organized religious bodies, and noted church figures were among the most zealous leaders—Beecher, Edwards, Armstrong, and bishops Asbury, Alonzo Potter of Pennsylvania, and John Hopkins of Vermont. The Methodists, Baptists, Presbyterians, and Episcopalians were especially active, with the Congregationalists following closely, but more inclined toward temperance than teetotalism. As the movement progressed conventions were held by the various societies for the purpose of consolidating and agreeing upon the nature of the temperance pledge; disagreement over the kinds of liquors to be banned in the pledge often snarled their business but did not dampen their ardor. And new and devastating ways of attacking "John Barleycorn" were always byproducts of these conventions.

Although the movement drew its heaviest support from the church, it also marshaled forces from other quarters. The lyceum, the schoolroom, and the press made valuable contributions to the reform effort. While prominent clergymen such as Beecher and Asbury railed at liquor from the pulpit, colorful temperance lecturers such as John B. Gough and John

[41] John Allen Krout, *The Origins of Prohibition* (New York, 1925), pp. 128–129.

H. W. Hawkins exhorted drinkers from the lyceum platform, and educational leaders such as Eliphalet Nott and Heman Humphrey gathered converts through classroom lectures and published addresses. The leaders were skilled in the techniques of argument, appeal, and propaganda, and made frequent use of revivalistic and evangelistic methods. The usual instruments of attack were expository argument and cold statistics, and the tactic of battle for the most part, "moral suasion." The press annually printed hundreds of thousands of tracts, leaflets, almanacs, and broadsides. As the temperance societies multiplied, the number of monthly and quarterly temperance journals increased, enjoying a wide circulation throughout the United States. The public interest in temperance literature did not escape the notice of enterprising publishers, who by the middle of the century realized tidy profits from the flood of temperance annuals and cold-water gift books they poured on the market. There was a noticeable absence of fiction in the earliest literature of protest, but short fiction was to come in great abundance after the way was made clear for it in the late thirties. The lingering disapproval of novels that had its origin in the early puritan days clouded their use until the forties and fifties, and even then, when they did appear, they were usually accompanied by a prefatory apology of one sort or another.

In 1836 it was necessary to regroup the forces of the Cold-Water Army. Some dissension had arisen among its leaders over ways and means of promulgating the war on intoxicants. Societies could not keep agreement as to what constituted "spiritous liquors." The liberal elements, although dedicated adherents to the cause, were not convinced that wine and malt beverages were harmful; the right-wing radicals struck for banning "all that can intoxicate." Also, readers of the reams of temperance propaganda that fell from the presses every month were beginning to tire of dull fact and dry argument. Clearly, it was time to recognize and do something about two ideas that had begun to circulate among the reformers since the early thirties: complete eradication of drink through prohibition, and acceptance of "products of fancy" as a propaganda weapon for the Cold-Water arsenal. A lull of public interest in the reform movement during 1835 spurred the leaders to action.

On August 4, 1836, three hundred and forty-eight delegates from nineteen American states and several Canadian territories met at Saratoga Springs, New York, for the second annual convention of the American Temperance Union.[42] The main purpose of the convention was to reorganize and enlarge the parent society, the United States Temperance Union, so that

[42] A full account of the Saratoga convention appears in *The Origins of Prohibition*, pp. 153–156.

any local society in the United States or Canada could become an affiliate and thus help to strengthen the movement. General John H. Cocke, a wealthy Virginia slaveowner and Bible Society promoter, was elected president; Edward C. Delavan of Albany was appointed chairman of the executive committee. The first major issue to come before Delavan's committee was the official wording of the pledge. During the early sessions of the convention a contingent headed by the extremists Lyman Beecher and Justin Edwards had gathered backing to have all intoxicants including wine and beer placed under the pledge's ban. Delavan favored ultraism over temperance but the matter required delicate handling by the executive committee, since a number of the delegates were not in favor of having the commitment extend to wine and malt beverages. After lengthy discussion the issue was finally resolved by wording the pledge in such a way that the obligation to abstain was voluntary rather than mandatory. Both sides were placated, but the teetotalers had in effect scored a moral victory. The intended meaning of "total abstinence" was clearly apparent, and with the adoption of the pledge, the way was opened for the march toward legal coercion that culminated in the passage of the famous Maine Liquor Law some fifteen years later.

With the blueprint thus drawn for prohibition, a second notable item was considered by the convention delegates. It was a recommendation that official sanction be given to prose fiction and other "light" literature as propaganda material for the movement. Again there was some resistance by conservatives to this proposed innovation, but whether it was a compromise to those who had lost out on the matter of the pledge, or simply that the assembled reformers were wearied by the heated debates in other sessions and were anxious to return home, the recommendation was brought quickly to a vote and passed. Thus "temperance fiction" [43] was given the formal stamp of approval, and it proved to be one of the most remarkable genres ever to appear in American literature. During the next two decades scores of writers, including Timothy Shay Arthur, earned a place in literary history because they influenced the development of the lurid narrative that came to be known as the temperance novel. Not the least of these writers was Walt Whitman, who published one called *Franklin Evans* in 1842.

Four years after the Saratoga convention, an event occurred in Baltimore that added a new chapter to the history of temperance societies and revitalized public interest in the movement. On an April evening

[43] For an interesting discussion of temperance fiction see "Ten Thousand and One Nights in a Barroom" in H. R. Brown, *The Sentimental Novel in America 1789–1860* (Durham, N. C., 1940), pp. 201–240.

in 1840 six jovial companions—William K. Mitchell, David Anderson, John F. Hoss, James McCurley, Archibald Campbell, and George Steers—met at Chase's Tavern in Baltimore for their weekly session of cards and drinking. As the evening wore on the game lost its zest and the conversation its sparkle, until one of their number remembered that a temperance lecture was to be given at a nearby church. It was humorously suggested that they send a committee to attend the lecture and report back with the findings. The suggestion was taken and a deputation left for the church where they listened for more than an hour to the speaker, Mathew Hale Smith, who lectured eloquently on the evils of alcohol. At the conclusion the listeners, stimulated now by Smith's evangelism, hurried back to the tavern. An enthusiastic discussion followed concerning the principle of total abstinence and the change it could work in their lives. What started out as a lark became a serious consideration of the good that might come from the formation of a temperance society.

In the small hours of the morning the six companions agreed to pledge themselves to total abstinence. To insure their intentions they banded together officially as a society obligated to a commitment drawn up by William Mitchell:

We whose names are annexed, desirous of forming a society for our mutual benefit, to guard against a pernicious practice, which is injurious to our health, standing and families, do pledge ourselves as gentlemen, that we will not drink any spiritous or malt liquors, wine or cider.[44]

They named their new organization the "Washington Temperance Society" and advertised themselves as "reformed drunkards." They set out immediately to rescue other helpless victims through what they called "experience" meetings. From the start the campaign was successful; the Washingtonians had discovered a new weapon against "Prince Alcohol" and "Demon Rum." It was the use of testimonials or confessions by reformed drunkards concerning their misadventures with strong drink. The spectacle of a former inebriate relating in minute detail the history of his degeneracy and miraculous redemption had a powerful emotional effect upon the crowded audiences that assembled to hear him. Until the Washingtonians began their meetings, the drunkard had been considered a lost soul, and the reformers spent their energies trying to turn the moderate drinker from his erring ways. Now it became evident that there was hope for the heavy imbiber, and what was

[44] The Washingtonian pledge was one of the best known of many famous temperance commitments. Arthur printed it verbatim as part of a dialogue in "The Broken Merchant," one of the tales in *Six Nights with the Washingtonians* (Philadelphia, 1842). See page 16 of the 1865 edition published by T. B. Peterson and Brothers.

more appealing, through his testimonial it was obvious that he was trying to save himself. The image of
the fallen saved was irresistible to the public. Between
April and December more than a thousand local
members joined the Washingtonians. As the work of
the former Chase Tavern tipplers continued, the con-
tagion spread to New York, Boston, and other large
cities. By 1842 there were Washingtonian groups in
New Jersey, Virginia, Ohio, Kentucky, Tennessee,
Indiana, and Illinois. In less than two years the
reformation of six Baltimore public house habitués
had resulted in the greatest revival movement of the
Temperance Crusade.

The stir created by the Washingtonians acted as a
catalyst on the older temperance groups. They renewed their efforts to suppress alcohol by increasing
their agitation for legal prohibition. Since the early
thirties various kinds of legislative action had been
urged upon governing bodies at both the state and
local levels. Most states had liquor laws of one sort
or another, usually tempered by local option, but
licensing in general proved to be ineffectual. Even
the notorious "Fifteen-Gallon Law" passed by the
Massachusetts legislature in 1838 was at best a nui-
sance law designed to restrict the retailer as well as
the consumer. It was the most drastic measure
adopted thus far, but it did not achieve prohibition.
The law established that liquor could not be retailed

in quantities less than fifteen gallons, and that the entire amount had to be delivered and carried away all at once. Few consumers had the cash or the capacity to cope with such a quantity "all at once"; yet the law still permitted the retail and individual purchase of intoxicants; so it proved unsatisfactory to both the liquor interests and the teetotalers. In 1842 it was repealed.

The first genuine prohibitory law resulted from the work of Neal Dow, a Maine reformer who conducted an unusually vigorous campaign against alcohol throughout New England and especially in his home state. Dow came from Quaker origins, made a fortune in the lumber business (where he first became aware of the economic as well as social disasters of drinking among his lumberjacks), and spent most of his adult life fighting to make Maine a dry state. In 1851 he succeeded, when as Mayor of Portland he gathered sufficient political power in the legislature to force the passage of the "Maine Liquor Law," a bill that forbade the manufacture and sale of liquor anywhere within the borders of Maine. For a half dozen years after its enactment, the law was the center of a heated controversy. It was argued on a variety of legal grounds, including the question of its constitutionality, and it gave rise to a sizable body of polemical literature. The Maine Law was legal coercion. That it was roundly debated is at once a manifestation of the fallacy of trying to legislate morality and the length to which the reformers were willing to go. Dow's achievement represents a chapter in the "legal phase" of the movement's history, and the stormy aftermath provided T. S. Arthur with the occasion for his *Ten Nights in a Bar-Room.*

The Civil War temporarily slackened the advance of the temperance movement, but in the postwar decades new phases and campaigns developed. The Cold-Water Army gained a contingent of "crusaders in crinoline" whose activities provided some of the most colorful moments of the whole movement. The bands of praying women who rallied to the cause were the forerunners of the women's temperance societies and the antisaloon leagues that battled the "monster drink" in the second half of the century. Other reform agencies evolved and other temperance tactics were adopted, but they belong to an era beyond the concern of this essay. The fifty years from 1830 to 1880 is the period that forms the backdrop for the work of Timothy Shay Arthur. Viewed from the vantage point of the present, this half century of the temperance movement has all the aspects of a *tableau vivant.* Its grouped figures in various poses were the dedicated societies, the singular groups of Washingtonians and women crusaders, and from time to time, the individual heroes and heroines such as Lyman Beecher, Neal Dow, Frances Willard, and

Carry Nation. There is much to provoke a smile in the soul-saving, devil-chasing antics of these reformers, but one must admire the relentless determination with which they fought the liquor traffic. If nothing else, they were ingenious in finding ways to spill the "cup of confusion."

4

Arthur first gained recognition as a temperance writer in 1840 soon after he had been hired by General Duff Green to edit the *Baltimore Merchant*. The *Merchant* was a campaign daily established by Green to support his friend William Henry Harrison for president, and Green's main interest was in editorializing his candidate; the gathering and reporting of local news he left to Arthur. Early in the spring of 1840 Arthur learned of the newly formed Washington Temperance Society and their "experience" meetings. Word circulated around Baltimore that these meetings offered something different from the usual lecture, so in the course of his reporting work Arthur visited one of the Washingtonian gatherings to see at first hand what took place in their meeting hall at the corner of Lombard and Hanover Streets. The testimonials he witnessed that first evening deeply moved him. For six successive nights he returned to cover the activities of the Washingtonians, and each following day he reported in the *Merchant* what he had seen and heard. His articles were the first to inform the nation about the Baltimore society of reformed drunkards, and other newspapers picked them up and reprinted them.

Two years after these earliest reports appeared in the *Merchant,* Arthur took advantage of the widespread public interest in the Washingtonians by issuing his series of six small pamphlets based on certain testimonials that he had previously witnessed at their meetings. The Washingtonian excitement had reached fever pitch and it was a strategic time to release them. The tales were thinly fictionalized adaptations of his newspaper accounts, individually titled "The Broken Merchant," "The Experience Meeting," "The Tavern Keeper," "The Drunkard's Wife," "The Widow's Son," and "The Moderate Drinker." The six themes were aptly chosen. The standard appeals against drink—its threat to the home and business, its degrading influence on the seller, its danger for the casual drinker—were effectively presented, along with an interest-catching sketch that described the new technique of salvation used by the Washingtonians.

Released separately by publishers Louis Godey and Morton McMichael of Philadelphia in 1842, later the same year the pamphlets were collected and published as the book *Six Nights with the Washingtonians: A Series of Original Temperance Tales.* With

only minor changes in the title, seven editions of the
tales were printed in the next few years, and by 1850
the book had sold 175,000 copies. Five years later it
was still selling at a rate that encouraged T. B. Peterson and Brothers to bring out an expensive edition
illustrated with nine engravings from George Cruik-
shank's famous series of temperance drawings called
"The Bottle." In some ways the work was more important to Arthur's career than *Ten Nights in a Bar-
Room.* It associated him directly with an event in the
history of the reform movement, it established him in
the front ranks of the "temperance tractarians" along
with such popular propagandists as Hartford's "sweet
singer," Lydia Sigourney, and Boston's scholar-re-
former, Lucius Manlius Sargent, and it gave him his
first best-seller.

Toward the end of the forties the temperance reformers, always anxious to promote their cause, and
the American publishers, always eager to sell books,
joined forces; the issue of their union was the temperance annual. After the solid success of *Six Nights
with the Washingtonians,* Arthur could turn his attention to the blossoming temperance annual business
and expect a warm reception. In 1847 he succeeded
in publishing a temperance tale in *The Fountain, A
Gift: "To stir up the pure mind by way of remem-
brance." The Fountain* was one of the better annuals
designed to point out "the virtue of temperance and

the evils of smoking and gambling." [45] He had joined respectable company; the annual contained pieces by Horace Greeley, C. M. Kirkland, Seba Smith, and John Greenleaf Whittier.

In 1850 he wrote for *The National Temperance Offering*, one of the best of the special-occasion annuals, containing selections by the giants of the movement—Lyman Beecher, Father Mathew, and H. Hastings Weld. The year 1850 seems to have been Arthur's *annus mirabilis*. He became the editor of *The Sons of Temperance Offering, The Temperance Offering*, and then in rapid succession, *The Crystal Fount, Friendship's Offering, The Moss Rose, The Passion Flower*, and a score more under at least a dozen different publishers' imprints. This flurry of temperance-annual writing and editing further enlarged his position as the "prose laureate of teetotalism." From 1850 until 1854 he continued to edit and pour out antiliquor propaganda, gathering national attention and a substantial fortune, as well as earning a permanent place in the history of the movement.

Arthur's publication of *Ten Nights in a Bar-Room* in 1854 came at the height of the nationwide reaction against the use of legal coercion to control the manufacture and sale of liquor. The novel clearly supported the prohibitionists and urged total abstinence. Arthur

[45] Ralph Thompson, *American Literary Annuals and Gift Books 1825–1865* (New York, 1936), p. 120.

worked his theme around a time-sequence device
which had proved successful in *Six Nights with the
Washingtonians,* a device that carried the reader
through a series of elapsed intervals enabling him to
see the devastation wrought by drink on all walks of
life over a period of time. *Ten Nights in a Bar-Room*
collected only a handful of enthusiastic reviews during the first year or two after its publication, but by
1860 it was on its way to becoming a popular classic.

The Civil War and his own long siege of illness
during the sixties temporarily halted Arthur's temperance activity, but early in the seventies he renewed his attack on drink with *Three Years in a Man-
Trap* (1872), a novel that lashed out at saloons and
rum sellers. The postwar era saw a sharp increase in
the number of liquor-dispensing establishments in the
United States, despite the restrictions imposed by
prohibitionary statutes. The temperance statisticians
lost little time in turning this fact into compilations
that roused the guardians of sobriety. They assembled
figures, largely associated with urban areas, that
proved saloons were the latest menace to the welfare
of society. A typical example was the report that the
great city of Boston prior to the mid-century "had one
licensed grogshop for every twenty-one males sixteen
years of age or older," [46] and that this ratio had nearly
tripled by 1870. Such statistics shook Arthur's faith in
legal coercion and he set out to disprove them by

[46] *Freedom's Ferment,* p. 321.

investigating conditions in his home city of Philadelphia. To his dismay he discovered that the city of brotherly love had "six or seven thousand saloons and dram-shops." He resolved to do something about the "deadly ulcer that is eating steadily down toward the vitals of the people." [47] The result was *Three Years in a Man-Trap*, advertised by the publisher J. M. Stoddart as "a sequel to *Ten Nights in a Bar-Room*," in which the author "grapples again with the monster intemperance, but in a new field, and with enemies more thoroughly disciplined and organized." [48] The "new" field was the big city saloon (those "nurseries of vice and crime"), rather than the quiet country inn; the "disciplined and organized" enemy was the liquor interest—the brewers, distillers, and saloon proprietors who had learned how to circumvent social and political pressures with counteractions of their own. *Three Years in a Man-Trap* is notable for the profusion of stereotyped temperance blasts Arthur crowds into it, and like the typical temperance novel of the eighteen fifties, it is a phantasmagoria of shocking and sensational incidents. Arthur was sixty-three years old when he wrote it, but despite waning energies and failing sight, he managed to write five more lengthy works castigating liquor before he died.

In the same year (1872) Stoddart and Company

[47] T. S. Arthur, *Three Years in a Man-Trap* (Dayton, Ohio, 1872), p. 3.
[48] *Three Years in a Man-Trap*, p. 3.

published Arthur's *Woman to the Rescue. A Story of the New Crusade.* The novel publicized the activities of the bands of militant females who shortly after the Civil War began to invade taverns and public houses bent upon saving the patrons through prayer. A good many befuddled minds in those early days were doubtless sobered by the prospect of a group of determined women, kneeling in the sawdust amid the brass cuspidors, praying and singing by turns for the lost souls at the bar. The tactic was dramatic, and for a time, effective; but as the novelty wore off and the drinking continued, the frenzied ladies adopted measures that brought them afoul of the law. With a ferocity belying their former meekness they turned to destruction, smashing bottles and glasses, driving out customers with their parasols, and frequently leaving the interior of a saloon a shambles. One of the most famous of these righteous avengers was Carry Nation, whose antics created a national sensation when, at the turn of the century, she made sorties on saloons throughout Kansas, a prohibition state, conducting what she called her "hatchetations." Armed with a hatchet and resolutely believing she had the right to destroy property since saloons were illegal in Kansas, she went on wrecking expeditions that caused her to be arrested, imprisoned, and on several occasions, beaten and shot at.

Arthur recognized the narrative value of the

women's crusade; the martyrdom suffered by a few groups of the praying women made excellent grist for the temperance fiction mill. He placed the setting for *Woman to the Rescue* in Delhi, "a beautiful town in the centre of a rich agricultural region," presumably in Ohio where the crusade was said to have started.[49] The story presents repeated scenes of misery and degradation caused by the evil work of saloons and culminates in a graphic picture of the praying women who succeed in drying up Delhi. The early efforts of women like those Arthur describes led eventually to the formation of the Women's National Christian Temperance Union. Under the capable direction of Frances Willard and her cohorts, Mrs. Annie Wittenmyer of Philadelphia, Mrs. Mary C. Johnson of Brooklyn, and Mrs. Mary A. Ingham of Cleveland, the organization expanded to become international in the eighties. In 1910 Miss Willard was elected to the American Hall of Fame for her work in behalf of temperance.

Three years after the appearance of *Woman to the Rescue*, Arthur published *Danger; or, Wounded in the House of a Friend* (1875). It was less successful than his other books, partly because it had no particular historical connotation and partly because its theme of "caution" was tediously familiar to the pub-

[49] T. S. Arthur, *Woman to the Rescue. A Story of the New Crusade* (New York, 1872), p. 18.

lic. It warned against social or moderate drinking. The moderate drinker was the reformers' problem child. His sins did not invariably lead to debauchery and wantonness, his professional and social standings were not always blighted by his casual glass, and he frequently embarrassed the principle of abstention by living a happy and normal life. He was a source of frustration for those who predicted a dire fate for anyone who touched a drop of the fiery liquid. Nonetheless, social drinking received constant rebuke in tracts and journals. The teetotalers cried their alarms over the use of alcohol for any occasion. They held to the platform of "no compromise" wherever stimulants might enter the household. Even the medicine cabinet and the pantry were not free of censure. The temperance mother was expected to nurse her children through colds and colic without the aid of certain old-fashioned remedies, and the temperance father was expected to deny himself such delectables as rum cake and brandy pudding. The monster drink, as every good reformer knew, had subtle ways of capturing his victim. Arthur wrote *Danger* "as an argument against what is called the temperate use of liquor, and as an exhibition of the fearful disasters that flow from our social drinking customs." [50]

In 1877 Arthur delivered another blast at saloons

[50] T. S. Arthur, *Danger; or, Wounded in the House of a Friend* (New York, 1875), p. 4.

in *The Bar-Rooms at Brantly; or, The Great Hotel Speculation.* The theme was inspired by public interest in the "temperance coffee-houses" and "friendly inns" that appeared in the seventies. To provide the nondrinking traveler with accommodations free of the noise and indignities of a taproom, many "clear-headed merchants" turned their establishments into "dry hotels." The first of these apparently appeared in Philadelphia in 1874, when Joshua L. Baily converted his dining room into "The Workingmen's Central Coffee-House," which served food but no drink to travelers and local workmen.[51] The idea gained popularity among temperance men, and by 1880 there were several thousand such eating and sleeping places in the United States. To meet this new development the liquor people spent great sums of money to make their bars and hotels even more attractive by installing lavish furnishings and appointments. The growth of transportation systems led some speculators to build plush resort hotels in isolated regions where the anticipated extension of travel facilities failed to materialize; when bankruptcy followed, such cases became scandals for the newspapers. Arthur saw an opportunity to praise the temperance houses and at the same time to warn against the dangers of speculation, so he wrote the Brantly story. It is told by an

[51] T. S. Arthur, *Grappling with the Monster; or, The Curse and Cure of Strong Drink* (New York, 1877), pp. 273–274.

elderly philanthropist who spends his time and fortune blocking the attempts of certain citizens of
Brantly (a cold-water town) to open a drinking
house. He succeeds until a group of wealthy speculators from New York manage to evade his obstacles.
They start construction on a fabulous new hotel with
velvet and crystal drinking rooms, but they encounter
financial difficulties that interrupt its completion and
disaster follows for the investors. The final coup is
accomplished a few weeks later, when an accidental
fire (it is no accident but the hand of the Lord)
destroys the hotel, and Brantly returns once more to
its friendly, old-fashioned "Fountain Inn."

Also in 1877 Arthur gathered a compendium of
temperance information of the kind widely distributed after the Civil War. The ramifications of the
Temperance Movement were varied and diversified;
there was a lively market for inexpensive books that
could be used by ministers, lecturers, and propagandists in general as sources of statistical and historical
information. Arthur compiled in *Grappling with the
Monster; or, The Curse and Cure of Strong Drink* a
potpourri of facts, records, articles, and historical accounts of the leaders of the movement. He included
arguments and debates over the use of alcohol as a
food or a medicine and discussions of the physiolog-
ical and psychological problems of alcoholism. The
book is noteworthy for the light it sheds on such

topics as inebriate asylums, reformatory homes and clubs, temperance literature, licensing problems, temperance inns, and the women's crusade. It is loosely arranged in a chronological order paralleling the development of the movement and divides its attention equally between the curse of drinking and its cure.

Arthur's last gallant effort to promote the antiliquor cause occurred in 1881 when he published *Saved as by Fire*. He was seventy-two and a little out of touch with the main stream of the movement, but he could write from the experience of almost half a century of service. The shelves of his study were lined with several hundred of his own books, a goodly number of them written in the interest of temperance; he was satisfied that not a single book on his shelves had gone out to the public without its moral purpose. *Saved as by Fire* proved to be little more than a benediction to fifty years of sermonizing on the subject of temperance. It told of the fall of "one of nature's noble creatures" and his rescue from Demon Rum through "moral suasion." The plot, familiar now to the point of tedium, followed the first-tumbler-to-the-tomb formula, but with diminishing success, since postwar audiences preferred more realism and less pious romance in their fiction. Perhaps the publisher signaled both the end of a unique era of social reform and the final gesture of one of its greatest champions when he remarked that in *Saved as by Fire* Arthur "lifted the subject of temperance into the region of spiritual laws and forces." [52]

III: *Ten Nights in a Bar-Room*

The publisher of the first edition of *Ten Nights in a Bar-Room* announced in his preface, "this new temperance volume, by Mr. Arthur, comes in just at the right time, when the subject of restrictive laws is agitating the whole country . . ." The time was 1854, three years after Neal Dow had successfully petitioned the Maine state legislature to pass a prohibitionary statute. Since 1837 Dow had worked vigorously to drive liquor out of his state; his efforts were rewarded on June 2, 1851, when Governor John Hubbard signed into law a statute that was virtually of Dow's own design. It banned the manufacture and sale of intoxicating liquors anywhere within the limits of the state boundaries. In addition, it authorized peace officers and magistrates to issue search and seizure warrants upon the complaint of three persons and insured enforcement of the law by awarding all fines to the prosecutors. [53]

The Maine Law was the ultimate in liquor control. As it was clearly a coercive measure the liquor forces lost no time in raising the question of its constitution-

[52] T. S. Arthur, *Saved as by Fire* (New York, 1881), p. v.
[53] *Origins of Prohibition*, p. 295.

ality. Even among the dedicated reformers there were many who preferred the slow progress and frequent failures of moral suasion to the potential dangers of legal coercion. But the mild protests of the more cautious were drowned out by the powerful voices of zealots like Beecher and Dow. After two centuries of ineffectual licensing and regulatory legislation, temperance sentiment turned inevitably toward prohibitory laws. In most of his fiction Arthur employed moral suasion, but after 1850 he was convinced that "there is but one cure: *Total Abstinence*, by the help of God, for the individual, and *Prohibition* for the State." [54]

Dow's victory in Maine encouraged reformers in other states to stump for similar laws, but the opponents of liquor legislation were not idle. By 1854 counterpropagandists were able to cast a shadow on the Maine Law. In a letter he sent to Arthur some years later Dow recalled that "in every part of the country, reports were industriously circulated that the law was inoperative for good, and that liquors were sold in Maine as freely and in as large quantities as before the law." [55] Dow went on to demonstrate that the reports were false, but his enemies did not stop with mere reports. They borrowed a leaf from

---

[54] *Grappling with the Monster,* p. 320.
[55] Arthur printed the complete text of Dow's letter in *Grappling with the Monster,* pp. 312–320.

Dow's own book of political tactics and counter-attacked from that quarter: "For some years after the enactment of the law, it entered largely into the politics of the State. Candidates were nominated by one party or the other with reference to their proclivities for rum or their hostility to it, and the people were determined in their votes, one way or the other, by this Consideration."

When "dry" candidates continued to win at the polls, opponents of the law pressed the battle along other lines. They argued that the law jeopardized the rights of free enterprise and the individual consumer. The issue was carried to the Supreme Court where four justices rendered opinions favorable to the law. Chief Justice Roger Taney declared:

If any State deems the retail and internal traffic in ardent spirits injurious to its citizens, and calculated to produce idleness, vice, and debauchery, I see nothing in the Constitution of the United States to prevent it from regulating the traffic, or from prohibiting it altogether, if it thinks proper.[56]

He was supported in his view by Justices John McLean, John Catron, and Robert Grier. But despite pronouncements on the legality of the law by members of the highest court in the land the battle continued. Indeed, the issue was debated for a full

[56] *Grappling with the Monster*, p. 307.

generation after the passage of the Maine Law. Not until Congress passed the Eighteenth Amendment in 1920 did the reformers achieve full victory; and even then the matter was not finally resolved, for only thirteen years later, in 1933, another Congress turned back a century of reforming effort with the passage of the Twenty-First Amendment.

The motives that led to the Maine legislation were deeply rooted in social concerns and aspirations common to most of the other nineteenth-century reforms. Collectively they represent a quickening of the national conscience over domestic problems that stood in the way of realizing the American democratic dream. Temperance reformers felt impelled to resist an evil that enslaved the individual, violated the sanctity of the family, and in general weakened the social order the reformers sought to perfect. When half a century of persuasive methods failed, the reformers were convinced that legal coercion was the last resort.

Ten Nights in a Bar-Room was written deliberately to support legal coercion and was occasioned by the reaction that threatened the Maine Law. Its thesis is unmistakably total abstinence, made certain by legal means. As one long experienced in the propaganda techniques of temperance reform, Arthur confounds all honest opposition to his thesis with chapter after chapter of the most tearful and horrifying events (which he assures us are "infinitely less than the reality"), until he is ready to allow his central character, the redeemed Joe Morgan, to announce:

The accursed traffic must cease among us. You must cut off the fountain, if you would dry up the stream. If you would save the young, the weak, and the innocent—on you God has laid the solemn duty of their protection—you must cover them from the temptor . . . Let us resolve, this night, that from henceforth, the traffic shall cease in Cedarville.

And the good citizens of Cedarville corroborate the wisdom of the good citizens of Maine by adopting for their town measures inspired by the Maine Law:

Be it resolved by the inhabitants of Cedarville, That from this day henceforth, no more intoxicating drink shall be sold within the limits of the corporation.

Resolved, further, That all the liquors in the Sickle and Sheaf be forthwith destroyed, and that a fund be raised to pay the creditors of Simon Slade therefor, should they demand compensation.

Resolved, That in closing up all other places where liquor is sold, regard shall be had for the right of property which the law secures to every man.

Resolved, That with the consent of the legal authorities, all the liquor for sale in Cedarville be destroyed; provided the owners thereof be paid its full value out of a fund specially raised for that purpose.

Without apology or hesitancy Arthur thus boldly

championed prohibition by law, a stand not yet openly advocated by his fellow temperance novelists. Though later in the fifties other writers followed, he was the first to lift his pen on behalf of Dow and in the face of a large opposition to the Maine Law.

2

Arthur wrote the major portion of *Ten Nights in a Bar-Room* during the fall of 1852 and the winter of 1853, while he was living on South Tenth Street in Philadelphia. In a second floor room that served as both a study and an office for conducting the business affairs of his *Home Magazine,* he devoted the morning hours of each working day to the writing of the novel and the numerous pieces of fiction that went into his periodical. The novel was still unfinished when he moved to Girard Street late in 1853, but the narrow, three-story, red brick house on South Tenth has been established by tradition as the birthplace of *Ten Nights in a Bar-Room.* It is presently one of Philadelphia's minor literary landmarks, where, as one historian of the city observed, "annually a number of disagreeable-looking people reverently visit it." [57]

Ten Nights in a Bar-Room was first published in 1854 under the combined imprints of Lippincott, Grambo and Company, and J. W. Bradley. Bradley

[57] Struthers Burt, *Philadelphia. Holy Experiment* (London, n.d.), p. 103.

had subsidiaries at Auburn, New York (H. A. Yates) and at New Haven, Connecticut (M. Bradley), so the first edition of the novel appeared simultaneously in these two cities when it was released in Philadelphia. In the same year two additional printings were released, one bearing the joint imprint of L. P. Crown in Boston and J. W. Bradley in Philadelphia, and another carrying only Bradley's name. Arthur never altered or revised the original text, so edition designations can only be determined on the basis of imprint and copyright. The pages of all the early issues were printed from the same stereotype plates cast in the shop of L. Johnson and Company in Philadelphia.

The original edition carries Arthur's name on the entry page as that of the copyright holder, but Arthur seems to have had an arrangement with J. W. Bradley whereby either could issue the novel at his own discretion. Between 1856 and 1858 agitation over the Maine Law increased, and Bradley seized the opportunity to gather additional profits from the novel by releasing it in a gift-book edition in 1857. Bradley printed it from the original plates but added a new preface and substituted his own name on the entry page. The double frontispieces by Van Ingen and the illustrations by Rea, the work of Philadelphia engravers that had appeared in the earlier editions, were retained, and the novel was published by John E. Potter and Company.

In 1882 Arthur prepared the last edition in which he had an active hand during his lifetime. It was printed from reset type and bound in the traditional gift-book style. Aside from punctuation changes there were no alterations in the text. Porter and Coates of Philadelphia published the work and Arthur was listed as the copyright holder. At the time of this edition the accumulated sales of the novel in the United States were reported to be in excess of 100,000 copies.[58] This figure was greatly increased in the 1890's, after the copyright expired and the religious press and the publishers of "cheapbacks" flooded the market with inexpensive editions. By 1900 the American sales ran close to a million copies. With the arrival of a new century, however, active interest in the novel declined. It was still in print as late as 1928 in a much reduced pamphlet form, presumably selling to church groups and die-hard temperance advocates, but its thin trickle of sales disappeared altogether after the repeal of prohibition.

Between 1854 and 1874 *Ten Nights in a Bar-Room* was widely circulated by temperance groups in England, Scotland, and Sweden. Pirated editions were printed in London and Edinburgh, some of which were sold in bookseller's shops on the continent. Nearly a century later the rare-book hunter, I. R.

[58] J. C. Derby, *Fifty Years Among Authors, Books and Publishers* (New York, 1884), p. 719.

Brussel, discovered a roving book-peddler still optimistically offering for sale on his pushcart in an Amsterdam, Holland, market place the English edition of *Ten Nights in a Bar-Room*.[59] Temperance societies contributed in great measure to the spread of Arthur's name and fame, but the individual admirer of Arthur and his cause seems not to have died out entirely. In 1952, on the eve of the centennial anniversary of *Ten Nights in a Bar-Room*, the late Samuel Schoonover, teacher, temperance worker, and philanthropist, provided a footnote to the history of Arthur and his book, when a national magazine disclosed that his will contained a provision that the schools of Stroudsburg, Pennsylvania, were to receive $25,000 from his estate on the condition that "they always keep on the school library shelves ten copies of the famed novel, *Ten Nights in a Bar-Room*, by Timothy Shay Arthur." [60]

The vogue of the temperance novel disappeared after the Civil War, but Arthur's novel retained its lease on life through another medium. *Ten Nights in a Bar-Room* was adapted for the stage in 1858 by William W. Pratt, the New York impresario-playwright. It was first produced at the National Theater

[59] David Dempsey, "A Gumshoe in the World of Books," *New York Times Book Review*, April 16, 1950, p. 38.

[60] "Ten Volumes for a School Library," *Life*, March 17, 1952, pp. 63–64.

in New York City on August 23, 1858. Pratt kept the general plot but eliminated most of the minor episodes. He refashioned Arthur's character Harry Grimes into a traditional Yankee comic figure, Sample Swichel—"a Yankee tippler very much alive," and added a female counterpart, Mehitable Cartwright—"a sentimental Yankee girl." The changes provided comic relief but did not detract from the temperance message. The drama was performed as a tragedy for a time, but it gradually took on the character of a melodrama, as the barnstorming stock companies of the eighties and nineties played it with a lighter touch when they carried it into countless opera houses and town halls throughout the country. It became a popular item in the repertory of these theatrical groups along with such other favorites as *The Octoroon, East Lynne,* and *The Ticket-of-Leave Man.* Late in the century American theater audiences applauded moving performances of *Ten Nights in a Bar-Room* by such well-known character actors as Joseph Jefferson and John Kelly in the role of the drunkard Joe Morgan. After 1864 various songs and recitations were introduced into the play, including the famous temperance poem, "Come Home, Father," by Henry Clay Work, the Illinois song writer who wrote for Christy's Minstrels. Arthur's novel, Pratt's play version, and Work's poem have gradually blurred into one image in American folklore, so that a hundred years after *Ten Nights in a Bar-Room* first appeared, the peculiar title connotes less of the early nineteenth-century era of reform than a later nineteenth-century old-fashioned montage, distinguished by a mellow mixture of paper-mache realism, smoking kerosene stage lamps, and the tearful strains of "Father, dear father, come home with me now." Doubtless the play version of the novel helped to perpetuate this image of *Ten Nights in a Bar-Room,* just as the "Tom Shows" did for *Uncle Tom's Cabin.*

Quite apart from its value as legend and myth, *Ten Nights in a Bar-Room* deserves its place in American literary history as the classic example of the temperance novel genre. All the characteristics common to the type are happily met in this one work—the belabored thesis, the step-by-step decline of the inebriate, the lurid episodes of horror and death, the martyred innocents, and the all-pervading atmosphere of sanctimonious piety. For nearly three decades temperance novels provided part of the literary fare of a people grappling with enormous social problems. During this period every conceivable angle that promised a solution to the problem of excessive drinking was covered by the temperance writers. If the literature of protest in the era of temperance reform never reached a high level of literary art, it was at least successful as a highly developed form of propaganda. Moreover, buried in the mass of this literature is the essence of young America's utopian hope for "the design of Heaven to establish a powerful nation . . . where all the energies of man might find full scope and excitement, on purpose to show the world by one great successful experiment of what man is capable." [61] As the chief example of a genre that expresses one of the strongest motifs in the "design of Heaven," *Ten Nights in a Bar-Room* is an enduring social document, one that seems to have gained rather than lost significance, as it passed through the transforming processes of burlesque and parody.

DONALD A. KOCH
Simpson College
May 1964

[61] Constance Rourke, *Trumpets of Jubilee* (New York, 1927), p. 31.

NOTE ON THE TEXT

Though there were numerous reprintings of *Ten Nights in a Bar-Room* during and after Arthur's lifetime, he never made any alterations in the text of the first edition of 1854. At least four issues were struck from the original plates by 1857 and as many more from reset type by 1885. The John Harvard Library facsimile edition reproduces an 1854 printing discussed in the Introduction which bears the imprint of L. P. Crown in Boston and J. W. Bradley in Philadelphia.

D. A. K.

TEN NIGHTS IN A BAR-ROOM

VAN INGEN

SICKLE & SHEAF
BY
SIMON SLADE

TEN NIGHTS
IN A
BARROOM

VAN INGEN

Ten Nights in a Bar-Room,

AND WHAT I SAW THERE.

By T. S. ARTHUR.

BOSTON:

L. P. CROWN & CO., 61 CORNHILL.

PHILADELPHIA:

J. W. BRADLEY, 48 N. FOURTH ST.

1854.

PUBLISHER'S PREFACE.

THIS new temperance volume, by Mr. Arthur, comes in just at the right time, when the subject of restrictive laws is agitating the whole country, and good and true men everywhere are gathering up their strength for a prolonged and unflinching contest. It will prove a powerful auxiliary in the cause.

"Ten Nights in a Bar-Room" gives a series of sharply drawn sketches of scenes, some of them touching in the extreme, and some dark and terrible. Step by step the author traces the downward course of the tempting vender and his infatuated victims, until both are involved in hopeless ruin. The book is marred by no exaggerations, but exhibits the actualities of bar-room life, and the consequences flowing therefrom, with a severe simplicity, and adherence to truth, that gives to every picture a Daguerrean vividness.

3

CONTENTS.

TEN NIGHTS IN A BAR-ROOM.

NIGHT THE FIRST.

The "Sickle and Sheaf."

Ten years ago, business required me to pass a day in
Cedarville. It was late in the afternoon when the stage
set me down at the "Sickle and Sheaf," a new tavern,
just opened by a new landlord, in a new house, built
with the special end of providing "accommodations for
man and beast." As I stepped from the dusty old vehicle in which I had been jolted along a rough road for
some thirty miles, feeling tired and hungry, the good-
natured face of Simon Slade, the landlord, beaming as
it did with a hearty welcome, was really a pleasant sight
to see, and the grasp of his hand was like that of a true
friend.

I felt, as I entered the new and neatly furnished
sitting-room adjoining the bar, that I had indeed found
a comfortable resting-place after my wearisome journey.

"All as nice as a new pin," said I, approvingly, as I
glanced around the room, up to the ceiling—white as

the driven snow—and over the handsomely carpeted floor. "Haven't seen any thing so inviting as this. How long have you been open?"

"Only a few months," answered the gratified landlord. "But we are not yet in good going order. It takes time, you know, to bring every thing into the right shape. Have you dined yet?"

"No. Every thing looked so dirty at the stage-house where we stopped to get dinner, that I couldn't venture upon the experiment of eating. How long before your supper will be ready?"

"In an hour," replied the landlord.

"That will do. Let me have a nice piece of tender steak, and the loss of dinner will soon be forgotten."

"You shall have that, cooked fit for an alderman," said the landlord. "I call my wife the best cook in Cedarville."

As he spoke, a neatly dressed girl, about sixteen years of age, with rather an attractive countenance, passed through the room.

"My daughter," said the landlord, as she vanished through the door. There was a sparkle of pride in the father's eyes, and a certain tenderness in the tones of his voice, as he said—"My daughter," that told me she was very dear to him.

"You are a happy man to have so fair a child," said I, speaking more in compliment than with a careful choice of words.

"I am a happy man," was the landlord's smiling answer; his fair, round face, unwrinkled by a line of care or trouble, beaming with self-satisfaction. "I have always been a happy man, and always expect to be. Simon Slade takes the world as it comes, and takes it easy. My son, sir"—he added, as a boy in his twelfth year, came in. "Speak to the gentleman."

The boy lifted to mine a pair of deep blue eyes, from which innocence beamed, as he offered me his hand, and said, respectfully—"How do you do, sir?" I could not but remark the girl-like beauty of his face, in which the hardier firmness of the boy's character was already visible.

"What is your name?" I asked.

"Frank, sir."

"Frank is his name," said the landlord—"we called him after his uncle. Frank and Flora—the names sound pleasant to our ears. But, you know, parents are apt to be a little partial and over fond."

"Better that extreme than its opposite," I remarked.

"Just what I always say. Frank, my son"—the landlord spoke to the boy, "there's some one in the bar. You can wait on him as well as I can."

The lad glided from the room, in ready obedience.

"A handy boy that, sir; a very handy boy. Almost as good in the bar as a man. He mixes a toddy or a punch just as well as I can."

"But," I suggested, "are you not a little afraid of placing one so young in the way of temptation."

"Temptation!" The open brows of Simon Slade contracted a little. "No, sir!" he replied, emphatically. "The till is safer under his care than it would be in that of one man in ten. The boy comes, sir, of honest parents. Simon Slade never wronged anybody out of a farthing."

"Oh," said I, quickly, "you altogether misapprehend me. I had no reference to the till, but to the bottle."

The landlord's brows were instantly unbent, and a broad smile circled over his good-humoured face.

"Is that all? Nothing to fear, I can assure you. Frank has no taste for liquor, and might pour it out for months without a drop finding its way to his lips. Nothing to apprehend there, sir—nothing."

I saw that further suggestions of danger would be useless, and so remained silent. The arrival of a traveller called away the landlord, and I was left alone for observation and reflection. The bar adjoined the neat sitting-room, and I could see, through the open door, the customer upon whom the lad was attending. He was a well-dressed young man—or rather boy, for he did not appear to be over nineteen years of age— with a fine, intelligent face, that was already slightly marred by sensual indulgence. He raised the glass to his lips, with a quick, almost eager motion, and drained it at a single draught.

"Just right," said he, tossing a sixpence to the young bar-tender. "You are first-rate at a brandy-toddy. Never drank a better in my life."

The lad's smiling face told that he was gratified by the compliment. To me the sight was painful, for I saw that this youthful tippler was on dangerous ground.

"Who is that young man in the bar?" I asked, a few minutes afterward, on being rejoined by the landlord.

Simon Slade stepped to the door and looked into the bar for a moment. Two or three men were there by this time; but he was at no loss in answering my question.

"Oh, that's a son of Judge Hammond, who lives in the large brick house just as you enter the village. Willy Hammond, as everybody familiarly calls him, is about the finest young man in our neighbourhood. There is nothing proud or put-on about him—nothing— even if his father is a judge, and rich into the bargain. Every one, gentle or simple, likes Willy Hammond. And then he is such good company. Always so cheerful, and always with a pleasant story on his tongue. And he's so high-spirited withal, and so honourable. Willy Hammond would lose his right hand rather than be guilty of a mean action."

"Landlord!" The voice came loud from the road in front of the house, and Simon Slade again left me to answer the demands of some new comer. I went into the bar-room, in order to take a closer observation of

Willy Hammond, in whom an interest, not unmingled
with concern, had already been awakened in my mind.
I found him engaged in a pleasant conversation with a
plain-looking farmer, whose homely, terse, common
sense was quite as conspicuous as his fine play of words
and lively fancy. The farmer was a substantial con-
servative, and young Hammond a warm admirer of new
ideas and the quicker adaptation of means to ends. I
soon saw that his mental powers were developed beyond
his years, while his personal qualities were strongly attractive. I understood better, after being a silent listener and observer for ten minutes, why the landlord
had spoken of him so warmly.

"Take a brandy-toddy, Mr. H———?" said Hammond, after the discussion closed, good humouredly.
"Frank, our junior bar-keeper here, beats his father,
in that line."

"I don't care if I do," returned the farmer; and the
two passed up to the bar.

"Now, Frank, my boy, don't belie my praises," said
the young man; "do your handsomest."

"Two brandy-toddies, did you say?" Frank made the
inquiry with quite a professional air.

"Just what I did say; and let them be equal to
Jove's nectar."

Pleased at this familiarity, the boy went briskly to
his work of mixing the tempting compound, while Hammond looked on with an approving smile.

" There," said the latter, as Frank passed the glasses across the counter, "if you don't call that first-rate, you're no judge." And he handed one of them to the farmer, who tasted the agreeable draught, and praised its flavour. As before, I noticed that Hammond drank eagerly, like one athirst—emptying his glass without once taking it from his lips.

Soon after the bar-room was empty; and then I walked around the premises, in company with the land-lord, and listened to his praise of every thing and his plans and purposes for the future. The house, yard, garden, and out-buildings were in the most perfect order; presenting, in the whole, a model of a village tavern.

" Whatever I do, sir," said the talkative Simon Slade, "I like to do well. I wasn't just raised to tavern-keep-ing, you must know; but I'm one who can turn his hand to almost any thing."

" What was your business?" I inquired.

" I'm a miller, sir, by trade," he answered—"and a better miller, though I say it myself, is not to be found in Bolton county. I've followed milling these twenty years, and made some little money. But I got tired of hard work, and determined to lead an easier life. So I sold my mill, and built this house with the money. I always thought I'd like tavern-keeping. It's an easy life; and, if rightly seen after, one in which a man is sure to make money."

" You were still doing a fair business with your mill?"

"Oh yes. Whatever I do, I do right. Last year, I put by a thousand dollars above all expenses, which is not bad, I can assure you, for a mere grist mill. If the present owner comes out even, he'll do well!"

"How is that?"

"Oh, he's no miller. Give him the best wheat that is grown, and he'll ruin it in grinding. He takes the life out of every grain. I don't believe he'll keep half the custom that I transferred with the mill."

"A thousand dollars, clear profit, in so useful a business, ought to have satisfied you," said I.

"There you and I differ," answered the landlord. "Every man desires to make as much money as possible, and with the least labour. I hope to make two or three thousand dollars a year, over and above all expenses, at tavern-keeping. My bar alone ought to yield me that sum. A man with a wife and children very naturally tries to do as well by them as possible."

"Very true; but," I ventured to suggest, "will this be doing as well by them as if you had kept on at the mill?"

"Two or three thousand dollars a year against one thousand! Where are your figures, man?"

"There may be something beyond the money to take into the account," said I.

"What?" inquired Slade, with a kind of half credulity.

"Consider the different influences of the two callings in life—that of a miller and a tavern-keeper."

"Well! say on."

"Will your children be as safe from temptation here as in their former home?"

"Just as safe," was the unhesitating answer. "Why not?"

I was about to speak of the alluring glass in the case of Frank, but remembering that I had already expressed a fear in that direction, felt that to do so again would be useless, and so kept silent.

"A tavern-keeper," said Slade, "is just as respectable as a miller—in fact, the very people who used to call me 'Simon,' or 'Neighbour Dustycoat,' now say 'Landlord,' or Mr. Slade, and treat me in every way more as if I were an equal than ever they did before."

"The change," said I, "may be due to the fact of your giving evidence of possessing some means. Men are very apt to be courteous to those who have property. The building of the tavern has, without doubt, contributed to the new estimation in which you are held."

"That isn't all," replied the landlord. "It is because I am keeping a good tavern, and thus materially advancing the interests of Cedarville, that some of our best people look at me with different eyes."

"Advancing the interests of Cedarville! In what way?" I did not apprehend his meaning.

"A good tavern always draws people to a place, while a miserable old tumbledown of an affair, badly kept, such as we have had for years, as surely repels them. You can generally tell something about the condition of a town by looking at its taverns. If they are well kept, and doing a good business, you will hardly be wrong in the conclusion that the place is thriving. Why, already, since I built and opened the 'Sickle and Sheaf,' property has advanced over twenty per cent. along the whole street, and not less than five new houses have been commenced."

"Other causes, besides the simple opening of a new tavern, may have contributed to this result," said I.

"None of which I am aware. I was talking with Judge Hammond only yesterday—he owns a great deal of ground on the street—and he did not hesitate to say, that the building and opening of a good tavern here had increased the value of his property at least five thousand dollars. He said, moreover, that he thought the people of Cedarville ought to present me with a silver pitcher; and that, for one, he would contribute ten dollars for the purpose."

The ringing of the supper bell here interrupted further conversation; and with the best of appetites, I took my way to the room, where a plentiful meal was spread. As I entered, I met the wife of Simon Slade, just passing out, after seeing that every thing was in order. I had not observed her before; and now could not help remarking that she had a flushed, excited countenance, as if she had been over a hot fire, and was both worried and fatigued. And there was, moreover, a peculiar expression of the mouth, never observed in one whose mind is entirely at ease—an expression that once seen is never forgotten. The face stamped itself, instantly, on my memory; and I can even now recall it with almost the original distinctness. How strongly it contrasted with that of her smiling, self-satisfied husband, who took his place at the head of his table with an air of conscious importance. I was too hungry to talk much, and so found greater enjoyment in eating than in conversation. The landlord had a more chatty guest by his side, and I left them to entertain each other, while I did ample justice to the excellent food with which the table was liberally provided.

After supper I went to the sitting-room, and remained there until the lamps were lighted. A newspaper occupied my time for perhaps half an hour; then the buzz of voices from the adjoining bar-room, which had been increasing for some time, attracted my attention, and I went in there to see and hear what was passing. The first person upon whom my eyes rested was young Hammond, who sat talking with a man older than himself by several years. At a glance, I saw that this man could only associate himself with Willy Hammond as a tempter. Unscrupulous selfishness was written all over his sinister countenance; and I wondered that it did not strike every one, as it did me, with instant repulsion. There could not be, I felt certain, any common ground

of association, for two such persons, but the dead level
of a village bar-room. I afterward learned, during the
evening, that this man's name was Harvey Green, and
that he was an occasional visitor at Cedarville, remaining
a few days, or a few weeks at a time, as appeared to suit
his fancy, and having no ostensible business or special
acquaintance with anybody in the village.

"There is one thing about him," remarked Simon
Slade, in answering some question that I put in reference
to the man, "that I don't object to; he has plenty of
money, and is not at all niggardly in spending it. He
used to come here, so he told me, about once in five or
six months; but his stay at the miserably kept tavern,
the only one then in Cedarville, was so uncomfortable,
that he had pretty well made up his mind never to visit
us again. Now, however, he has engaged one of my
best rooms, for which he pays me by the year, and I am
to charge him full board for the time he occupies it. He
says that there is something about Cedarville that always attracts him; and that his health is better while
here than it is anywhere, except South during the winter season. He'll not leave less than two or three hundred dollars a year in our village—there is one item, for
you, of advantage to a place in having a good tavern."

"What is his business?" I asked. "Is he engaged
in any trading operations?"

The landlord shrugged his shoulders, and looked slightly mysterious, as he answered—

"I never inquire about the business of a guest. My calling is to entertain strangers. If they are pleased with my house, and pay my bills on presentation, I have no right to seek further. As a miller, I never asked a customer whether he raised, bought, or stole his wheat. It was my business to grind it, and I took care to do it well. Beyond that, it was all his own affair. And so it will be in my new calling. I shall mind my own business and keep my own place."

Besides young Hammond and this Harvey Green, there were, in the bar-room, when I entered, four others besides the landlord. Among these was a Judge Lyman, —so he was addressed—a man between forty and fifty years of age, who had a few weeks before received the Democratic nomination for member of Congress. He was very talkative and very affable, and soon formed a kind of centre of attraction to the bar-room circle. Among other topics of conversation that came up was the new tavern, introduced by the landlord, in whose mind it was, very naturally, the uppermost thought.

"The only wonder to me is," said Judge Lyman, "that nobody had wit enough to see the advantage of a good tavern in Cedarville ten years ago, or enterprise enough to start one. I give our friend Slade the credit of being a shrewd, far-seeing man; and, mark my word for it, in ten years from to-day he will be the richest man in the county."

"Nonsense—Ho! ho!" Simon Slade laughed outright. "The richest man! You forget Judge Hammond."

"No, not even Judge Hammond, with all deference for our clever friend Willy"—and Judge Lyman smiled pleasantly on the young man.

"If he gets richer, somebody will be poorer!" The individual who uttered these words had not spoken before; and I turned to look at him more closely. A glance showed him to be one of a class seen in all bar-rooms; a poor, broken-down inebriate, with the inward power of resistance gone—conscious of having no man's respect, and giving respect to none. There was a shrewd twinkle in his eyes, as he fixed them on Slade, that gave added force to the peculiar tone in which his brief, but telling sentence was uttered. I noticed a slight contraction on the landlord's ample forehead, the first evidence I had yet seen of ruffled feelings. The remark, thrown in so untimely, (or, timely, some will say,) and with a kind of prophetic malice, produced a temporary pause in the conversation. No one answered, or questioned the intruder, who, I could perceive, silently enjoyed the effect of his words. But soon the obstructed current ran on again.

"If our excellent friend, Mr. Slade," said Harvey Green, "is not the richest man in Cedarville at the end of ten years, he will at least enjoy the satisfaction of having made his town richer."

"A true word that," replied Judge Lyman—"as true a word as ever was spoken. What a dead-and-alive place this has been until within the last few months. All vigorous growth had stopped, and we were actually going to seed."

"And the graveyard too"—muttered the individual who had before disturbed the self-satisfied harmony of the company, remarking upon the closing sentence of Harvey Green. "Come, landlord," he added, as he strode across to the bar, speaking in a changed, reckless sort of a way, "fix me up a good hot whisky-punch, and do it right; and there's another sixpence toward the fortune you are bound to make. It's the last one left— not a copper more in my pockets"—and he turned them inside-out, with a half-solemn, half-ludicrous air. "I send it to keep company in your till with four others that have found their way into that snug place since morning, and which will be lonesome without their little friend."

I looked at Simon Slade, his eyes rested on mine for a moment or two, and then sunk beneath my earnest gaze. I saw that his countenance flushed, and that his motions were slightly confused. The incident, it was plain, did not awaken agreeable thoughts. Once I saw his hand move toward the sixpence, that lay upon the counter; but, whether to push it back, or draw it toward the till, I could not determine. The whisky-punch was in due time ready, and with it the man retired to a table across the room, and sat down to enjoy the tempting beverage. As he did so, the landlord quietly swept the poor unfortunate's last sixpence into his drawer. The influence of this strong potation was to render the man a little more talkative. To the free conversation passing around him he lent an attentive ear, dropping in a word, now and then, that always told upon the company like a well-directed blow. At last, Slade lost all patience with him, and said, a little fretfully,—

"Look here, Joe Morgan, if you will be ill-natured, pray go somewhere else, and not interrupt good feeling among gentlemen."

"Got my last sixpence," retorted Joe, turning his pockets inside-out again. "No more use for me here to-night. That's the way of the world. How apt a scholar is our good friend Dustycoat, in this new school! Well, he was a good miller—no one ever disputed that—and it's plain to see that he is going to make a good land-lord. I thought his heart was a little too soft; but the indurating process has begun; and, in less than ten years, if it isn't as hard as one of his old millstones, Joe Morgan is no prophet. Oh, you needn't knit your brows so, friend Simon, we're old friends; and friends are privileged to speak plain."

"I wish you'd go home. You're not yourself, to-night," said the landlord, a little coaxingly—for he saw that nothing was to be gained by quarrelling with Morgan. "Maybe my heart *is* growing harder," he added, with affected-good humour; "and it is time, perhaps. One of my weaknesses, I have heard even you say, was being too woman-hearted."

"No danger of that now," retorted Joe Morgan. "I've known a good many landlords in my time, but can't remember one that was troubled with the disease that once afflicted you."

Just at this moment the outer door was pushed open with a slow, hesitating motion; then a little pale face peered in, and a pair of soft blue eyes went searching about the room. Conversation was instantly hushed, and every face, excited with interest, turned toward the child, who had now stepped through the door. She was not over ten years of age; but it moved the heart to look upon the saddened expression of her young countenance, and the forced bravery therein, that scarcely overcame the native timidity so touchingly visible.

"Father!" I have never heard this word spoken in a voice that sent such a thrill along every nerve. It was full of sorrowful love—full of a tender concern that had its origin too deep for the heart of a child. As she spoke, the little one sprang across the room, and laying her hands upon the arm of Joe Morgan, lifted her eyes, that were ready to gush over with tears, to his face.

"Come, father! won't you come home?" I hear that low, pleading voice even now, and my heart gives a quicker throb. Poor child! Darkly shadowed was the sky that bent gloomily over thy young life.

Morgan arose, and suffered the child to lead him from the room. He seemed passive in her hands. I noticed that he thrust his fingers nervously into his pocket, and that a troubled look went over his face as they were withdrawn. His last sixpence was in the till of Simon Slade!

The first man who spoke was Harvey Green, and this not for a minute after the father and his child had vanished through the door.

"If I was in your place, landlord"—his voice was cold and unfeeling—"I'd pitch that fellow out of the bar-room the next time he stepped through the door. He's no business here, in the first place; and, in the second, he doesn't know how to behave himself. There's no telling how much a vagabond like him injures a respectable house."

"I wish he would stay away," said Simon, with a perplexed air.

"I'd *make* him stay away," answered Green.

"That may be easier said than done," remarked Judge Lyman. "Our friend keeps a public-house, and can't just say who shall or who shall not come into it."

"But such a fellow has no business here. He's a good-for-nothing sot. If I kept a tavern, I'd refuse to sell him liquor."

"That you might do," said Judge Lyman—"and I presume your hint will not be lost on our friend Slade."

"He will have liquor, so long as he can get a cent to

buy it with," remarked one of the company; "and I don't see why our landlord here, who has gone to so much expense to fit up a tavern, shouldn't have the sale of it as well as anybody else. Joe talks a little freely sometimes; but no one can say that he is quarrelsome. You've got to take him as he is, that's all."

"I'm one," retorted Harvey Green, with a slightly ruffled manner, "who is never disposed to take people as they are when they choose to render themselves disagreeable. If I was Mr. Slade, as I remarked in the beginning, I'd pitch that fellow into the road the next time he put his foot over my door-step."

"Not if I were present," remarked the other coolly.

Green was on his feet in a moment; and I saw, from the flash of his eyes, that he was a man of evil passions. Moving a pace or two in the direction of the other, he said sharply—

"What is that, sir?"

The individual against whom his anger was so suddenly aroused was dressed plainly, and had the appearance of a working-man. He was stout and muscular.

"I presume you heard my words. They were spoken distinctly," he replied, not moving from where he sat, nor seeming to be in the least disturbed. But there was cool defiance in the tones of his voice and in the steady look of his eyes.

"You're an impertinent fellow, and I'm half tempted to chastise you."

Green had scarcely finished the sentence, ere he was lying at full length upon the floor! The other had sprung upon him like a tiger, and with one blow from his heavy fist, struck him down as if he had been a child. For a moment or two, Green lay stunned and bewildered—then, starting up with a savage cry, that sounded more bestial than human, he drew a long knife from a concealed sheath, and attempted to stab his assailant; but the murderous purpose was not accomplished, for the other man, who had superior strength and coolness, saw the design, and with a well-directed blow almost broke the arm of Green, causing the knife to leave his hand and glide far across the room.

" I'm half tempted to wring your neck off," exclaimed the man, whose name was Lyon, now much excited; and seizing Green by the throat, he strangled him until his face grew black. "Draw a knife on me, ha! You murdering villain!" And he gripped him tighter.

Judge Lyman and the landlord now interfered, and rescued Green from the hands of his fully aroused antagonist. For some time they stood growling at each other, like two parted dogs, struggling to get free, in order to renew the conflict, but gradually cooled off. In a little while Judge Lyman drew Green aside, and the two men left the bar-room together. In the door, as they were retiring, the former slightly nodded to Willy Hammond, who soon followed them, going into the sitting-room; and from thence, as I could perceive, up-stairs, to an apartment above.

"Not after much good," I heard Lyon mutter to him-self. "If Judge Hammond don't look a little closer after that boy of his, he'll be sorry for it, that's all."

"Who is this Green?" I asked of Lyon, finding my-self alone with him in the bar-room, soon after.

"A black-leg, I take it," was his unhesitating answer.

"Does Judge Lyman suspect his real character?"

"I don't know any thing about that; but, I wouldn't be afraid to bet ten dollars, that if you could look in upon them now, you would find cards in their hands."

"What a school, and what teachers for the youth who just went with them!" I could not help remarking.

"Willy Hammond?"

"Yes."

"You may well say that. What can his father be thinking about to leave him exposed to such influences!"

"He's one of the few who are in raptures about this tavern, because its erection has slightly increased the value of his property about here; but, if he is not the loser of fifty per cent. for every one gained, before ten years go by, I'm very much in error."

"How so?"

"It will prove, I fear, the open door to ruin for his son."

"That's bad," said I.

"Bad! It is awful to think of. There is not a finer

young man in the country; nor one with better mind and heart than Willy Hammond. So much the sadder will be his destruction. Ah, sir! this tavern-keeping is a curse to any place."

"But I thought, just now, that you spoke in favour of letting even the poor drunkard's money go into our landlord's till, in order to encourage his commendable enterprise in opening so good a tavern."

"We all speak with covert irony sometimes," answered the man, "as I did then. Poor Joe Morgan! He is an old and early friend of Simon Slade. They were boys together, and worked as millers under the same roof for many years. In fact, Joe's father owned the mill, and the two learned their trade with him. When old Morgan died, the mill came into Joe's hands. It was in rather a worn-out condition, and Joe went in debt for some pretty thorough repairs and additions of machinery. By and by, Simon Slade, who was hired by Joe to run the mill, received a couple of thousand dollars at the death of an aunt. This sum enabled him to buy a share in the mill, which Morgan was very glad to sell in order to get clear of his debt. Time passed on, and Joe left his milling interest almost entirely in the care of Slade, who, it must be said in his favour, did not neglect the business. But it somehow happened— I will not say unfairly—that, at the end of ten years, Joe Morgan no longer owned a share in the mill. The whole property was in the hands of Slade. People did

not much wonder at this; for while Slade was always
to be found at the mill, industrious, active, and attentive to customers, Morgan was rarely seen on the premises. You would oftener find him in the woods, with a
gun over his shoulder, or sitting by a trout brook, or
lounging at the tavern. And yet everybody liked Joe;
for he was companionable, quick-witted, and very kind-
hearted. He would say sharp things, sometimes, when
people manifested little meannesses; but there was so
much honey in his gall, that bitterness rarely predo-
minated.

"A year or two before his ownership in the mill
ceased, Morgan married one of the sweetest girls in our
town—Fanny Ellis, that was her name, and she could
have had her pick of the young men. Everybody affected to wonder at her choice; and yet nobody really
did wonder, for Joe was an attractive young man, take
him as you would, and just the one to win the heart of
a girl like Fanny. What if he had been seen, now and
then, a little the worse for drink! What if he showed
more fondness for pleasure than for business! Fanny
did not look into the future with doubt or fear. She
believed that her love was strong enough to win him
from all evil allurements; and, as for this world's goods,
they were matters in which her maiden fancies rarely
busied themselves.

"Well. Dark days came for her, poor soul! And
yet, in all the darkness of her earthly lot, she has never,

it is said, been any thing but a loving, forbearing, self-denying wife to Morgan. And he—fallen as he is, and powerless in the grasp of the monster intemperance—has never, I am sure, hurt her with a cruel word. Had he added these, her heart would, long ere this, have broken. Poor Joe Morgan! Poor Fanny! Oh, what a curse is this drink!"

The man, warming with his theme, had spoken with an eloquence I had not expected from his lips. Slightly overmastered by his feelings, he paused for a moment or two, and then added.

"It was unfortunate for Joe, at least, that Slade sold his mill, and became a tavern-keeper; for Joe had a sure berth, and wages regularly paid. He didn't always stick to his work, but would go off on a spree every now and then; but Slade bore with all this, and worked harder himself to make up for his hand's shortcoming. And no matter what deficiency the little store-room at home might show, Fanny Morgan never found her meal barrel empty without knowing where to get it replenished.

"But, after Slade sold the mill, a sad change took place. The new owner was little disposed to pay wages to a hand who would not give him all his time during working hours; and in less than two weeks from the day he took possession, Morgan was discharged. Since then, he has been working about at one odd job and another, earning scarcely enough to buy the liquor it

requires to feed the inordinate thirst that is consuming
him. I am not disposed to blame Simon Slade for the
wrong-doing of Morgan; but here is a simple fact in the
case—if he had kept on at the useful calling of a miller,
he would have saved this man's family from want, suffering, and a lower deep of misery than that into
which they have already fallen. I merely state it, and
you can draw your own conclusion. It is one of the
many facts, on the other side of this tavern question,
which it will do no harm to mention. I have noted a
good many facts besides, and one is, that before Slade
opened the "Sickle and Sheaf," he did all in his power
to save his early friend from the curse of intemperance;
now he has become his tempter. Heretofore, it was his
hand that provided the means for his family to live in
some small degree of comfort; now he takes the poor
pittance the wretched man earns, and dropping it in his
till, forgets the wife and children at home who are
hungry for the bread this money should have purchased.

"Joe Morgan, fallen as he is, sir, is no fool. His
mind sees quickly yet; and he rarely utters a sentiment
that is not full of meaning. When he spoke of Slade's
heart growing as hard in ten years as one of his old mill-
stones, he was not uttering words at random, nor merely
indulging in a harsh sentiment, little caring whether it
were closely applicable or not. That the indurating
process had begun, he, alas! was too sadly conscious."

The landlord had been absent from the room for

some time. He left soon after Judge Lyman, Harvey Green, and Willy Hammond withdrew, and I did not see him again during the evening. His son Frank was left to attend at the bar; no very hard task, for not more than half a dozen called in to drink from the time Morgan left until the bar was closed.

While Mr. Lyon was giving me the brief history just recorded, I noticed a little incident that caused a troubled feeling to pervade my mind. After a man, for whom the landlord's son had prepared a fancy drink, had nearly emptied his glass, he sat it down upon the counter and went out. A tablespoonful or two remained in the glass, and I noticed Frank, after smelling at it two or three times, put the glass to his lips and sip the sweetened liquor. The flavour proved agreeable; for after tasting it, he raised the glass again and drained every drop.

"Frank!" I heard a low voice, in a warning tone, pronounce the name, and glancing toward a door partly opened, that led from the inside of the bar to the yard, I saw the face of Mrs. Slade. It had the same troubled expression I had noticed before, but now blended with more of anxiety.

The boy went out at the call of his mother; and when a new customer entered, I noticed that Flora, the daughter, came in to wait upon him. I noticed, too, that while she poured out the liquor, there was a heightened colour on her face, in which I fancied that I saw

a tinge of shame. It is certain that she was not in the
least gracious to the person on whom she was waiting;
and that there was little heart in her manner of per-
forming the task.

Ten o'clock found me alone and musing in the bar-
room over the occurrences of the evening. Of all the
incidents, that of the entrace of Joe Morgan's child
kept the most prominent place in my thoughts. The
picture of that mournful little face was ever before me;
and I seemed all the while to hear the word "Father,"
uttered so touchingly, and yet with such a world of
childish tenderness. And the man, who would have
opposed the most stubborn resistance to his fellow men,
had they sought to force him from the room, going pas-
sively, almost meekly out, led by that little child—I
could not, for a time, turn my thoughts from the image
thereof! And then thought bore me to the wretched
home, back to which the gentle, loving child had taken
her father, and my heart grew faint in me as imagination busied itself with all the misery there.

And Willy Hammond. The little that I had heard
and seen of him greatly interested me in his favour.
Ah! upon what dangerous ground was he treading.
How many pitfalls awaited his feet—how near they were
to the brink of a fearful precipice, down which to fall
was certain destruction. How beautiful had been his
life-promise! How fair the opening day of his exist-
ence! Alas! the clouds were gathering already, and

the low rumble of the distant thunder presaged the
coming of a fearful tempest. Was there none to warn
him of the danger? Alas! all might now come too
late, for so few who enter the path in which his steps were
treading will hearken to friendly counsel, or heed the
solemn warning. Where was he now? This question
recurred over and over again. He had left the bar-
room with Judge Lyman and Green early in the evening, and had not made his appearance since. Who and
what was Green? And Judge Lyman, was he a man
of principle? One with whom it was safe to trust a youth
like Willy Hammond?

While I mused thus, the bar-room door opened, and a
man past the prime of life, with a somewhat florid face,
which gave a strong relief to the gray, almost white hair
that, suffered to grow freely, was pushed back, and lay
in heavy masses on his coat collar, entered with a hasty
step. He was almost venerable in appearance; yet,
there was in his dark, quick eyes the brightness of un-
quenched loves, the fires of which were kindled at the
altars of selfishness and sensuality. This I saw at a
glance. There was a look of concern on his face, as
he threw his eyes around the bar-room; and he seemed
disappointed, I thought, at finding it empty.

"Is Simon Slade here?"

As I answered in the negative, Mrs. Slade entered
through the door that opened from the yard, and stood
behind the counter.

" Ah, Mrs. Slade ! Good evening, madam !" he said.

" Good evening, Judge Hammond."

" Is your husband at home ?"

" I believe he is," answered Mrs. Slade. " I think he's somewhere about the house."

" Ask him to step here, will you ?"

Mrs. Slade went out. Nearly five minutes went by, during which time Judge Hammond paced the floor of the bar-room uneasily. Then the landlord made his appearance. The free, open, manly, self-satisfied expression of his countenance, which I had remarked on alighting from the stage in the afternoon, was gone. I noticed at once the change, for it was striking. He did not look steadily into the face of Judge Hammond, who asked him in a low voice, if his son had been there during the evening.

" He was here," said Slade.

" When ?"

" He came in some time after dark and stayed, maybe, an hour."

" And hasn't been here since ?"

" It's nearly two hours since he left the bar-room," replied the landlord.

Judge Hammond seemed perplexed. There was a degree of evasion in Slade's manner that he could hardly help noticing. To me it was all apparent, for I had lively suspicions that made my observation acute.

Judge Hammond crossed his arms behind him, and took three or four strides about the floor.

"Was Judge Lyman here to-night?" he then asked.

"He was," answered Slade.

"Did he and Willy go out together?"

The question seemed an unexpected one for the landlord. Slade appeared slightly confused, and did not answer promptly.

"I—I rather think they did," he said, after a brief hesitation.

"Ah, well! Perhaps he is at Judge Lyman's. I will call over there."

And Judge Hammond left the bar-room.

"Would you like to retire, sir?" said the landlord, now turning to me, with a forced smile—I saw that it was forced.

"If you please," I answered.

He lit a candle and conducted me to my room, where, overwearied with the day's exertion, I soon fell asleep, and did not awake until the sun was shining brightly into my windows.

I remained at the village a portion of the day, but saw nothing of the parties in whom the incidents of the previous evening had awakened a lively interest. At four o'clock I left in the stage, and did not visit Cedarville again for a year.

NIGHT THE SECOND.

The Changes of a Year.

A cordial grasp of the hand and a few words of hearty welcome greeted me as I alighted from the stage at the "Sickle and Sheaf," on my next visit to Cedarville. At the first glance, I saw no change in the countenance, manner, or general bearing of Simon Slade, the landlord. With him, the year seemed to have passed like a pleasant summer day. His face was round, and full, and rosy, and his eyes sparkled with that good-humour which flows from intense self-satisfaction. Every thing about him seemed to say—"All right with myself and the world."

I had scarcely expected this. From what I saw during my last brief sojourn at the "Sickle and Sheaf," the inference was natural, that elements had been called into activity, which must produce changes adverse to those pleasant states of mind that threw an almost perpetual sunshine over the landlord's countenance. How many hundred of times had I thought of Joe Morgan and Willy Hammond—of Frank, and the temptations to which a bar-room exposed him. The heart of Slade

4

must, indeed, be as hard as one of his old mill-stones, if he could remain an unmoved witness of the corruption and degradation of these.

" My fears have outrun the actual progress of things," said I to myself, with a sense of relief, as I mused alone in the still neatly arranged sitting-room, after the land-lord, who sat and chatted for a few minutes, had left me. "There is, I am willing to believe, a basis of good in this man's character, which has led him to remove, as far as possible, the more palpable evils that ever attach themselves to a house of public entertainment. He had but entered on the business last year. There was much to be learned, pondered, and corrected. Experience, I doubt not, has led to many important changes in the manner of conducting the establishment, and especially in what pertains to the bar."

As I thought thus, my eyes glanced through the half open door, and rested on the face of Simon Slade. He was standing behind his bar—evidently alone in the room—with his head bent in a musing attitude. At first I was in some doubt as to the identity of the singularly changed countenance. Two deep perpendicular seams lay sharply defined on his forehead—the arch of his eyebrows was gone, and from each corner of his compressed lips, lines were seen reaching halfway to the chin. Blending with a slightly troubled expression, was a strongly marked selfishness, evidently brooding over the consummation of its purpose. For some moments I sat gazing on this face, half doubting at times if it were really that of Simon Slade. Suddenly, a gleam flashed over it—an ejaculation was uttered, and one clenched hand brought down, with a sharp stroke, into the open palm of the other. The landlord's mind had reached a conclusion, and was resolved upon action. There were no warm rays in the gleam of light that irradiated his countenance—at least none for my heart, which felt under them an almost icy coldness.

"Just the man I was thinking about," I heard the landlord say, as some one entered the bar, while his whole manner underwent a sudden change.

"The old saying is true," was answered in a voice, the tones of which were familiar to my ears.

"Thinking of the old Harry?" said Slade.

"Yes."

"True, literally, in the present case," I heard the landlord remark, though in a much lower tone; "for, if you are not the devil himself, you can't be farther removed than a second cousin."

A low, gurgling laugh met this little sally. There was something in it so unlike a human laugh, that it caused my blood to trickle, for a moment, coldly along my veins.

I heard nothing more except the murmur of voices in the bar, for a hand shut the partly opened door that led from the sitting-room.

Whose was that voice? I recalled its tones, and tried

to fix in my thought the person to whom it belonged, but was unable to do so. I was not very long in doubt, for on stepping out upon the porch in front of the tavern, the well-remembered face of Harvey Green presented itself. He stood in the bar-room door, and was talking earnestly to Slade, whose back was toward me. I saw that he recognised me, although I had not passed a word with him on the occasion of my former visit; and there was a lighting up of his countenance as if about to speak—but I withdrew my eyes from his face to avoid the unwelcome greeting. When I looked at him again, I saw that he was regarding me with a sinister glance, which was instantly withdrawn. In what broad, black characters was the word TEMPTER written on his face! How was it possible for any one to look thereon, and not read the warning inscription!

Soon after, he withdrew into the bar-room, and the landlord came and took a seat near me on the porch.

"How is the Sickle and Sheaf coming on?" I inquired.

"First-rate," was the answer—"First-rate."

"As well as you expected?"

"Better."

"Satisfied with your experiment."

"Perfectly. Couldn't get me back to the rumbling old mill again, if you were to make me a present of it."

"What of the mill?" I asked. "How does the new owner come on?"

"About as I thought it would be."

"Not doing very well?"

"How could it be expected, when he didn't know enough of the milling business to grind a bushel of wheat right. He lost half of the custom I transferred to him in less than three months. Then he broke his main shaft, and it took over three weeks to get in a new one. Half of his remaining customers discovered by this time, that they could get far better meal from their grain at Harwood's mill near Lynwood, and so did not care to trouble him any more. The upshot of the whole matter is, he broke down next, and had to sell the mill at a heavy loss."

"Who has it now?"

"Judge Hammond is the purchaser."

"He is going to rent it, I suppose?"

"No; I believe he means to turn it into some kind of a factory—and, I rather think, will connect therewith a distillery. This is a fine grain-growing country, as you know. If he does set up a distillery, he'll make a fine thing of it. Grain has been too low in this section for some years: this all the farmers have felt, and they are very much pleased at the idea. It will help them wonderfully. I always thought my mill a great thing for the farmers; but what I did for them was a mere song compared to the advantage of an extensive distillery."

"Judge Hammond is one of your richest men?"

"Yes—the richest in the county. And what is

4*

more, he's a shrewd, far-seeing man, and knows how to multiply his riches."

"How is his son Willy coming on?"

"Oh! first-rate."

The landlord's eyes fell under the searching look I bent upon him.

"How old is he now?"

"Just twenty."

"A critical age," I remarked.

"So people say; but I didn't find it so," answered Slade, a little distantly.

"The impulses within and the temptations without, are the measure of its dangers. At his age, you were, no doubt, daily employed at hard work."

"I was, and no mistake."

"Thousands and hundred of thousands are indebted to useful work, occupying many hours through each day, and leaving them with wearied bodies at night, for their safe passage from yielding youth to firm, resisting manhood. It might not be with you as it is now, had leisure and freedom to go in and out when you pleased, been offered at the age of nineteen."

"I can't tell as to that," said the landlord, shrugging his shoulders. "But I don't see that Willy Hammond is in any especial danger. He is a young man with many admirable qualities—is social—liberal—generous almost to a fault—but has good common sense, and wit enough, I take it, to keep out of harm's way."

A man passing the house at the moment, gave Simon Slade an opportunity to break off a conversation, that was not, I could see, altogether agreeable. As he left me, I arose and stepped into the bar-room. Frank, the landlord's son, was behind the bar. He had grown considerably in the year—and from a rather delicate, innocent-looking boy, to a stout, bold lad. His face was rounder, and had a gross, sensual expression, that showed itself particularly about the mouth. The man Green was standing beside the bar talking to him, and I noticed that Frank laughed heartily, at some low, half obscene remarks that he was making. In the midst of these, Flora, the sister of Frank, a really beautiful girl, came in to get something from the bar. Green spoke to her familiarly, and Flora answered him with a perceptibly heightening colour.

I glanced toward Frank, half expecting to see an indignant flush on his young face. But no—he looked on with a smile! "Ah!" thought I, "have the boy's pure impulses so soon died out in this fatal atmosphere? Can he bear to see those evil eyes—he knows they are evil—rest upon the face of his sister? or to hear those lips, only a moment since polluted with vile words, address her with the familiarity of a friend?"

"Fine girl, that sister of yours, Frank! Fine girl!" said Green, after Flora had withdrawn—speaking of her with about as much respect in his voice as if he were praising a fleet racer or favourite hound.

The boy smiled, with a pleased air.

"I must try and find her a good husband, Frank. I wonder if she wouldn't have me?"

"You'd better ask her," said the boy, laughing.

"I would, if I thought there was any chance for me."

"Nothing like trying. Faint heart never won fair lady," returned Frank, more with the air of a man than a boy. How fast he was growing old!

"A banter, by George!" exclaimed Green, slapping his hands together. "You're a great boy, Frank! a great boy! I shall have to talk to your father about you. Coming on too fast. Have to be put back in your lessons—hey!"

And Green winked at the boy, and shook his finger at him. Frank laughed in a pleased way, as he replied—

"I guess I'll do."

"I guess you will," said Green, as, satisfied with his colloquy, he turned off and left the bar-room.

"Have something to drink, sir?" inquired Frank, addressing me in a bold, free way.

I shook my head.

"Here's a newspaper," he added.

I took the paper and sat down—not to read, but to observe. Two or three men soon came in, and spoke in a very familiar way to Frank, who was presently busy setting out the liquors they had called for. Their conversation, interlarded with much that was profane and vulgar, was of horses, horse-racing, gunning, and the like, to all of which the young bar-keeper lent an attentive ear, putting in a word now and then, and showing an intelligence in such matters quite beyond his age. In the midst thereof, Mr. Slade made his appearance. His presence caused a marked change in Frank, who retired from his place among the men, a step or two outside of the bar, and did not make a remark while his father remained. It was plain from this, that Mr. Slade was not only aware of Frank's dangerous precocity, but had already marked his forwardness by rebuke.

So far, all that I had seen and heard impressed me unfavourably, notwithstanding the declaration of Simon Slade, that every thing about the "Sickle and Sheaf" was coming on "first-rate," and that he was "perfectly satisfied" with his experiment. Why, even if the man had gained, in money, fifty thousand dollars by tavern-keeping in a year, he had lost a jewel in the innocence of his boy that was beyond all valuation. "Perfectly satisfied?" Impossible! He was not perfectly satisfied. How could he be? The look thrown upon Frank when he entered the bar-room, and saw him "hale fellow, well met," with three or four idle, profane, drinking customers, contradicted that assertion.

After supper, I took a seat in the bar-room, to see how life moved on in that place of rendezvous for the surface-population of Cedarville. Interest enough in the characters I had met there a year before remained, for me to choose this way of spending the time, instead of visiting at the house of a gentleman who had kindly invited me to pass an evening with his family.

The bar-room custom, I soon found, had largely increased in a year. It now required, for a good part of the time, the active services of both the landlord and his son to meet the calls for liquor. What pained me most, was to see the large number of lads and young men who came in to lounge and drink; and there was scarcely one of them whose face did not show marks of sensuality, or whose language was not marred by obscenity, profanity, or vulgar slang. The subjects of conversation were varied enough, though politics was the most prominent. In regard to politics, I heard nothing in the least instructive; but only abuse of individuals and dogmatism on public measures. They were all exceedingly confident in assertion; but I listened in vain for exposition, or even for demonstrative facts. He who asseverated in the most positive manner, and swore the hardest, carried the day in the petty contests.

I noticed, early in the evening, and at a time when all the inmates of the room were in the best possible humour with themselves, the entrance of an elderly man, on whose face I instantly read a deep concern. It was one of those mild, yet strongly marked faces, that strike you at a glance. The forehead was broad, the eyes large and far back in their sockets, the lips full but firm. You saw evidences of a strong, but well balanced character. As he came in, I noticed a look of intelligence pass from one to another; and then the eyes of two or three were fixed upon a young man who was seated not far from me, with his back to the entrance, playing at dominoes. He had a glass of ale by his side. The old man searched about the room for some moments, before his glance rested upon the individual I have mentioned. My eyes were full upon his face, as he advanced toward him, yet unseen. Upon it was not a sign of angry excitement, but a most touching sorrow.

"Edward!" he said, as he laid his hand gently on the young man's shoulder. The latter started at the voice, and crimsoned deeply. A few moments he sat irresolute.

"Edward, my son!" It would have been a cold, hard heart indeed that softened not under the melting tenderness of these tones. The call was irresistible, and obedience a necessity. The powers of evil had, yet, too feeble a grasp on the young man's heart to hold him in thrall. Rising with a half-reluctant manner, and with a shamefacedness that it was impossible to conceal, he retired as quietly as possible. The notice of only a few in the bar-room was attracted by the incident.

"I can tell you what," I heard the individual, with whom the young man had been playing at dominos, remark—himself not twenty years of age—"if my old man were to make a fool of himself in this way—sneaking around after me in bar-rooms—he'd get only his trouble for his pains. I'd like to see him try it, though! There'd be a nice time of it, I guess. Wouldn't I creep off with him, as meek as a lamb! Ho! ho!"

"Who is that old gentleman who came in just now?" I inquired of the person who thus commented on the incident which had just occurred.

"Mr. Hargrove is his name."

"And that was his son?"

"Yes; and I'm only sorry he doesn't possess a little more spirit."

"How old is he?"

"About twenty."

"Not of legal age, then?"

"He's old enough to be his own master."

"The law says differently," I suggested.

In answer, the young man cursed the law, snapping his fingers in its imaginary face as he did so.

"At least you will admit," said I, "that Edward Hargrove, in the use of a liberty to go where he pleases, and do what he pleases, exhibits but small discretion."

"I will admit no such thing. What harm is there, I would like to know, in a social little game such as we were playing? There were no stakes—we were not gambling."

I pointed to the half-emptied glass of ale left by young Hargrove.

"Oh! oh!" half sneered, half laughed a man, twice the age of the one I had addressed, who sat near by, listening to our conversation. I looked at him for a moment, and then said—

"The great danger lies there, without doubt. If it were only a glass of ale and a game of dominos—but it doesn't stop there, and well the young man's father knows it."

"Perhaps he does," was answered. "I remember him in his younger days; and a pretty high boy he was. He didn't stop at a glass of ale and a game at dominos; not he! I've seen him as drunk as a lord many a time; and many a time at a horse-race, or cock-fight, betting with the bravest. I was only a boy, though a pretty old boy; but I can tell you, Hargrove was no saint."

"I wonder not, then, that he is anxious for his son," was my remark. "He knows well the lurking dangers in the path he seems inclined to enter."

"I don't see that they have done him much harm. He sowed his wild oats—then got married, and settled down into a good, substantial citizen. A little too religious and pharisaical, I always thought; but upright in his dealings. He had his pleasures in early life, as was befitting the season of youth—why not let his son taste of the same agreeable fruit? He's wrong, sir—wrong! And I've said as much to Ned. I only wish the boy had showed the right spunk this evening, and told the old man to go home about his business."

"So do I," chimed in the young disciple in this bad school. "It's what I'd say to my old man, in double-quick time, if he was to come hunting after me."

"He knows better than to do that," said the other, in a way that let me deeper into the young man's character.

"Indeed he does. He's tried his hand on me once or twice during the last year, but found it wouldn't do, no how; Tom Peters is out of his leading-strings."

"And can drink his glass with any one, and not be a grain the worse for it."

"Exactly, old boy!" said Peters, slapping his pre-ceptor on the knee. "Exactly! I'm not one of your weak-headed ones. Oh no!"

"Look here, Joe Morgan!"—the half angry voice of Simon Slade now rung through the bar-room,—"just take yourself off home!"

I had not observed the entrance of this person. He was standing at the bar, with an emptied glass in his hand. A year had made no improvement in his appear-ance. On the contrary, his clothes were more worn and tattered; his countenance more sadly marred. What he had said to irritate the landlord, I know not; but Slade's face was fiery with passion, and his eyes glared threat-eningly at the poor besotted one, who showed not the least inclination to obey.

"Off with you, I say! And never show your face here again. I won't have such low vagabonds as you are about my house. If you can't keep decent and stay decent, don't intrude yourself here."

"A rum-seller talk of decency!" retorted Morgan. "Pah! You were a decent man once, and a good miller into the bargain. But that time's past and gone. Decency died out when you exchanged the pick and facing-hammer for the glass and muddler. Decency! Pah! How you talk! As if it were any more decent to sell rum than to drink it."

There was so much of biting contempt in the tones, as well as the words of the half intoxicated man, that Slade, who had himself been drinking rather more freely than usual, was angered beyond self-control. Catching up an empty glass from the counter, he hurled it with all his strength at the head of Joe Morgan. The missive just grazed one of his temples, and flew by on its dangerous course. The quick sharp cry of a child startled the air, followed by exclamations of alarm and horror from many voices.

"It's Joe Morgan's child!" "He's killed her!" "Good heavens!" Such were the exclamations that rang through the room. I was among the first to reach the spot where a little girl, just gliding in through the door, had been struck on the forehead by the glass, which had cut a deep gash, and stunned her into insensibility. The blood flowed instantly from the wound, and covered her face, which presented a shocking appearance. As I lifted her from the floor, upon which she had fallen, Morgan, into whose very soul the piercing cry of his child had penetrated, stood by my side, and grappled his arms around her insensible form, uttering as he did so heart-touching moans and lamentations.

"What's the matter? Oh, what's the matter?"   It was a woman's voice, speaking in frightened tones.

"It's nothing! Just go out, will you, Ann!" I heard the landlord say.

But his wife—it was Mrs. Slade—having heard the shrieks of pain and terror uttered by Morgan's child, had come running into the bar-room—heeded not his words, but pressed forward into the little group that stood around the bleeding girl.

"Run for Doctor Green, Frank," she cried in an imperative voice, the moment her eyes rested on the little one's bloody face.

Frank came around from behind the bar, in obedience to the word; but his father gave a partial countermand, and he stood still. Upon observing which, his mother repeated the order, even more emphatically.

"Why don't you jump, you young rascal!" exclaimed Harvey Green. "The child may be dead before the doctor can get here."

Frank hesitated no longer, but disappeared instantly through the door.

"Poor, poor child!" Almost sobbed Mrs. Slade, as she lifted the insensible form from my arms. "How did it happen? Who struck her?"

"Who? Curse him! Who but Simon Slade?" answered Joe Morgan, through his clenched teeth.

The look of anguish, mingled with bitter reproach,

instantly thrown upon the landlord by his wife, can hardly be forgotten by any who saw it that night.

"Oh, Simon! Simon! And has it come to this already?" What a world of bitter memories, and sad forebodings of evil, did that little sentence express. "To this already"—Ah! In the downward way, how rapidly the steps do tread—how fast the progress!

"Bring me a basin of water, and a towel, quickly!" she now exclaimed.

The water was brought, and in a little while the face of the child lay pure and white as snow against her bosom. The wound from which the blood had flowed so freely was found on the upper part of the forehead, a little to the side, and extending several inches back, along the top of the head. As soon as the blood stains were wiped away, and the effusion partially stopped, Mrs. Slade carried the still insensible body into the next room, whither the distressed, and now completely sobered father, accompanied her. I went with them, but Slade remained behind.

The arrival of the doctor was soon followed by the restoration of life to the inanimate body. He happened to be at home, and came instantly. He had just taken the last stitch in the wound, which required to be drawn together, and was applying strips of adhesive plaster, when the hurried entrance of some one caused me to look up. What an apparition met my eyes! A woman stood in the door, with a face in which maternal anxiety and terror blended fearfully. Her countenance was like ashes—her eyes straining wildly—her lips apart, while the panting breath almost hissed through them.

"Joe! Joe! What is it? Where is Mary? Is she dead?" were her eager inquiries.

"No, Fanny," answered Joe Morgan, starting up from where he was actually kneeling by the side of the reviving little one, and going quickly to his wife. "She's better now. It's a bad hurt, but the doctor says it's nothing dangerous. Poor, dear child!"

The pale face of the mother grew paler—she gasped—caught for breath two or three times—a low shudder ran through her frame—and then she lay white and pulseless in the arms of her husband. As the doctor applied restoratives, I had opportunity to note more particularly the appearance of Mrs. Morgan. Her person was very slender, and her face so attenuated that it might almost be called shadowy. Her hair, which was a rich chestnut brown, with a slight golden lustre, had fallen from her comb, and now lay all over her neck and bosom in beautiful luxuriance. Back from her full temples it had been smoothed away by the hand of Morgan, that all the while moved over her brow and temples with a caressing motion that I saw was unconscious, and which revealed the tenderness of feeling with which, debased as he was, he regarded the wife of his youth, and the long suffering companion of his later and evil days. Her dress was plain and coarse, but clean and

well fitting; and about her whole person was an air of
neatness and taste. She could not now be called beautiful; yet in her marred features—marred by suffering and
grief—were many lineaments of beauty; and much that
told of a pure, true woman's heart beating in her bosom.
Life came slowly back to the stilled heart, and it was
nearly half an hour before the circle of motion was fully
restored.

Then, the twain, with their child, tenderly borne in
the arms of her father, went sadly homeward, leaving
more than one heart heavier for their visit.

I saw more of the landlord's wife on this occasion than
before. She had acted with a promptness and humanity
that impressed me very favourably. It was plain, from
her exclamations on learning that her husband's hand
inflicted the blow that came so near destroying the child's
life, that her faith for good in the tavern-keeping
experiment had never been strong. I had already
inferred as much. Her face, the few times I had seen
her, wore a troubled look; and I could never forget its
expression, nor her anxious, warning voice, when she
discovered Frank sipping the dregs from a glass in the
bar-room.

It is rarely, I believe, that wives consent freely to
the opening of taverns by their husbands; and the determination on the part of the latter to do so, is not un-
frequently attended with a breach of confidence and good
feeling, never afterward fully healed. Men look close

to the money result; women to the moral consequences. I doubt if there be one dram-seller in ten, between whom and his wife there exists a good understanding—to say nothing of genuine affection. And, in the exceptional cases, it will generally be found that the wife is as mercenary, or careless of the public good, as her husband. I have known some women to set up grog-shops; but they were women of bad principles and worse hearts. I remember one case, where a woman, with a sober, church-going husband, opened a dram-shop. The husband opposed, remonstrated, begged, threatened—but all to no purpose. The wife, by working for the clothing stores, had earned and saved about three hundred dollars. The love of money, in the slow process of accumulation, had been awakened; and, in ministering to the depraved appetites of men who loved drink and neglected their families, she saw a quicker mode of acquiring the gold she coveted. And so the dram-shop was opened. And what was the result? The husband quit going to church. He had no heart for that; for, even on the Sabbath-day, the fiery stream was stayed not in his house. Next he began to tipple. Soon, alas! the subtle poison so pervaded his system that morbid desire came; and then he moved along quick-footed in the way to ruin. In less than three years, I think, from the time the grog-shop was opened by his wife, he was in a drunkard's grave. A year or two more, and the pit that was digged for others by the hands of the wife, she fell into herself.

Ever breathing an atmosphere, poisoned by the fumes of liquor, the love of tasting it was gradually formed, and she too, in the end, became a slave to the Demon of Drink. She died, at last, poor as a beggar in the street. Ah! this liquor-selling is the way to ruin; and they who open the gates, as well as those who enter the downward path, alike go to destruction. But this is digressing.

After Joe Morgan and his wife left the "Sickle and Sheaf," with that gentle child, who, as I afterward learned, had not, for a year or more, laid her little head to sleep until her father returned home—and who, if he stayed out beyond a certain hour, would go for him, and lead him back, a very angel of love and patience—I re-entered the bar-room, to see how life was passing there. Not one of all I had left in the room remained. The incident which had occurred was of so painful a nature, that no further unalloyed pleasure was to be had there during the evening, and so each had retired. In his little kingdom the landlord sat alone, his head resting on his hand, and his face shaded from the light. The whole aspect of the man was that of one in self-humiliation. As I entered he raised his head, and turned his face toward me. Its expression was painful.

"Rather an unfortunate affair," said he. "I'm angry with myself, and sorry for the poor child. But she'd no business here. As for Joe Morgan, it would take a saint to bear his tongue when once set a going by liquor. I wish he'd stay away from the house. Nobody wants his company. Oh dear!

The ejaculation, or rather groan, that closed the sentence, showed how little Slade was satisfied with himself, notwithstanding this feeble effort at self-justification.

"His thirst for liquor draws him hither," I remarked. "The attraction of your bar to his appetite is like that of the magnet to the needle. He cannot stay away."

"He *must* stay away!" exclaimed the landlord, with some vehemence of tone, striking his fist upon the table by which he sat. "He *must* stay away! There is scarcely an evening that he does not ruffle my temper, and mar good feelings in all the company. Just see what he provoked me to do this evening. I might have killed the child. It makes my blood run cold to think of it! Yes, sir—he must stay away. If no better can be done, I'll hire a man to stand at the door and keep him out."

"He never troubled you at the mill," said I. "No man was required at the mill door?"

"No!" And the landlord gave emphasis to the word by an oath, ejaculated with a heartiness that almost startled me. I had not heard him swear before. "No! the great trouble was to get him and keep him there, the good-for-nothing, idle fellow!"

"I'm afraid," I ventured to suggest, "that things don't go on quite so smoothly here as they did at the mill. Your customers are of a different class."

"I don't know about that; why not?" He did not just relish my remark.

"Between quiet, thrifty, substantial farmers, and drinking bar-room loungers, are many degrees of comparison."

"Excuse me, sir!" Simon Slade elevated his person. "The men who visit my bar-room, as a general thing, are quite as respectable, moral, and substantial as any who came to the mill—and I believe more so. The first people in the place, sir, are to be found here. Judge Lyman and Judge Hammond; Lawyer Wilks and Doctor Maynard; Mr. Grand and Mr. Lee; and dozens of others—all our first people. No, sir; you mustn't judge all by vagabonds like Joe Morgan."

There was a testy spirit manifested that I did not care to provoke. I could have met his assertion with facts and inferences of a character to startle any one occupying his position, who was in a calm, reflective state; but to argue with him then would have been worse than idle: and so I let him talk on until the excitement occasioned by my words died out for want of new fuel.

NIGHT THE THIRD.

Joe Morgan's Child.

" I DON'T see any thing of your very particular friend, Joe Morgan, this evening," said Harvey Green, leaning on the bar and speaking to Slade. It was the night succeeding that on which the painful and exciting scene with the child had occurred.

"No," was answered—and to the word was added a profane imprecation. "No; and if he'll just keep away from here, he may go to —— on a hard trotting horse and a porcupine saddle as fast as he pleases. He's tried my patience beyond endurance, and my mind is made up, that he gets no more drams at this bar. I've borne his vile tongue and seen my company annoyed by him just as long as I mean to stand it. Last night decided me. Suppose I'd killed that child?"

" You'd have had trouble then, and no mistake."

"Wouldn't I ? Blast her little picture! What business has she creeping in here every night ?"

" She must have a nice kind of a mother," remarked Green, with a cold sneer.

" I don't know what she is now," said Slade, a slight touch of feeling in his voice—"heart-broken, I suppose.

I couldn't look at her last night; it made me sick. But, there was a time when Fanny Morgan was the loveliest and best woman in Cedarville. I'll say that for her. Oh dear! What a life her miserable husband has caused her to lead."

"Better that he were dead and out of the way."

"Better a thousand times," answered Slade. "If he'd only fall down some night and break his neck, it would be a blessing to his family."

"And to you in particular," laughed Green.

"You may be sure it wouldn't cost me a large sum for mourning," was the unfeeling response.

Let us leave the bar-room of the "Sickle and Sheaf," and its cold-hearted inmates, and look in upon the family of Joe Morgan, and see how it is in the home of the poor inebriate. We will pass by a quick transition.

"Joe!" The thin white hand of Mrs. Morgan clasps the arm of her husband, who has arisen up suddenly, and now stands by the partly opened door. "Don't go out to-night, Joe. Please, don't go out."

"Father!" A feeble voice calls from the corner of an old settee, where little Mary lies with her head bandaged.

"Well, I won't then!" is replied—not angrily, nor even fretfully—but in a kind voice.

"Come and sit by me, father." How tenderly, yet how full of concern is that low, sweet voice. "Come, won't you?"

" Yes, dear."

" Now hold my hand, father."

Joe takes the hand of little Mary, that instantly
tightens upon his.

" You won't go away and leave me to-night, will you,
father?   Say you won't."

" How very hot your hand is, dear.   Does your head
ache?"

" A little; but it will soon feel better."

Up into the swollen and disfigured face of the fallen
father, the large, earnest blue eyes of the child are
raised.   She does not see the marred lineaments; but,
only the beloved countenance of her parent.

" Dear father!"

" What, love?"

" I wish you'd promise me something."

" What, dear?"

" Will you promise?"

" I can't say until I hear your request.   If I can
promise, I will."

" Oh! you can promise—you can, father!"

How the large blue eyes dance and sparkle.

" What is it, love?"

" That you'll never go into Simon Slade's bar any
more."

The child raises herself, evidently with a painful
effort; and leans nearer to her father.

Joe shakes his head, and poor Mary drops back upon

her pillow with a sigh. Her lids fall, and the long lashes lie strongly relieved on her colourless cheeks.

"I won't go there to-night, dear. So let your heart be at rest."

Mary's lids unclose, and two round drops, released from their clasp, glide slowly over her face.

"Thank you, father—thank you. Mother will be so glad."

The eyes closed again; and the father moved uneasily. His heart is touched. There is a struggle within him. It is on his lips to say that he will never drink at the "Sickle and Sheaf" again; but resolution just lacks the force of utterance.

"Father!"

"Well, dear!"

"I don't think I'll be well enough to go out in two or three days. You know the doctor said that I would have to keep very still, for I had a great deal of fever."

"Yes, poor child."

"Now, won't you promise me one thing?"

"What is it, dear?"

"Not to go out in the evening until I get well."

Joe Morgan hesitated.

"Just promise me that, father. It won't be long. I shall be up again in a little while."

How well the father knows what is in the heart of his child. Her fears are all for him. Who is to go after her poor father, and lead him home when the darkness of inebriety is on his spirit, and external perception so dulled that not skill enough remains to shun the harm that lies in his path.

"Do promise just that, father, dear."

He cannot resist the pleading voice and look.

"I promise it, Mary; so shut your eyes now and go to sleep. I'm afraid this fever will increase."

"Oh! I'm so glad—so glad!"

Mary does not clasp her hands, nor show strong external signs of pleasure; but how full of a pure, unselfish joy is that low murmured ejaculation, spoken in the depths of her spirit, as well as syllabled by her tongue!

Mrs. Morgan has been no unconcerned witness of all this; but knowing the child's influence over her father, she has not ventured a word. More was to be gained, she was sure, by silence on her part; and so she has kept silent. Now she comes nearer to them, and says, as she lets a hand rest on the shoulder of her husband—

"You feel better for that promise, already; I know you do."

He looks up to her, and smiles faintly. He does feel better, but is hardly willing to acknowledge it.

Soon after Mary is sleeping. It does not escape the observation of Mrs. Morgan that her husband grows restless; for he gets up suddenly, every now and then,

and walks quickly across the room, as if in search of
something. Then sits down, listlessly—sighs—stretches
himself, and says—" Oh dear !" What shall she do for
him ? How is the want of his accustomed evening
stimulus to be met ? She thinks, and questions, and
grieves inwardly. Poor Joe Morgan! His wife understands his case, and pities him from her heart. But,
what can she do ? Go out and get him something to
drink ? " Oh, no ! no ! no ! Never !" She answered the
thought audibly almost, in the excitement of her feelings. An hour has passed—Joe's restlessness has increased instead of diminishing. What is to be done ?
Now Mrs. Morgan has left the room. She has resolved
upon something, for the case must be met. Ah ! here
she comes, after an absence of five minutes, bearing in
her hand a cup of strong coffee.

" It was kind and thoughtful in you, Fanny," says
Morgan, as with a gratified look he takes the cup. But
his hand trembles, and he spills a portion of the contents as he tries to raise it to his lips. How dreadfully
his nerves are shattered! Unnatural stimulants have
been applied so long, that all true vitality seems lost.

And now the hand of his wife is holding the cup to
his lips, and he drinks eagerly.

" This is dreadful—dreadful! Where will it end ?
What is to be done ?"

Fanny suppresses a sob, as she thus gives vent to her
troubled feelings. Twice, already, has her husband

been seized with the drunkard's madness; and, in the
nervous prostration consequent upon even a brief withdrawal of his usual strong stimulants, she sees the fearful precursor of another attack of this dreadful and
dangerous malady.   In the hope of supplying the needed
tone she has given him strong coffee; and this, for the
time, produces the effect desired. The restlessness is
allayed, and a quiet state of body and mind succeeds.
It needs but a suggestion to induce him to retire for the
night. After being a few minutes in bed, sleep steals
over him, and his heavy breathing tells that he is in the
world of dreams.

And now there comes a tap at the door.

"Come in," is answered.

The latch is lifted, the door swings open, and a woman enters.

"Mrs. Slade!" The name is uttered in a tone of
surprise.

"Fanny, how are you this evening?" Kindly,
yet half sadly, the words are said.

"Tolerable, I thank you."

The hands of the two women are clasped, and for a
few moments they gaze into each other's face. What
a world of tender commiseration is in that of Mrs.
Slade !

"How is little Mary to-night?"

"Not so well, I'm afraid. She has a good deal of
fever."

"Indeed! Oh, I'm sorry! Poor child! what a dreadful thing it was. Oh, Fanny! you don't know how it has troubled me. I've been intending to come around all day to see how she was, but couldn't get off until now."

"It came near killing her," said Mrs. Morgan.

"It's in God's mercy she escaped. The thought of it curdles the very blood in my veins. Poor child! is this her on the settee?"

"Yes."

Mrs. Slade takes a chair, and sitting by the sleeping child, gazes long upon her pale, sweet face. Now the lips of Mary part—words are murmured—what is she saying?

"No, no, mother; I can't go to bed yet. Father isn't home. And it's so dark. There's no one to lead him over the bridge. I'm not afraid. Don't—don't cry so, mother—I'm not afraid! Nothing will hurt me."

The child's face flushes. She moans, and throws her arms about uneasily. Hark again.

"I wish Mr. Slade wouldn't look so cross at me. He never did when I went to the mill. He doesn't take me on his knee now, and stroke my hair. Oh dear! I wish father wouldn't go there any more. Don't! don't, Mr. Slade. Oh! oh!"—the ejaculation prolonged into a frightened cry, "My head! my head!"

A few choking sobs are followed by low moans; and then the child breathes easily again. But the flush does not leave her cheek; and when Mrs. Slade, from whose eyes the tears come forth drop by drop, and roll down her face, touches it lightly, she finds it hot with fever.

"Has the doctor seen her to-day, Fanny?"

"No, ma'am."

"He should see her at once. I will go for him;" and Mrs. Slade starts up and goes quickly from the room. In a little while she returns with Doctor Green, who sits down and looks at the child for some moments with a sober, thoughtful face. Then he lays his fingers on her pulse and times its beat by his watch—shakes his head, and looks graver still.

"How long has she had fever?" he asks.

"All day."

"You should have sent for me earlier."

"Oh doctor! She is not dangerous, I hope?" Mrs. Morgan looks frightened.

"She's a sick child, madam."

"You've promised, father."—The dreamer is speaking again.—"I'm not well enough yet. Oh, don't go, father; don't! There! He's gone! Well, well! I'll try and walk there—I can sit down and rest by the way. Oh dear! How tired I am! Father! Father!"

The child starts up and looks about her wildly.

"Oh, mother, is it you?" And she sinks back upon her pillow, looking now inquiringly from face to face.

"Father—where is father?" she asks.

"Asleep, dear."

"Oh! Is he? I'm glad."

Her eyes close wearily.

"Do you feel any pain, Mary?" inquired the doctor.

"Yes, sir—in my head. It aches and beats so."

The cry of "Father" has reached the ears of Morgan, who is sleeping in the next room, and roused him into consciousness. He knows the doctor's voice. Why is he here at this late hour? "Do you feel any pain, Mary?" The question he hears distinctly, and the faintly uttered reply also. He is sober enough to have all his fears instantly excited. There is nothing in the world that he loves as he loves that child. And so he gets up and dresses himself as quickly as possible; the stimulus of anxiety giving tension to his relaxed nerves.

"Oh father!" The quick ears of Mary detect his entrance first, and a pleasant smile welcomes him.

"Is she very sick, doctor?" he asks, in a voice full of anxiety.

"She's a sick child, sir; you should have sent for me earlier." The doctor speaks rather sternly, and with a purpose to rebuke.

The reply stirs Morgan, and he seems to cower half-timidly under the words, as if they were blows. Mary has already grasped her father's hand, and holds on to it tightly.

After examining the case a little more closely, the doctor prepares some medicine, and, promising to call early in the morning, goes away. Mrs. Slade follows

soon after ; but, in parting with Mrs. Morgan, leaves
something in her hand, which, to the surprise of the latter,
proves to be a ten-dollar bill. The tears start to her
eyes; and she conceals the money in her bosom—mur-
muring a fervent " God bless her !"

A simple act of restitution is this on the part of
Mrs. Slade, prompted as well by humanity as a sense of
justice. With one hand her husband has taken the
bread from the family of his old friend, and thus with
the other she restores it.

And now Morgan and his wife are alone with their
sick child. Higher the fever rises, and partial delirium
seizes upon her over-excited brain. She talks for a time
almost incessantly. All her trouble is about her father;
and she is constantly referring to his promise not to go
out in the evening until she gets well. How tenderly
and touchingly she appeals to him; now looking up into
his face in partial recognition; and now calling anxiously after him, as if he had left her and was going away.

"You'll not forget your promise, will you, father?"
she says, speaking so calmly, that he thinks her mind
has ceased to wander.

"No, dear; I will not forget it," he answers, smooth-
ing her hair gently with his hand.

"You'll not go out in the evening again, until I get
well?"

"No, dear."

"Father !"

"What, love?"

"Stoop down closer; I don't want mother to hear; it will make her feel so bad."

The father bends his ear close to the lips of Mary. How he starts and shudders! What has she said?—only these brief words—

"I shall not get well, father; I'm going to die."

The groans, impossible to repress, that issued through the lips of Joe Morgan, startled the ears of his wife, and she came quickly to the bed-side.

"What is it? What is the matter, Joe?" she inquired with a look of anxiety.

"Hush, father. Don't tell her. I only said it to you." And Mary put a finger on her lips, and looked mysterious. "There, mother—you go away; you've got trouble enough, any how. Don't tell her, father."

But the words, which came to him like a prophecy, awoke such pangs of fear and remorse in the heart of Joe Morgan, that it was impossible for him to repress the signs of pain. For some moments he gazed at his wife—then stooping forward, suddenly, he buried his face in the bed-clothes, and sobbed bitterly.

A suggestion of the truth now flashed through the mind of Mrs. Morgan, sending a thrill of pain along every nerve. Ere she had time to recover herself, the low, sweet voice of Mary broke upon the hushed air of the room, and she sung—

"Jesus can make a dying bed
　　Feel soft as downy pillows are,
　While on his breast I lean my head,
　　And breathe my life out, sweetly, there."

It was impossible for Mrs. Morgan longer to repress
her feelings. As the softly breathed strain died away,
her sobs broke forth, and for a time she wept violently.

"There," said the child,—"I didn't mean to tell you.
I only told father, because—because he promised not to
go to the tavern any more until I got well; and I'm not
going to get well. So, you see, mother, he'll never go
again—never—never—never. Oh dear! how my head
pains. Mr. Slade threw it so hard. But it didn't strike
father; and I'm so glad. How it would have hurt him
—poor father! But he'll never go there any more; and
that will be so good, won't it, mother?"

A light broke over her face; but seeing that her
mother still wept, she said—

"Don't cry. Maybe I'll be better."

And then her eyes closed heavily, and she slept again.

"Joe," said Mrs. Morgan, after she had in a measure
recovered herself—she spoke firmly. "Joe, did you
hear what she said?"

Morgan only answered with a groan.

"Her mind wanders; and yet she may have spoken
only the truth."

He groaned again.

"If she should die, Joe—"

"Don't; oh, don't talk so, Fanny. She's not going to die. It's only because she's a little light-headed."

"Why is she light-headed, Joe?"

"It's the fever—only the fever, Fanny."

"It was the blow, and the wound on her head, that caused the fever. How do we know the extent of injury on the brain? Doctor Green looked very serious. I'm afraid, husband, that the worst is before us. I've borne and suffered a great deal—only God knows how much, —I pray that I may have strength to bear this trial also. Dear child! She is better fitted for heaven than for earth; and it may be that God is about to take her to himself. She's been a great comfort to me—and to you, Joe, more like a guardian angel than a child."

Mrs. Morgan had tried to speak very firmly; but as sentence followed sentence, her voice lost more and more of its even tone. With the closing words all self-control vanished; and she wept bitterly. What could her feeble erring husband do, but weep with her?

"Joe,"—Mrs. Morgan aroused herself as quickly as possible, for she had that to say which she feared she might not have the heart to utter—"Joe, if Mary dies, you cannot forget the cause of her death."

"Oh, Fanny! Fanny!"

"Nor the hand that struck the cruel blow."

"Forget it? Never! And if I forgive Simon Slade——"

"Nor the place where the blow was dealt," said Mrs. Morgan, interrupting him.

"Poor—poor child!" moaned the conscience-stricken man.

"Nor your promise, Joe—nor your promise given to our dying child."

"Father! Father! Dear father!" Mary's eyes suddenly unclosed, as she called her father eagerly.

"Here I am, love. What is it?" And Joe Morgan pressed up to the bed-side.

"Oh! it's you, father! I dreamed that you had gone out, and—and—but you won't, will you, dear father?"

"No, love—no."

"Never any more until I get well."

"I must go out to work, you know, Mary."

"At night, father. That's what I mean. You won't, will you?"

"No, dear, no."

A soft smile trembled over the child's face; her eye-lids drooped wearily, and she fell off into slumber again. She seemed not so restless as before—did not moan, nor throw herself about in her sleep.

"She's better, I think," said Morgan, as he bent over her, and listened to her softer breathing.

"It seems so," replied his wife. "And now, Joe, you must go to bed again. I will lie down here with Mary, and be ready to do any thing for her that she may want."

"I don't feel sleepy. I'm sure I couldn't close my eyes. So let me sit up with Mary. You are tired and worn out."

Mrs. Morgan looked earnestly into her husband's face. His eyes were unusually bright, and she noticed a slight nervous restlessness about his lips. She laid one of her hands on his, and perceived a slight tremor.

"You must go to bed," she spoke firmly. "I shall not let you sit up with Mary. So go at once." And she drew him almost by force into the next room.

"It's no use, Fanny. There's not a wink of sleep in my eyes. I shall lie awake anyhow. So do you get a little rest."

Even as he spoke there were nervous twitchings of his arms and shoulders; and as he entered the chamber, impelled by his wife, he stopped suddenly and said—

"What is that?"

"Where?" asked Mrs. Morgan.

"Oh, it's nothing—I see. Only one of my old boots. I thought it a great black cat."

Oh! what a shudder of despair seized upon the heart of the wretched wife. Too well she knew the fearful signs of that terrible madness from which, twice before, he had suffered. She could have looked on calmly and seen him die—but, "Not this—not this! Oh, Father in heaven!" she murmured, with such a heart-sinking that it seemed as if life itself would go out.

"Get into bed, Joe; get into bed as quickly as possible."

Morgan was now passive in the hands of his wife, and obeyed her almost like a child. He had turned down the bedclothes, and was about getting in, when he started back, with a look of disgust and alarm.

"There's nothing there, Joe. What's the matter with you?"

"I'm sure I don't know, Fanny," and his teeth rattled together, as he spoke. "I thought there was a great toad under the clothes."

"How foolish you are!"—yet tears were blinding her eyes as she said this. "It's only fancy. Get into bed and shut your eyes. I'll make you another cup of strong coffee. Perhaps that will do you good. You're only a little nervous. Mary's sickness has disturbed you."

Joe looked cautiously under the bedclothes, as he lifted them up still farther, and peered beneath.

"You know there's nothing in your bed; see!"

And Mrs. Morgan threw, with a single jerk, all the clothes upon the floor.

"There now! look for yourself. Now shut your eyes," she continued, as she spread the sheet and quilt over him, after his head was on the pillow. "Shut them tight and keep them so until I boil the water and make a cup of coffee. You know as well as I do that it's nothing but fancy."

Morgan closed his eyes firmly, and drew the clothes over his head.

"I'll be back in a very few minutes," said his wife,

going hurriedly to the door. Ere leaving, however, she partly turned her head and glanced back. There sat her husband, upright and staring fearfully.

"Don't, Fanny! don't go away!" he cried, in a frightened voice.

"Joe! Joe! why will you be so foolish? It's nothing but imagination. Now do lie down and shut your eyes. Keep them shut. There now."

And she laid a hand over his eyes, and pressed it down tightly.

"I wish Doctor Green was here," said the wretched man. "He could give me something."

"Shall I go for him?"

"Go, Fanny! Run over right quickly."

"But you won't keep in bed."

"Yes, I will. There now." And he drew the clothes over his face. "There; I'll lie just so until you come back. Now run, Fanny, and don't stay a minute."

Scarcely stopping to think, Mrs. Morgan went hurriedly from the room, and drawing an old shawl over her head, started with swift feet for the residence of Doctor Green, which was not very far away. The kind doctor understood, at a word, the sad condition of her husband, and promised to attend him immediately. Back she flew at even a wilder speed, her heart throbbing with vague apprehension. Oh! what a fearful cry was that which smote her ears as she came within a few paces of home. She knew the voice, changed as it was by terror, and a shudder almost palsied her heart. At a single bound she cleared the intervening space, and in the next moment was in the room where she had left her husband. But he was not there! With suspended breath, and feet that scarcely obeyed her will, she passed into the chamber where little Mary lay. Not here!

"Joe! husband!" she called in a faint voice.

"Here he is, mother." And now she saw that Joe had crept into the bed behind the sick child, and that her arm was drawn tightly around his neck.

"You won't let them hurt me, will you, dear?" said the poor, frightened victim of a terrible mania.

"Nothing will hurt you, father," answered Mary, in a voice that showed her mind to be clear, and fully conscious of her parent's true condition.

She had seen him thus before. Ah! what an experience for a child!

"You're an angel—my good angel, Mary," he murmured, in a voice yet trembling with fear. "Pray for me, my child. Oh, ask your Father in heaven to save me from these dreadful creatures. There now!" he cried, rising up suddenly, and looking toward the door. "Keep out! Go away! You can't come in here. This is Mary's room; and she's an angel. Ah, ha! I knew you wouldn't dare come in here—

"A single saint can put to flight,
    Ten thousand blustering sons of night."

He added in a half wandering way, yet with an assured voice, as he laid himself back upon his pillow, and drew the clothes over his head.

"Poor father!" sighed the child, as she gathered both arms about his neck. "I will be your good angel. Nothing shall hurt you here."

"I knew I would be safe where you were," he whispered back—"I knew it, and so I came. Kiss me, love."

How pure and fervent was the kiss laid instantly upon his lips! There was a power in it to remand the evil influences that were surrounding and pressing in upon him like a flood. All was quiet now, and Mrs. Morgan neither by word nor movement disturbed the solemn stillness that reigned in the apartment. In a few minutes the deepened breathing of her husband gave a blessed intimation that he was sinking into sleep. Oh, sleep! sleep! How tearfully, in times past, had she prayed that he might sleep; and yet no sleep came for hours and days—even though powerful opiates were given—until exhausted nature yielded, and then sleep had a long, long struggle with death. Now the sphere of his loving, innocent child seemed to have overcome, at least for the time, the evil influences that were getting possession even of his external senses. Yes, yes, he was sleeping! Oh, what a fervent "Thank God!" went up from the heart of his stricken wife.

Soon the quick ears of Mrs. Morgan detected the

doctor's approaching footsteps, and she met him at the door with a finger on her lips. A whispered word or two explained the better aspect of affairs, and the doctor said, encouragingly,

"That's good, if he will only sleep on."

"Do you think he will, doctor?" was asked anxiously.

"He may. But we cannot hope too strongly. It would be something very unusual."

Both passed noiselessly into the chamber. Morgan still slept, and by his deep breathing it was plain that he slept soundly. And Mary, too, was sleeping, her face now laid against her father's, and her arms still about his neck. The sight touched even the doctor's heart and moistened his eyes. For nearly half an hour he remained; and then, as Morgan continued to sleep, he left medicine to be given immediately, and went home, promising to call early in the morning.

It is now past midnight, and we leave the lonely, sad-hearted watcher with her sick ones.

———

I was sitting, with a newspaper in my hand—not reading, but musing—at the "Sickle and Sheaf," late in the evening marked by the incidents just detailed.

"Where's your mother?" I heard Simon Slade inquire. He had just entered an adjoining room.

"She's gone out somewhere," was answered by his daughter Flora.

"Where?"

"I don't know."

"How long has she been away?"

"More than an hour."

"And you don't know where she went to?"

"No, sir."

Nothing more was said, but I heard the landlord's heavy feet moving backward and forward across the room for some minutes.

"Why, Ann! where have you been?" The door of the next room had opened and shut.

"Where I wish you had been with me," was answered in a very firm voice.

"Where?"

"To Joe Morgan's."

"Humph!" Only this ejaculation met my ears. But something was said in a low voice, to which Mrs. Slade replied with some warmth,

"If you don't have his child's blood clinging for life to your garments, you may be thankful."

"What do you mean?" he asked, quickly.

"All that my words indicate. Little Mary is very ill!"

"Well, what of it."

"Much. The doctor thinks her in great danger. The cut on her head has thrown her into a violent fever, and she is delirious. Oh, Simon! if you had heard what I heard to-night."

" What ?" was asked in a growling tone.

" She is out of her mind, as I said, and talks a great deal. She talked about you."

" Of me! Well, what had she to say ?"

" She said—so pitifully—' I wish Mr. Slade wouldn't look so cross at me. He never did when I went to the mill. He doesn't take me on his knee now, and stroke my hair. Oh dear !' Poor child ! She was always so good."

" Did she say that ?" Slade seemed touched.

" Yes, and a great deal more. Once she screamed out, 'Oh don't! don't, Mr. Slade! don't ! My head! my head!' It made my very heart ache. I can never forget her pale, frightened face, nor her cry of fear. Simon—if she should die !"

There was a long silence.

" If we were only back to the mill." It was Mrs. Slade's voice.

"There, now! I don't want to hear that again," quickly spoke out the landlord. " I made a slave of myself long enough."

"You had at least a clear conscience," his wife answered.

" Do hush, will you !" Slade was now angry. " One would think, by the way you talk sometimes, that I had broken every command of the Decalogue."

" You will break hearts as well as commandments, if you keep on for a few years as you have begun—and ruin souls as well as fortunes."

Mrs. Slade spoke calmly, but with marked severity of tone.   Her husband answered with an oath, and then left the room, banging the door after him.   In the hush that followed I retired to my chamber, and lay for an hour awake, pondering on all I had just heard.   What a revelation was in that brief passage of words between the landlord and his excited companion!

NIGHT THE FOURTH.

Death of Little Mary Morgan.

"WHERE are you going, Ann?" It was the landlord's voice. Time—a little after dark.

"I'm going over to see Mrs. Morgan," answered his wife.

"What for?"

"I wish to go," was replied.

"Well, *I* don't wish you to go," said Slade, in a very decided way.

"I can't help that, Simon. Mary, I'm told, is dying, and Joe is in a dreadful way. I'm needed there—and so are you, as to that matter. There was a time when, if word came to you that Morgan or his family were in trouble——"

"Do hush, will you!" exclaimed the landlord, angrily. "I won't be preached to in this way any longer."

"Oh, well; then don't interfere with my movements, Simon; that's all I have to say. I'm needed over there, as I just said, and I'm going."

There were considerable odds against him, and Slade, perceiving this, turned off, muttering something that his wife did not hear, and she went on her way. A hurried walk brought her to the wretched home of the poor drunkard, whose wife met her at the door.

"How is Mary?" was the visitor's earnest inquiry.

Mrs. Morgan tried to answer the question; but, though her lips moved, no sounds issued therefrom.

Mrs. Slade pressed her hands tightly in both of hers; and then passed in with her to the room where the child lay. A glance sufficed to tell Mrs. Slade, that death had already laid his icy fingers upon her brow.

"How are you, dear?" she asked, as she bent over and kissed her.

"Better, I thank you?" replied Mary, in a low whisper.

Then she fixed her eyes upon her mother's face, with a look of inquiry.

"What is it, love?"

"Hasn't father waked up yet?"

"No, dear."

"Won't he wake up soon?"

"He's sleeping very soundly. I wouldn't like to disturb him."

"Oh, no; don't disturb him. I thought, maybe, he was awake."

And the child's lids drooped languidly, until the long lashes lay close against her cheeks.

There was silence for a little while, and then Mrs. Morgan said, in a half-whisper to Mrs. Slade,

"Oh, we've had such a dreadful time with poor Joe. He got in that terrible way again last night. I had to go for Doctor Green and leave him all alone. When I came back, he was in bed with Mary; and she, dear child! had her arms around his neck, and was trying to comfort him; and would you believe it, he went off to sleep, and slept in that way for a long time. The doctor came, and when he saw how it was, left some medicine for him, and went away. I was in such hopes that he would sleep it all off. But about twelve o'clock he started up, and sprung out of bed with an awful scream. Poor Mary! she too had fallen asleep. The cry wakened her, and frightened her dreadfully. She's been getting worse ever since, Mrs. Slade.

"Just as he was rushing out of the room, I caught him by the arm, and it took all my strength to hold him.

"'Father! father!' Mary called after him, as soon as she was awake enough to understand what was the matter—'Don't go out, father; there's nothing here.'

"He looked back toward the bed, in a frightful way.

"'See, father!' and the dear child turned down the quilt and sheet, in order to convince him that nothing was in the bed. 'I'm here,' she added. 'I'm not afraid. Come, father. If there's nothing here to hurt me, there's nothing to hurt you.'

"There was something so assuring in this, that Joe took a step or two toward the bed, looking sharply into it as he did so. From the bed his eyes wandered up to the ceiling, and the old look of terror came into his face.

" ' There it is now ! Jump out of bed, quick ! Jump out, Mary !' he cried. ' See ! it's right over your head.'

" Mary showed no sign of fear as she lifted her eyes to the ceiling, and gazed steadily, for a few moments, in that direction.

" ' There's nothing there, father,' said she, in a confident voice.

" ' It's gone now,' Joe spoke in a tone of relief. ' Your angel-look drove it away. Aha ! There it is now, creeping along the floor !' he suddenly exclaimed, fearfully; starting away from where he stood.

" ' Here, father ! Here !' Mary called to him, and he sprung into the bed again ; while she gathered her arms about him tightly, saying, in a low, soothing voice, —' Nothing can harm you here, father.'

" Without a moment's delay, I gave him the morphine left by Doctor Green. He took it eagerly, and then crouched down in the bed, while Mary continued to assure him of perfect safety. So long as he was clearly conscious as to where he was, he remained perfectly still. But, as soon as partial slumber came, he would scream out, and spring from the bed in terror, and then it would take us several minutes to quiet him again. Six times during the night did this occur; and as often, Mary coaxed him back. The morphine I continued to give, as the doctor had directed. By morning, the opiates had

done their work, and he was sleeping soundly.   When
the doctor came, we removed him to his own bed.   He
is still asleep; and I begin to feel uneasy, lest he should
never awake again.   I have heard of this happening."

"See if father isn't awake," said Mary, raising her
head from the pillow.   She had not heard what passed
between her mother and Mrs. Slade, for the conversation
was carried on in low voices.

Mrs. Morgan stepped to the door, and looked into the
room where her husband lay.

"He is still asleep, dear," she remarked, coming back
to the bed.

"Oh! I wish he was awake.   I want to see him so
much.   Won't you call him, mother?"

"I have called him a good many times.   But you
know the doctor gave him opium.   He can't wake up yet."

"He's been sleeping a very long time; don't you
think so, mother?"

"Yes, dear, it does seem a long time.   But it's best
for him.   He'll be better when he wakes."

Mary closed her eyes, wearily.   How deathly white
was her face—how sunken her eyes—how sharply contracted her features!

"I've given her up, Mrs. Slade," said Mrs. Morgan,
in a low, rough, choking whisper, as she leaned nearer
to her friend.   "I've given her up!   The worst is over;
but, oh! it seemed as though my heart would break in
the struggle.   Dear child!   In all the darkness of my

way, she has helped and comforted me. Without her, it would have been the blackness of darkness."

"Father! father!" The voice of Mary broke out with a startling quickness.

Mrs. Morgan turned to the bed, and laying her hand on Mary's arm said—

"He's still sound asleep, dear."

"No, he isn't, mother. I heard him move. Won't you go in and see if he is awake?"

In order to satisfy the child, her mother left the room. To her surprise, she met the eyes of her husband as she entered the chamber where he lay. He looked at her calmly.

"What does Mary want with me?" he asked.

"She wishes to see you. She's called you so many, many times. Shall I bring her in here?"

"No. I'll get up and dress myself."

"I wouldn't do that. You've been sick."

"Oh, no. I don't feel sick."

"Father! father!" The clear, earnest voice of Mary was heard calling.

"I'm coming, dear," answered Morgan.

"Come quick, father, won't you?"

"Yes, love." And Morgan got up and dressed himself—but with unsteady hands, and every sign of nervous prostration. In a little while, with the assistance of his wife, he was ready, and, supported by her, came tottering into the room where Mary was lying.

" Oh, father !"—What a light broke over her countenance.—" I've been waiting for you so long. I thought you were never going to wake up. Kiss me, father."

" What can I do for you, Mary?" asked Morgan, tenderly, as he laid his face down upon the pillow beside her.

" Nothing, father. I don't wish for any thing. I only wanted to see you."

" I'm here, now, love."

" Dear father !" How earnestly, yet tenderly she spoke, laying her small hand upon his face. " You've always been good to me, father."

" Oh, no. I've never been good to anybody," sobbed the weak, broken-spirited man, as he raised himself from the pillow.

How deeply touched was Mrs. Slade, as she sat, the silent witness of this scene !

" You haven't been good to yourself, father—but you've always been good to us."

" Don't, Mary ! don't say any thing about that," interposed Morgan. " Say that I've been very bad—very wicked. Oh, Mary, dear ! I only wish that I was as good as you are ; I'd like to die, then, and go right away from this evil world. I wish there was no liquor to drink —no taverns—no bar-rooms. Oh dear ! Oh dear ! I wish I was dead."

And the weak, trembling, half-palsied man laid his face again upon the pillow beside his child, and sobbed aloud.

What an oppressive silence reigned for a time through the room!

"Father." The stillness was broken by Mary. Her voice was clear and even. "Father, I want to tell you something?"

"What is it, Mary?"

"There'll be nobody to go for you, father." The child's lips now quivered, and tears filled into her eyes.

"Don't talk about that, Mary. I'm not going out in the evening any more until you get well. Don't you remember I promised?"

"But, father"—She hesitated.

"What, dear?"

"I'm going away to leave you and mother."

"Oh, no—no—no, Mary! Don't say that."—The poor man's voice was broken.—"Don't say that! We can't let you go, dear."

"God has called me." The child's voice had a solemn tone, and her eyes turned reverently upward.

"I wish he would call me! Oh, I wish he would call me!" groaned Morgan, hiding his face in his hands. "What shall I do when you are gone? Oh dear! Oh dear!"

"Father!" Mary spoke calmly again. "You are not ready to go yet. God will let you live here longer, that you may get ready."

"How can I get ready without you to help me, Mary? My angel child!"

"Haven't I tried to help you, father, oh, so many times?" said Mary.

"Yes—yes—you've always tried."

"But it wasn't any use. You would go out—you would go to the tavern. It seemed almost as if you couldn't help it."

Morgan groaned in spirit.

"Maybe I can help you better, father, after I die. I love you so much, that I am sure God will let me come to you, and stay with you always, and be your angel. Don't you think he will, mother?"

But Mrs. Morgan's heart was too full. She did not even try to answer, but sat, with streaming eyes, gazing upon her child's face.

"Father, I dreamed something about you, while I slept to-day." Mary again turned to her father.

"What was it, dear?"

"I thought it was night, and that I was still sick. You promised not to go out again until I was well. But you did go out; and I thought you went over to Mr. Slade's tavern. When I knew this, I felt as strong as when I was well, and I got up and dressed myself, and started out after you. But I hadn't gone far, before I met Mr. Slade's great bull-dog Nero, and he growled at me so dreadfully that I was frightened and ran back home. Then I started again, and went away round by Mr. Mason's. But there was Nero in the road, and this time he caught my dress in his mouth and tore a great piece out of the skirt. I ran back again, and he chased me all the way home. Just as I got to the door, I looked around, and there was Mr. Slade, setting Nero on me. As soon as I saw Mr. Slade, though he looked at me very wicked, I lost all my fear, and turning around, I walked past Nero, who showed his teeth, and growled as fiercely as ever, but didn't touch me. Then Mr. Slade tried to stop me. But I didn't mind him, and kept right on, until I came to the tavern, and there you stood in the door. And you were dressed so nice. You had on a new hat and a new coat; and your boots were new, and polished just like Judge Hammond's. I said—'O father! is this you?' And then you took me up in your arms and kissed me, and said—'Yes, Mary, I am your real father. Not old Joe Morgan—but Mr. Morgan now.' It seemed all so strange, that I looked into the bar-room to see who was there. But it wasn't a bar-room any longer; but a store full of goods. The sign of the Sickle and Sheaf was taken down; and over the door I now read your name, father. Oh! I was so glad, that I awoke—and then I cried all to myself, for it was only a dream."

The last words were said very mournfully, and with a drooping of Mary's lids, until the tear-gemmed lashes lay close upon her cheeks. Another period of deep silence followed—for the oppressed listeners gave no utterance to what was in their hearts. Feeling was too strong for speech. Nearly five minutes glided away, and then Mary whispered the name of her father, but without opening her eyes.

Morgan answered, and bent down his ear.

"You will only have mother left," she said—"only mother. And she cries so much when you are away."

"I won't leave her, Mary, only when I go to work," said Morgan, whispering back to the child. "And I'll never go out at night any more."

"Yes; you promised me that."

"And I'll promise more."

"What, father?"

"Never to go into a tavern again."

"Never!"

"No, never. And I'll promise still more."

"Father?"

"Never to drink a drop of liquor as long as I live."

"Oh, father! dear, dear father!" And with a cry of joy Mary started up and flung herself upon his breast. Morgan drew his arms tightly around her, and sat for a long time, with his lips pressed to her cheek—while she lay against his bosom as still as death. As death? Yes; for, when the father unclasped his arms, the spirit of his child was with the angels of the resurrection!

It was my fourth evening in the bar-room of the "Sickle and Sheaf." The company was not large, nor in very gay spirits. All had heard of little Mary's illness; which followed so quickly on the blow from the tumbler, that none hesitated about connecting the one with the other. So regular had been the child's visits, and so gently exerted, yet powerful, her influence over her father, that most of the frequenters at the "Sickle and Sheaf" had felt for her a more than common interest; which the cruel treatment she received, and the subsequent illness, materially heightened.

"Joe Morgan hasn't turned up this evening," remarked some one.

"And isn't likely to for a while," was answered.

"Why not?" inquired the first speaker.

"They say, the man with the poker is after him."

"Oh, dear! that's dreadful. It's the second or third chase, isn't it?"

"Yes."

"He'll be likely to catch him this time."

"I shouldn't wonder."

"Poor devil! It won't be much matter. His family will be a great deal better without him."

"It will be a blessing to them if he dies."

"Miserable, drunken wretch!" muttered Harvey Green, who was present. "He's only in the way of everybody. The sooner he's off, the better."

The landlord said nothing. He stood leaning across the bar, looking more sober than usual.

"That was rather an unlucky affair of yours, Simon. They say the child is going to die."

"Who says so?" Slade started, scowled, and threw a quick glance upon the speaker.

"Doctor Green."

"Nonsense! Doctor Green never said any such thing."

"Yes, he did, though."

"Who heard him?"

"I did."

"You did?"

"Yes."

"He wasn't in earnest?" A slight paleness overspread the countenance of the landlord.

"He was, though. They had an awful time there last night."

"Where?"

"At Joe Morgan's. Joe has the mania, and Mrs. Morgan was alone with him and her sick girl all night."

"He deserves to have it; that's all I've got to say." Slade tried to speak with a kind of rough indifference.

"That's pretty hard talk," said one of the company.

"I don't care if it is. It's the truth. What else could he expect?"

"A man like Joe is to be pitied," remarked the other.

"I pity his family," said Slade.

"Especially little Mary." The words were uttered tauntingly, and produced murmurs of satisfaction throughout the room.

Slade started back from where he stood, in an impatient manner, saying something that I did not hear.

"Look here, Simon, I heard some strong suggestions over at Lawyer Phillip's office to-day."

Slade turned his eyes upon the speaker.

"If that child should die, you'll probably have to stand a trial for manslaughter."

"No—girl-slaughter," said Harvey Green, with a cold, inhuman chuckle.

"But, I'm in earnest," said the other. "Mr. Phillips said that a case could be made out of it."

"It was only an accident, and all the lawyers in Christendom can't make any thing more of it," remarked Green, taking the side of the landlord, and speaking with more gravity than before.

"Hardly an accident," was replied.

"He didn't throw at the girl."

"No matter. He threw a heavy tumbler at her father's head. The intention was to do an injury; and the law will not stop to make any nice discriminations in regard to the individual upon whom the injury was wrought. Moreover, who is prepared to say, that he didn't aim at the girl?"

"Any man who intimates such a thing is a cursed liar!" exclaimed the landlord, half maddened by the suggestion.

"I won't throw a tumbler at your head," coolly remarked the individual whose plain speaking had so irritated Simon Slade. "Throwing tumblers I never thought a very creditable kind of argument—though, with some men, when cornered, it is a favourite mode of settling a question. Now, as for our friend the land-lord, I am sorry to say, that his new business doesn't seem to have improved either his manners or his temper a great deal. As a miller, he was one of the best-tem-pered men in the world, and wouldn't have harmed a kitten. But, now, he can swear, and bluster, and throw glasses at people's heads, and all that sort of·thing, with the best of brawling rowdies. I'm afraid he's taking lessons in a bad school—I am."

"I don't think you have any right to insult a man in his own house," answered Slade, in a voice dropped to a lower key than the one in which he had before spoken.

"I had no intention to insult you," said the other. "I was only speaking suppositiously, and in view of your position on a trial for manslaughter, when I sug-gested, that no one could prove, or say, that you didn't mean to strike little Mary, when you threw the tumbler."

"Well, I didn't mean to strike her ; and I don't be-lieve there is a man in this bar-room who thinks that I did—not one."

"I'm sure I do not," said the individual with whom he was in controversy. "Nor I"—Nor I"—went round the room.

"But, as I wished to set forth," was continued, "the case will not be so plain a one when it finds its way into court, and twelve men, to each of whom you may be a stranger, come to sit in judgment upon the act. The slightest twist in the evidence, the prepossessions of a witness, or the bad tact of the prosecution, may cause things to look so dark on your side as to leave you but little chance. For my part, if the child should die, I think your chances for a term in the state's prison are as eight to ten; and I should call that pretty close cutting."

I looked attentively at the man who said this, all the while he was speaking, but could not clearly make out whether he were altogether in earnest, or merely trying to worry the mind of Slade. That he was successful in accomplishing the latter, was very plain; for the landlord's countenance steadily lost colour, and became overcast with alarm. With that evil delight which some men take in giving pain, others, seeing Slade's anxious looks, joined in the persecution, and soon made the landlord's case look black enough; and the landlord himself almost as frightened as a criminal just under arrest.

"It's bad business, and no mistake," said one.

"Yes, bad enough. I wouldn't be in his shoes for his coat," remarked another.

"For his coat? No, not for his whole wardrobe," said a third.

"Nor for the Sickle and Sheaf thrown into the bargain," added a fourth.

"It will be a clear case of manslaughter, and no mistake. What is the penalty?"

"From two to ten years in the penitentiary," was readily answered.

"They'll give him five, I reckon."

"No—not more than two. It will be hard to prove malicious intention."

"I don't know that. I've heard him curse the girl and threaten her many a time. Haven't you?"

"Yes"—"Yes"—"I have, often," ran around the bar-room.

"You'd better hang me at once," said Slade, affecting to laugh.

At this moment, the door behind Slade opened, and I saw his wife's anxious face thrust in for a moment. She said something to her husband, who uttered a low ejaculation of surprise, and went out quickly.

"What's the matter now?" asked one of another.

"I shouldn't wonder if little Mary Morgan was dead," was suggested.

"I heard her say dead," remarked one who was standing near the bar.

"What's the matter, Frank?" inquired several voices, as the landlord's son came in through the door out of which his father had passed.

"Mary Morgan is dead," answered the boy.

"Poor child! Poor child!" sighed one, in genuine

regret at the not unlooked for intelligence. "Her trouble is over."

And there was not one present, but Harvey Green, who did not utter some word of pity or sympathy. He shrugged his shoulders, and looked as much of contempt and indifference as he thought it prudent to express.

"See here, boys," spoke out one of the company, "can't we do something for poor Mrs. Morgan? Can't we make up a purse for her?"

"That's it," was quickly responded; "I'm good for three dollars; and there they are," drawing out the money and laying it upon the counter.

"And here are five to go with them," said I, quickly stepping forward, and placing a five-dollar bill along side of the first contribution.

"Here are five more," added a third individual. And so it went on, until thirty dollars were paid down for the benefit of Mrs. Morgan.

"Into whose hands shall this be placed?" was next asked.

"Let me suggest Mrs. Slade," said I. "To my certain knowledge, she has been with Mrs. Morgan to-night. I know that she feels in her a true woman's interest."

"Just the person," was answered. "Frank, tell your mother we would like to see her. Ask her to step into the sitting-room."

In a few moments the boy came back, and said that

his mother would see us in the next room, into which we all passed. Mrs. Slade stood near the table, on which burned a lamp. I noticed that her eyes were red, and that there was on her countenance a troubled and sorrowful expression.

"We have just heard," said one of the company, "that little Mary Morgan is dead."

"Yes—it is too true," answered Mrs. Slade, mournfully. "I have just left there. Poor child! she has passed from an evil world."

"Evil it has indeed been to her," was remarked.

"You may well say that. And yet, amid all the evil, she has been an angel of mercy. Her last thought in dying was of her miserable father. For him, at any time, she would have laid down her life willingly."

"Her mother must be nearly broken-hearted. Mary is the last of her children."

"And yet the child's death may prove a blessing to her."

"How so?"

"Her father promised Mary, just at the last moment —solemnly promised her—that, henceforth, he would never taste liquor. That was all her trouble. That was the thorn in her dying pillow. But he plucked it out, and she went to sleep, lying against his heart. Oh, gentlemen! it was the most touching sight I ever saw."

All present seemed deeply moved.

"They are very poor and wretched," was said.

"Poor and miserable enough," answered Mrs. Slade.

"We have just been taking up a collection for Mrs. Morgan. Here is the money, Mrs. Slade—thirty dollars—we place it in your hands for her benefit. Do with it, for her, as you may see best."

"Oh, gentlemen!" What a quick gleam went over the face of Mrs. Slade. "I thank you, from my heart, in the name of that unhappy one, for this act of true benevolence. To you the sacrifice has been small; to her the benefit will be great indeed. A new life will, I trust, be commenced by her husband, and this timely aid will be something to rest upon, until he can get into better employment than he now has. Oh, gentlemen! let me urge on you, one and all, to make common cause in favour of Joe Morgan. His purposes are good now; he means to keep his promise to his dying child—means to reform his life. Let the good impulses that led to this act of relief, further prompt you to watch over him, and, if you see him about going astray, to lead him kindly back into the right path. Never—oh! never encourage him to drink; but rather take the glass from his hand, if his own appetite lead him aside, and by all the persuasive influence you possess, induce him to go out from the place of temptation.

"Pardon my boldness in saying so much," added Mrs. Slade, recollecting herself, and colouring deeply as she did so. "My feelings have led me away."

And she took the money from the table where it had been placed, and retired toward the door.

"You have spoken well, madam," was answered. "And we thank you for reminding us of our duty."

"One word more—and forgive the earnest heart from which it comes"—said Mrs. Slade, in a voice that trembled on the words she uttered. "I cannot help speaking, gentlemen! Think if some of you be not entering the road wherein Joe Morgan has so long been walking. Save him, in heaven's name!—but see that ye do not yourselves become cast-aways!"

As she said this, she glided through the door, and it closed after her.

"I don't know what her husband would say to that," was remarked after a few moments of surprised silence.

"I don't care what *he* would say; but I'll tell you what *I* will say," spoke out a man whom I had several times noticed as rather a free tippler. "The old lady has given us capital advice, and I mean to take it, for one. I'm going to try to save Joe Morgan, and—myself too. I've already entered the road she referred to; but I'm going to turn back. So good-night to you all; and if Simon Slade gets no more of my sixpences, he may thank his wife for it—God bless her!"

And the man drew his hat with a jerk over his forehead, and left immediately.

This seemed the signal for dispersion, and all retired —not by way of the bar-room, but out into the hall, and through the door leading upon the porch that ran along in front of the house. Soon after the bar was closed, and a dead silence reigned throughout the house. I saw no more of Slade that night. Early in the morning, I left Cedarville; the landlord looked very sober when he bade me good-by through the stage-door, and wished me a pleasant journey.

NIGHT THE FIFTH.

Some of the Consequences of Tavern-Keeping.

NEARLY five years glided away before business again called me to Cedarville. I knew little of what passed there in the interval, except that Simon Slade had actually been indicted for manslaughter, in causing the death of Morgan's child. He did not stand a trial, however, Judge Lyman having used his influence, successfully, in getting the indictment quashed. The judge, some people said, interested himself in Slade more than was just seemly—especially, as he had, on several occasions, in the discharge of his official duties, displayed what seemed an over-righteous indignation against individuals arraigned for petty offences. The impression made upon me by Judge Lyman had not been favourable. He seemed a cold, selfish, scheming man of the world. That he was an unscrupulous politician, was plain to me, in a single evening's observation of his sayings and doings among the common herd of a village barroom.

As the stage rolled, with a gay flourish of our driver's bugle, into the village, I noted here and there familiar objects, and marked the varied evidences of change.

Our way was past the elegant residence and grounds of Judge Hammond, the most beautiful and highly cultivated in Cedarville. At least, such it was regarded at the time of my previous visit. But, the moment my eyes rested upon the dwelling and its varied surroundings, I perceived an altered aspect. Was it the simple work of time? or, had familiarity with other and more elegantly arranged suburban homes, marred this in my eyes by involuntary contrast? Or had the hand of cultivation really been stayed, and the marring fingers of neglect suffered undisturbed to trace on every thing disfiguring characters?

Such questions were in my thoughts, when I saw a man in the large portico of the dwelling, the ample columns of which, capped in rich Corinthian, gave the edifice the aspect of a Grecian temple. He stood leaning against one of the columns—his hat off, and his long gray hair thrown back and resting lightly on his neck and shoulders. His head was bent down upon his breast, and he seemed in deep abstraction. Just as the coach swept by, he looked up, and in the changed features I recognised Judge Hammond. His complexion was still florid, but his face had grown thin, and his eyes were sunken. Trouble was written in every lineament. Trouble? How inadequately does the word express my meaning! Ah! at a single glance, what a volume of suffering was opened to the gazer's eye. Not lightly had the foot of time rested there, as if treading on

odorous flowers, but heavily, and with iron-shod heel.
This I saw at a glance ; and then, only the image of the
man was present to my inner vision, for the swiftly rolling stage-coach had borne me onward past the altered
home of the wealthiest denizen of Cedarville. In a few
minutes our driver reined up before the "Sickle and
Sheaf," and as I stepped to the ground, a rotund, coarse,
red-faced man, whom I failed to recognise as Simon
Slade until he spoke, grasped my hand, and pronounced
my name. I could not but contrast, in thought, his appearance with what it was when I first saw him, some
six years previously; nor help saying to myself—

" So much for tavern-keeping !"

As marked a change was visible everywhere in and
around the "Sickle and Sheaf." It, too, had grown
larger by additions of wings and rooms ; but it had also
grown coarser in growing larger. When built, all the
doors were painted white, and the shutters green, giving
to the house a neat, even tasteful appearance. But the
white and green had given place to a dark, dirty brown,
that to my eyes was particularly unattractive. The bar-
room had been extended, and now a polished brass rod,
or railing, embellished the counter, and sundry orna-
mental attractions had been given to the shelving behind
the bar—such as mirrors, gilding, etc. Pictures, too,
were hung upon the walls, or more accurately speaking,
coarse coloured lithographs, the subjects of which, if not
really obscene, were flashing, or vulgar. In the sitting-

room, next to the bar, I noticed little change of objects, but much in their condition. The carpet, chairs, and tables were the same in fact, but far from being the same in appearance. The room had a close, greasy odour, and looked as if it had not been thoroughly swept and dusted for a week.

A smart young Irishman was in the bar, and handed me the book in which passenger's names were registered. After I had recorded mine, he directed my trunk to be carried to the room designated as the one I was to occupy. I followed the porter, who conducted me to the chamber which had been mine at previous visits. Here, too, were evidences of change; but not for the better. Then the room was as sweet and clean as it could be; the sheets and pillow-cases as white as snow, and the furniture shining with polish. Now all was dusty and dingy, the air foul, and the bed linen scarcely whiter than tow. No curtain made softer the light as it came through the window; nor would the shutters entirely keep out the glare, for several of the slats were broken. A feeling of disgust came over me, at the close smell and foul appearance of every thing; so, after washing my hands and face, and brushing the dust from my clothes, I went down-stairs. The sitting-room was scarcely more attractive than my chamber; so I went out upon the porch and took a chair. Several loungers were here; hearty, strong-looking, but lazy fellows, who, if they had any thing to do, liked idling better than working. One of them had leaned his chair back against the wall of the house, and was swinging his legs with a half circular motion, and humming "Old Folks at Home." Another sat astride of his chair, with his face turned toward, and his chin resting upon, the back. He was in too lazy a condition of body and mind for motion or singing. A third had slidden down in his chair, until he sat on his back, while his feet were elevated above his head, and resting against one of the pillars that supported the porch; while a fourth lay stretched out on a bench, sleeping, his hat over his face to protect him from buzzing and biting flies.

Though all but the sleeping man eyed me, inquisitively, as I took my place among them, not one changed his position. The rolling of eyeballs cost but little exertion; and with that effort they were contented.

"Hallo! who's that?" one of these loungers suddenly exclaimed, as a man went swiftly by in a light sulky; and he started up, and gazed down the road, seeking to penetrate the cloud of dust which the fleet rider had swept up with hoofs and wheels.

"I didn't see." The sleeping man aroused himself, rubbed his eyes, and gazed along the road.

"Who was it, Matthew?" The Irish bar-keeper now stood in the door.

"Willy Hammond," was answered by Matthew.

"Indeed! Is that his new three hundred dollar horse?"

"Yes."

"My! but he's a screamer!"

"Isn't he! Most as fast as his young master."

"Hardly," said one of the men, laughing. "I don't think any thing in creation can beat Hammond. He goes it, with a perfect rush."

"Doesn't he! Well; you may say what you please of him, he's as good-hearted a fellow as ever walked; and generous to a fault."

"His old dad will agree with you in the last remark," said Matthew.

"No doubt of that, for he has to stand the bills," was answered.

"Yes, whether he will or no, for I rather think Willy has, somehow or other, got the upper hand of him."

"In what way?"

"It's Hammond and Son, over at the mill and distillery."

"I know; but what of that?"

"Willy was made the business man—ostensibly—in order, as the old man thought, to get him to feel the responsibility of the new position, and thus tame him down."

"Tame *him* down! Oh, dear! It will take more than business to do that. The curb was applied too late."

"As the old gentleman has already discovered, I'm thinking, to his sorrow."

" He never comes here any more; does he, Matthew?"

" Who ?"

" Judge Hammond."

" Oh, dear, no. He and Slade had all sorts of a quarrel about a year ago, and he's never darkened our doors since."

" It was something about Willy and——." The speaker did not mention any name, but winked knowingly and tossed his head toward the entrance of the house, to indicate some member of Slade's family.

" I believe so."

" D'ye think Willy really likes her ?"

Matthew shrugged his shoulders, but made no answer.

" She's a nice girl," was remarked in an under tone, " and good enough for Hammond's son any day; though, if she were my daughter, I'd rather see her in Jericho than fond of his company."

" He'll have plenty of money to give her. She can live like a queen."

" For how long ?"

" Hush !" came from the lips of Matthew. " There she is now."

I looked up and saw, at a short distance from the house, and approaching, a young lady, in whose sweet, modest face, I at once recognised Flora Slade. Five years had developed her into beautiful woman. In her alone, of all that appertained to Simon Slade, there was no deterioration. Her eyes were as mild and pure as when first I met her at gentle sixteen, and her father said " My daughter," with such a mingling of pride and affection in his tone. She passed near where I was sitting, and entered the house. A closer view showed me some marks of thought and suffering; but they only heightened the attractions of her face. I failed not to observe the air of respect with which all returned her slight nod and smile of recognition.

" She's a nice girl, and no mistake—the flower of this flock," was said, as soon as she passed into the house.

" Too good for Willy Hammond, in my opinion," said Matthew. " Clever and generous as people call him."

" Just my opinion," was responded. " She's as pure and good, almost, as an angel; and he ?—I can tell you what—he's not the clear thing. He knows a little too much of the world—on its bad side, I mean."

The appearance of Slade put an end to this conversation. A second observation of his person and countenance did not remove the first unfavourable impression. His face had grown decidedly bad in expression, as well as gross and sensual. The odour of his breath, as he took a chair close to where I was sitting, was that of one who drank habitually and freely; and the red, swimming eyes evidenced, too surely, a rapid progress toward the sad condition of a confirmed inebriate. There was, too, a certain thickness of speech, that gave another corroborating sign of evil progress.

" Have you seen any thing of Frank this afternoon ?"

he inquired of Matthew, after we had passed a few
words.

"Nothing," was the bar-keeper's answer.

"I saw him with Tom Wilkins as I came over," said
one of the men who was sitting in the porch.

"What was he doing with Tom Wilkins?" said Slade,
in a fretted tone of voice. "He doesn't seem very
choice of his company."

"They were gunning."

"Gunning!"

"Yes. They both had fowling-pieces. I wasn't
near enough to ask where they were going."

This information disturbed Slade a good deal. After
muttering to himself for a little while, he started up and
went into the house.

"And I could have told him a little more, had I been
so inclined," said the individual who mentioned the fact
that Frank was with Tom Wilkins.

"What more?" inquired Matthew.

"There was a buggy in the case; and a champagne
basket. What the latter contained you can easily guess."

"Whose buggy?"

"I don't know any thing about the buggy; but if
'Lightfoot' doesn't sink in value a hundred dollars or so
before sundown, call me a false prophet."

"Oh, no," said Matthew, incredulously. "Frank
wouldn't do an outrageous thing like that. Lightfoot
won't be in a condition to drive for a month to come."

"I don't care. She's out now; and the way she was putting it down when I saw her, would have made a loco-motive look cloudy."

"Where did he get her?" was inquired.

"She's been in the six-acre field, over by Mason's Bridge, for the last week or so," Matthew answered. "Well; all I have to say," he added, "is that Frank ought to be slung up and well horsewhipped. I never saw such a young rascal. He cares for no good, and fears no evil. He's the worst boy I ever saw."

"It would hardly do for you to call him a boy to his face," said one of the men, laughing.

"I don't have much to say to him in any way," re-plied Matthew, "for I know very well, that if we ever do get into a regular quarrel, there'll be a hard time of it. The same house will not hold us afterward—that's certain. So I steer clear of the young reprobate."

"I wonder his father don't put him to some business," was remarked. "The idle life he now leads will be his ruin."

"He was behind the bar for a year or two."

"Yes; and was smart at mixing a glass—but——"

"Was himself becoming too good a customer?"

"Precisely. He got drunk as a fool before reaching his fifteenth year."

"Good gracious!" I exclaimed, involuntarily.

"It's true, sir," said the last speaker, turning to me. "I never saw any thing like it. And this wasn't all.

Bar-room talk, as you maybe know, isn't the most refined and virtuous in the world. I wouldn't like my son
to hear much of it. Frank was always an eager listener
to every thing that was said, and in a very short time
became an adept in slang and profanity. I'm no saint
myself; but it's often made my blood run cold to hear
him swear."

"I pity his mother," said I; for my thought turned
naturally to Mrs. Slade.

"You may well do that," was answered. "I doubt
if Cedarville holds a sadder heart. It was a dark day
for her, let me tell you, when Simon Slade sold his mill
and built this tavern. She was opposed to it in the
beginning."

"I have inferred as much."

"I know it," said the man. "My wife has been in-
timate with her for years. Indeed, they have always
been like sisters. I remember very well her coming to
our house, about the time the mill was sold, and crying
about it as if her heart would break. She saw nothing
but trouble and sorrow ahead. Tavern-keeping she had
always regarded as a low business; and the change from
a respectable miller to a lazy tavern-keeper, as she expressed it, was presented to her mind as something disgraceful. I remember, very well, trying to argue the
point with her—assuming that it was quite as respectable
to keep tavern as to do any thing else; but I might as
well have talked to the wind. She was always a pleasant,

hopeful, cheerful woman before that time; but, really, I don't think I've seen a true smile on her face since."

"That was a great deal for a man to lose," said I.

"What?" he inquired, not clearly understanding me.

"The cheerful face of his wife."

"The face was but an index of her heart," said he.

"So much the worse."

"True enough for that. Yes, it was a great deal to lose."

"What has he gained that will make up for this?"

The man shrugged his shoulders.

"What has he gained?" I repeated. "Can you figure it up?"

"He's a richer man, for one thing."

"Happier?"

There was another shrug of the shoulders. "I wouldn't like to say that."

"How much richer?"

"Oh, a great deal. Somebody was saying, only yesterday, that he couldn't be worth less than thirty thousand dollars."

"Indeed? So much."

"Yes."

"How has he managed to accumulate so rapidly?"

"His bar has a large run of custom. And, you know, that pays wonderfully."

"He must have sold a great deal of liquor in six years."

" And he has. I don't think I'm wrong in saying, that in the six years which have gone by since the 'Sickle and Sheaf' was opened, more liquor has been drank than in the previous twenty years."

" Say forty," remarked a man who had been a listener to what we said.

" Let it be forty then," was the according answer.

"How comes this?" I inquired. "You had a tavern here before the Sickle and Sheaf was opened."

" I know we had, and several places besides where liquor was sold. But, everybody far and near knew Simon Slade the miller, and everybody liked him. He was a good miller, and a cheerful, social, chatty sort of a man, putting everybody in a good humour who came near him. So it became the talk everywhere, when he built this house, which he fitted up nicer than any thing that had been seen in these parts. Judge Hammond, Judge Lyman, Lawyer Wilson, and all the big-bugs of the place at once patronised the new tavern; and, of course, everybody else did the same. So, you can easily see how he got such a run."

" It was thought in the beginning," said I, " that the new tavern was going to do wonders for Cedarville."

" Yes," answered the man laughing, "and so it has."

" In what respect?"

" Oh, in many. It has made some men richer, and some poorer."

" Who has it made poorer?"

"Dozens of people. You may always take it for granted, when you see a tavern-keeper, who has a good run at his bar, getting rich, that a great many people are getting poor."

"How so?" I wished to hear in what way the man, who was himself, as was plain to see, a good customer at somebody's bar, reasoned on the subject.

"He does not add to the general wealth. He produces nothing. He takes money from his customers, but gives them no article of value in return—nothing that can be called property, personal or real. He is just so much richer and they just so much poorer for the exchange. Is it not so?"

I readily assented to the position as true, and then said—

"Who, in particular, is poorer?"

"Judge Hammond, for one."

"Indeed! I thought the advance in his property, in consequence of the building of this tavern, was so great, that he was reaping a rich pecuniary harvest."

"There was a slight advance in property along the street after the Sickle and Sheaf was opened, and Judge Hammond was benefited thereby. Interested parties made a good deal of noise about it; but it didn't amount to much, I believe."

"What has caused the judge to grow poorer?"

"The opening of this tavern, as I just said."

"In what way did it affect him?"

"He was among Slade's warmest supporters, as soon as he felt the advance in the price of building lots; called him one of the most enterprising men in Cedarville—a real benefactor to the place—and all that stuff. To set a good example of patronage, he came over every day and took his glass of brandy, and encouraged everybody else that he could influence to do the same. Among those who followed his example was his son Willy. There was not, let me tell you, in all the country for twenty miles around, a finer young man than Willy, nor one of so much promise, when this man-trap"—he let his voice fall, and glanced around, as he thus designated Slade's tavern—"was opened; and now, there is not one dashing more recklessly along the road to ruin. When too late, his father saw that his son was corrupted, and that the company he kept was of a dangerous character. Two reasons led him to purchase Slade's old mill, and turn it into a factory and a distillery. Of course, he had to make a heavy outlay for additional buildings, machinery, and distilling apparatus. The reasons influencing him were the prospect of realizing a large amount of money, especially in distilling, and the hope of saving Willy, by getting him closely engaged and interested in business. To accomplish, more certainly, the latter end, he unwisely transferred to his son, as his own capital, twenty thousand dollars, and then formed with him a regular copartnership—giving Willy an active business control.

"But the experiment, sir," added the man, emphatically, "has proved a failure. I heard yesterdy, that both mill and distillery were to be shut up, and offered for sale."

"They did not prove as money-making as was anticipated?"

"No, not under Willy Hammond's management. He had made too many bad acquaintances—men who clung to him because he had plenty of money at his command, and spent it as freely as water. One half of his time he was away from the mill, and while there, didn't half attend to business. I've heard it said—and I don't much doubt its truth—that he's squandered his twenty thousand dollars, and a great deal more besides."

"How is that possible?"

"Well; people talk, and not always at random. There's been a man staying here, most of his time, for the last four or five years, named Green. He does not do any thing, and don't seem to have any friends in the neighbourhood. Nobody knows where he came from, and he is not at all communicative on that head himself. Well, this man became acquainted with young Hammond after Willy got to visiting the bar here, and attached himself to him at once. They have, to all appearance, been fast friends ever since; riding about, or going off on gunning or fishing excursions almost every day, and secluding themselves somewhere nearly every evening. That man, Green, sir, it is whispered, is a

gambler; and I believe it. Granted, and there is no
longer a mystery as to what Willy does with his own
and his father's money."

I readily assented to this view of the case.

"And so assuming that Green is a gambler," said I,
"he has grown richer, in consequence of the opening
of a new and more attractive tavern in Cedarville."

"Yes, and Cedarville is so much the poorer for all
his gains; for I've never heard of his buying a foot of
ground, or in any way encouraging productive industry.
He's only a blood-sucker."

"It is worse than the mere abstraction of money,"
I remarked; "he corrupts his victims, at the same time
that he robs them."

"True."

"Willy Hammond may not be his only victim," I
suggested.

"Nor is he, in my opinion. I've been coming to this
bar, nightly, for a good many years—a sorry confession
for a man to make, I must own," he added, with a slight
tinge of shame; "but so it is. Well, as I was saying,
I've been coming to this bar, nightly, for a good many
years, and I generally see all that is going on around
me. Among the regular visitors are at least half a
dozen young men, belonging to our best families—who
have been raised with care, and well educated. That
their presence here is unknown to their friends, I am
quite certain—or, at least, unknown and unsuspected by

some of them. They do not drink a great deal yet; but all try a glass or two. Toward nine o'clock, often at an earlier hour, you will see one and another of them go quietly out of the bar, through the sitting-room, preceded, or soon followed, by Green and Slade. At any hour of the night, up to one or two, and sometimes three o'clock, you can see light streaming through the rent in a curtain drawn before a particular window, which I know to be in the room of Harvey Green. These are facts, sir; and you can draw your own conclusion. I think it a very serious matter."

"Why does Slade go out with these young men?" I inquired. "Do you think he gambles, also?"

"If he isn't a kind of a stool-pigeon for Harvey Green, then I'm mistaken again."

"Hardly. He cannot, already, have become so utterly unprincipled."

"It's a bad school, sir, this tavern-keeping," said the man.

"I readily grant you that."

"And it's nearly seven years since he commenced to take lessons. A great deal may be learned, sir, of good or evil, in seven years, especially if any interest be taken in the studies."

"True."

"And it's true in this case, you may depend upon it. Simon Slade is not the man he was, seven years ago. Anybody with half an eye can see that. He's grown selfish, grasping, unscrupulous, and passionate. There could hardly be a greater difference between men than exists between Simon Slade the tavern-keeper, and Simon Slade the miller."

"And intemperate, also ?" I suggested.

"He's beginning to take a little too much," was answered.

"In that case, he'll scarcely be as well off five years hence as he is now."

"He's at the top of the wheel, some of us think."

"What has led to this opinion ?"

"He's beginning to neglect his house, for one thing."

"A bad sign."

"And there is another sign. Heretofore, he has always been on hand, with the cash, when desirable property went off, under forced sale, at a bargain. In the last three or four months, several great sacrifices have been made, but Simon Slade showed no inclination to buy. Put this fact against another,—week before last, he sold a house and lot in the town for five hundred dollars less than he paid for them, a year ago—and for just that sum less than their true value."

"How came that ?" I inquired.

"Ah! there's the question! He wanted money; though for what purpose, he has not intimated to any one, as far as I can learn."

"What do you think of it ?"

"Just this. He and Green have been hunting together in times past; but the professed gambler's instincts are too strong to let him spare even his friend in evil. They have commenced playing one against the other."

"Ah! you think so?"

"I do; and if I conjecture rightly, Simon Slade will be a poorer man, in a year from this time, than he is now."

Here our conversation was interrupted. Some one asked my talkative friend to go and take a drink, and he, nothing loath, left me without ceremony.

Very differently served was the supper I partook of on that evening, from the one set before me on the occasion of my first visit to the "Sickle and Sheaf." The table-cloth was not merely soiled, but offensively dirty; the plates, cups, and saucers, dingy and sticky; the knives and forks unpolished; and the food of a character to satisfy the appetite with a very few mouthfuls. Two greasy-looking Irish girls waited on the table, at which neither landlord nor landlady presided. I was really hungry when the supper-bell rang; but the craving of my stomach soon ceased in the atmosphere of the dining-room, and I was the first to leave the table.

Soon after the lamps were lighted, company began to assembly in the spacious bar-room, where were comfortable seats, with tables, newspapers, backgammon boards, dominoes, etc. The first act of nearly every one who came in, was to call for a glass of liquor; and sometimes the same individual drank two or three times in the course of half an hour, on the invitation of new-comers who were convivially inclined.

Most of those who came in were strangers to me. I was looking from face to face to see if any of the old company were present, when one countenance struck me as familiar. I was studying it, in order, if possible, to identify the person, when some one addressed him as "Judge."

Changed as the face was, I now recognised it as that of Judge Lyman. Five years had marred that face terribly. It seemed twice the former size; and all its bright expression was gone. The thickened and pro-truding eyelids half closed the leaden eyes, and the swollen lips and cheeks gave to his countenance a look of all-predominating sensuality. True manliness had bowed itself in debasing submission to the bestial. He talked loudly, and with a pompous dogmatism—mainly on political subjects—but talked only from memory; for any one could see, that thought came into but feeble activity. And yet, derationalized, so to speak, as he was, through drink, he had been chosen a representa-tive in Congress, at the previous election, on the anti-temperance ticket, and by a very handsome majority. He was the rum candidate; and the rum interest, aided by the easily swayed "indifferents," swept aside the claims of law, order, temperance, and good morals; and the district from which he was chosen as a National Legislator sent him up to the National Councils, and said in the act—" Look upon him we have chosen as our representative, and see in him a type of our principles, our quality, and our condition as a community."

Judge Lyman, around whom a little circle soon gathered, was very severe on the temperance party, which, for two years, had opposed his election, and which, at the last struggle, showed itself to be a rapidly growing organization. During the canvass, a paper was published by this party, in which his personal habits, character, and moral principles were discussed in the freest manner, and certainly not in a way to elevate him in the estimation of men whose opinion was of any value.

It was not much to be wondered at, that he assumed to think temperance issues at the polls were false issues; and that when temperance men sought to tamper with elections, the liberties of the people were in danger; nor that he prononnced the whole body of temperance men as selfish schemers and canting hypocrites.

" The next thing we will have," he exclaimed, warming with his theme, and speaking so loud that his voice sounded throughout the room, and arrested every one's attention, "will be laws to fine any man who takes a chew of tobacco or lights a cigar. Touch the liberties of the people in the smallest particular, and all guarantees are gone. The Stamp Act, against which our noble forefathers rebelled, was a light measure of oppression to that contemplated by these worse than fanatics."

"You are right there, judge; right for once in your life, if you (hic) were never right before!" exclaimed a battered looking specimen of humanity, who stood near the speaker, slapping Judge Lyman on the shoulder familiarly as he spoke. "There's no telling what they will do. There's (hic) my old uncle Josh Wilson, who's been keeper of the Poor-house these ten years. Well, they're going to turn him out, if ever they get the upper hand in Bolton county."

"If? That word involves a great deal, Harry?" said Lyman. "We mus'n't let them get the upper hand Every man has a duty to perform to his country in this matter, and every one must do his duty. But what have they got against your Uncle Joshua? What has he been doing to offend this righteous party?"

"They've nothing against him, (hic) I believe. Only, they say, they're not going to have a Poor-house in the county at all."

"What! Going to turn the poor wretches out to starve?" said one.

"Oh no! (hic)," and the fellow grinned, half shrewdly and half maliciously, as he answered—"no, not that. But, when they carry the day, there'll be no need of Poor-houses. At least, that's their talk—and I guess maybe there's something in it, for I never knew a man to go to the Poor-house, who hadn't (hic) rum to blame for his poverty. But, you see, I'm interested in this matter. I go for keeping up the Poor-house (hic); for

I guess I'm travelling that road, and I should'nt like to get to the last milestone (hic) and find no snug quarters—no Uncle Josh. You're safe for one vote, any how, old chap, on next election day!" And the man's broad hand slapped the member's shoulder again. "Huzza for the rummies! That's (hic) the ticket! Harry Grimes never deserts his friends. True as steel."

"You're a trump!" returned Judge Lyman, with low familiarity. "Never fear about the Poor-house and Uncle Josh. They're all safe."

"But look here, judge," resumed the man. "It isn't only the Poor-house, the jail is to go next."

"Indeed!"

"Yes, that's their talk; and I guess they ain't far out of the way neither. What takes men to jail? You can tell us something about that, judge, for you've jugged a good many in your time. Didn't pretty much all of 'em drink rum? (hic.)"

But the judge answered nothing.

"Silence (hic) gives consent," resumed Grimes. "And they say more; once give 'em the upper hand—and they're confident of beating us—and the Court-house will be to let. As for judges and lawyers, they'll starve, or go into some better business. So you see, (hic) judge, your liberties are in danger. But fight hard, old fellow; and if you must die, (hic) die game!"

How well judge Lyman relished this mode of pre-senting the case, was not very apparent; he was too

good a politician and office-seeker, to show any feeling
on the subject, and thus endanger a vote. Harry
Grimes's vote counted one, and a single vote, sometimes,
gained or lost an election.

"One of their gags," he said, laughing. "But I'm
too old a stager not to see the flimsiness of such preten-
sions. Poverty and crime have their origin in the corrupt heart, and their foundations are laid long and long
before the first step is taken on the road to inebriety.
It is easy to promise results; for only the few look at
causes, and trace them to their effects."

"Rum and ruin, (hic). Are they not cause and
effect?" asked Grimes.

"Sometimes they are," was the half extorted answer.

"Oh, Green! is that you?" exclaimed the judge, as
Harvey Green came in with a soft cat-like step. He
was, evidently, glad of a chance to get rid of his familiar friend and elector.

I turned my eyes upon the man, and read his face
closely. It was unchanged. The same cold, sinister
eye; the same chiselled mouth, so firm now, and now
yielding so elastically; the same smile "from the teeth
outward"—the same lines that revealed his heart's deep,
dark selfishness. If he had indulged in drink during
the five intervening years, it had not corrupted his blood,
nor added thereto a single degree of heat.

"Have you seen any thing of Hammond this evening?" asked Judge Lyman.

"I saw him an hour or two ago," answered Green.

"How does he like his new horse?"

"He's delighted with him."

"What was the price?"

"Three hundred dollars."

"Indeed!"

The judge had already arisen, and he and Green were now walking side by side across the bar-room floor.

"I want to speak a word with you," I heard Lyman say.

And then the two went out together. I saw no more of them during the evening.

Not long afterward, Willy Hammond came in. Ah! there was a sad change here; a change that in no way belied the words of Matthew the bar-keeper. He went up to the bar, and I heard him ask for Judge Lyman. The answer was in so low a voice, that it did not reach my ear.

With a quick, nervous motion, Hammond threw his hand toward a row of decanters on the shelf behind the bar-keeper, who immediately set one of them containing brandy before him. From this he poured a tumbler half full, and drank it off at a single draught, unmixed with water.

He then asked some further question, which I could not hear, manifesting, as it appeared, considerable excitement of mind. In answering him, Matthew glanced his eyes upward, as if indicating some room in the house. The young man then retired, hurridly, through the sitting-room.

"What's the matter with Willy Hammond to-night?" asked some one of the bar-keeper. "Who's he after in such a hurry?"

"He wants to see Judge Lyman," replied Matthew.

"Oh!"

"I guess they're after no good," was remarked.

"Not much, I'm afraid."

Two young men, well dressed, and with faces marked by intelligence, came in at the moment, drank at the bar, chatted a little while familiarly with the bar-keeper, and then quietly disappeared through the door leading into the sitting-room. I met the eyes of the man with whom I had talked during the afternoon, and his knowing wink brought to mind his suggestion, that in one of the upper rooms gambling went on nightly, and that some of the most promising young men of the town had been drawn, through the bar attraction, into this vortex of ruin. I felt a shudder creeping along my nerves.

The conversation that now went on among the company was of such an obscene and profane character, that, in disgust, I went out. The night was clear, the air soft, and the moon shining down brightly. I walked for some time in the porch, musing on what I had seen and heard; while a constant stream of visiters came pouring into the bar-room. Only a few of these remained. The larger portion went in quickly, took their glass, and then left, as if to avoid observation as much as possible.

Soon after I commenced walking in the porch I noticed an elderly lady go slowly by, who, in passing, slightly paused, and evidently tried to look through the bar-room door. The pause was but for an instant. In less than ten minutes she came back, again stopped—this time longer—and again moved off slowly, until she passed out of sight. I was yet thinking about her, when, on lifting my eyes from the ground, she was advancing along the road, but a few rods distant. I almost started at seeing her, for there no longer remained a doubt on my mind, that she was some trembling, heart-sick mother, in search of an erring son whose feet were in dangerous paths. Seeing me, she kept on, though lingeringly. She went but a short distance before returning; and this time, she moved in closer to the house, and reached a position that enabled her eyes to range through a large portion of the bar-room. A nearer inspection appeared to satisfy her. She retired with quicker steps; and did not again return during the evening.

Ah! what a commentary upon the uses of an attractive tavern was here! My heart ached, as I thought of all that unknown mother had suffered; and was doomed to suffer. I could not shut out the image of her drooping form as I lay upon my pillow that night; she even haunted me in my dreams.

NIGHT THE SIXTH.

More Consequences.

THE landlord did not make his appearance on the
next morning until nearly ten o'clock; and then he
looked like a man who had been on a debauch. It was
eleven before Harvey Green came down. Nothing
about him indicated the smallest deviation from the most
orderly habit. Clean shaved, with fresh linen, and a
face every line of which was smoothed into calmness, he
looked as if he had slept soundly on a quiet conscience,
and now hailed the new day with a tranquil spirit.

The first act of Slade was to go behind the bar and
take a stiff glass of brandy and water; the first act of
Green, to order beefsteak and coffee for his breakfast.
I noticed the meeting between the two men, on the appearance of Green. There was a slight reserve on the
part of Green, and an uneasy embarrassment on the
part of Slade. Not even the ghost of a smile was visible in either countenance. They spoke a few words together, and then separated as if from a sphere of mutual
repulsion. I did not observe them again in company
during the day.

"There's trouble over at the mill," was remarked
134

by a gentleman with whom I had some business transactions in the afternoon. He spoke to a person who
sat in his office.

" Ah! what's the matter?" said the other.

" All the hands were discharged at noon, and the mill
shut down."

"How comes that?"

" They've been losing money from the start."

" Rather bad practice, I should say."

" It involves some bad practices, no doubt."

" On Willy's part?"

" Yes. He is reported to have squandered the means
placed in his hands, after a shameless fashion."

" Is the loss heavy?"

" So it is said."

" How much?"

" Reaching to thirty or forty thousand dollars. But
this is rumour, and, of course, an exaggeration."

" Of course. No such loss as that could have been
made. But what was done with the money? How
could Willy have spent it. He dashes about a great
deal; buys fast horses, drinks rather freely, and all
that; but thirty or forty thousand dollars couldn't
escape in this way."

At the moment a swift trotting horse, bearing a light
sulky and a man, went by.

" There goes young Hammond's three hundred dollar animal," said the last speaker.

"It was Willy Hammond's yesterday. But there has been a change of ownership since then; I happen to know."

"Indeed."

"Yes. The man Green, who has been loafing about Cedarville for the last few years—after no good, I can well believe—came into possession to-day."

"Ah? Willy must be very fickle-minded. Does the possession of a coveted object so soon bring satiety?"

"There is something not clearly understood about the transaction. I saw Mr. Hammond during the forenoon, and he looked terribly distressed."

"The embarrassed condition of things at the mill readily accounts for this."

"True; but I think there are causes of trouble beyond the mere embarrassments."

"The dissolute, spendthrift habits of his son," was suggested. "These are sufficient to weigh down the father's spirits,—to bow him to the very dust."

"To speak out plainly," said the other, "I am afraid that the young man adds another vice to that of drinking and idleness."

"What?"

"Gaming."

"No!"

"There is little doubt of it in my mind. And it is further my opinion, that his fine horse, for which he paid three hundred dollars only a few days ago, has passed into the hands of this man Green, in payment of a debt contracted at the gaming table."

"You shock me. Surely, there can be no grounds for such a belief."

"I have, I am sorry to say, the gravest reasons for what I allege. That Green is a professional gambler, who was attracted here by the excellent company that assembled at the 'Sickle and Sheaf' in the beginning of the lazy miller's pauper-making experiment, I do not in the least question. Grant this, and take into account the fact that young Hammond has been much in his company, and you have sufficient cause for the most disastrous effects."

"If this be really so," observed the gentleman, over whose face a shadow of concern darkened, "then Willy Hammond may not be his only victim."

"And is not, you may rest assured. If rumour be true, other of our promising young men are being drawn into the whirling circles that narrow toward a vortex of ruin."

In corroboration of this, I mentioned the conversation I had held with one of the frequenters of Slade's bar-room, on this very subject; and also what I had myself observed on the previous evening.

The man, who had until now been sitting quietly in a chair, started up, exclaiming as he did so—

"Merciful heaven! I never dreamed of this! Whose sons are safe?"

"No man's," was the answer of the gentleman in whose office we were sitting—"No man's—while there are such open doors to ruin as you may find at the 'Sickle and Sheaf.' Did not you vote the anti-temperance ticket at the last election?"

"I did," was the answer; "and from principle."

"On what were your principles based?" was inquired.

"On the broad foundations of civil liberty."

"The liberty to do good or evil, just as the individual may choose?"

"I would not like to say that. There are certain evils against which there can be no legislation that would not do harm. No civil power in this country has the right to say what a citizen shall eat or drink."

"But may not the people, in any community, pass laws, through their delegated law-makers, restraining evil-minded persons from injuring the common good?"

"Oh, certainly—certainly."

"And are you prepared to affirm, that a drinking shop, where young men are corrupted—ay, destroyed, body and soul—does not work an injury to the common good?"

"Ah! but there must be houses of public entertainment."

"No one denies this. But can that be a really Christian community which provides for the moral debasement of strangers, at the same time that it entertains them? Is it necessary that, in giving rest and entertainment to the traveller, we also lead him into temptation ?"

" Yes—But—but——it is going too far to legislate on what we are to eat and drink. It is opening too wide a door for fanatical oppression. We must inculcate temperance as a right principle. We must teach our children the evils of intemperance, and send them out into the world as practical teachers of order, virtue, and sobriety. If we do this, the reform becomes radical, and in a few years there will be no bar-rooms, for none will crave the fiery poison."

" Of little value, my friend, will be, in far too many cases, your precepts, if temptation invites our sons at almost every step of their way through life. Thousands have fallen, and thousands are now tottering, soon to fall. Your sons are not safe ; nor are mine. We cannot tell the day nor the hour when they may weakly yield to the solicitation of some companion, and enter the wide open door of ruin. And are we wise and good citizens to commission men to do the evil work of enticement ? To encourage them to get gain in corrupting and destroying our children ? To hesitate over some vague ideal of human liberty, when the sword is among us, slaying our best and dearest ? Sir ! while you hold back from the work of staying the flood that is desolating our fairest homes, the black waters are approaching your own doors."

There was a startling emphasis in the tones with which

this last sentence was uttered; and I did not wonder at the look of anxious alarm that it called to the face of him whose fears it was meant to excite.

"What do you mean, sir?" was inquired.

"Simply, that your sons are in equal danger with others."

"And is that all?"

"They have been seen, of late, in the bar-room of the 'Sickle and Sheaf.'"

"Who says so?"

"Twice within a week I have seen them going in there," was answered.

"Good heavens! No!"

"It is true, my friend. But who is safe? If we dig pits, and conceal them from view, what marvel if our own children fall therein?"

"My sons going to a tavern!" The man seemed utterly confounded. "How *can* I believe it? You must be in error, sir."

"No. What I tell you is the simple truth. And if they go there——"

The man paused not to hear the conclusion of the sentence, but went hastily from the office.

"We are beginning to reap as we have sown," remarked the gentleman, turning to me as his agitated friend left the office. "As I told them in the commencement it would be, so it is happening. The want of a good tavern in Cedarville was over and over again alleged as one of the chief causes of our want of thrift, and when Slade opened the 'Sickle and Sheaf,' the man was almost glorified. The gentleman who has just left us failed not in laudation of the enterprising landlord; the more particularly, as the building of the new tavern advanced the price of ground on the street, and made him a few hundred dollars richer. Really, for a time, one might have thought, from the way people went on, that Simon Slade was going to make every man's fortune in Cedarville. But all that has been gained by a small advance in property, is as a grain of sand to a mountain, compared with the fearful demoralization that has followed."

I readily assented to this, for I had myself seen enough to justify the conclusion.

As I sat in the bar-room of the "Sickle and Sheaf" that evening, I noticed, soon after the lamps were lighted, the gentleman referred to in the above conversation, whose sons were represented as visitors to the bar, come in quietly, and look anxiously about the room. He spoke to no one, and, after satisfying himself that those he sought were not there, went out.

"What sent him here, I wonder?" muttered Slade, speaking partly to himself, and partly aside to Matthew, the bar-keeper.

"After the boys, I suppose," was answered.

"I guess the boys are old enough to take care of themselves."

"They ought to be," returned Matthew.

"And are," said Slade. "Have they been here this evening?"

"No, not yet."

While they yet talked together, two young men whom I had seen on the night before, and noticed particularly as showing signs of intelligence and respectability beyond the ordinary visiters at a bar-room, came in.

"John," I heard Slade say, in a low, confidential voice, to one of them, "your old man was here just now."

"No!" The young man looked startled—almost confounded.

"It's a fact. So you'd better keep shady."

"What did he want?"

"I don't know."

"What did he say?"

"Nothing. He just came in, looked around, and then went out."

"His face was dark as a thunder-cloud," remarked Matthew.

"Is No. 4 vacant?" inquired one of the young men.

"Yes."

"Send us up a bottle of wine and some cigars. And when Bill Harding and Harry Lee come in, tell them where they can find us."

"All right," said Matthew. "And now take a friend's advice and make yourselves scarce."

The young men left the room hastily. Scarcely had

they departed, ere I saw the same gentleman come in, whose anxious face had, a little while before, thrown its shadow over the apartment. He was the father in search of his sons. Again he glanced around, nervously; and this time appeared to be disappointed. As he entered, Slade went out.

"Have John and Wilson been here this evening?" he asked, coming up to the bar and addressing Matthew.

"They are not here," replied Matthew, evasively.

"But haven't they been here?"

"They *may* have been here; I only came in from my supper a little while ago."

"I thought I saw them entering, only a moment or two ago."

"They're not here, sir." Matthew shook his head and spoke firmly.

"Where is Mr. Slade?"

"In the house, somewhere."

"I wish you would ask him to step here."

Matthew went out, but in a little while came back with word that the landlord was not to be found.

"You are sure the boys are not here," said the man, with a doubting, dissatisfied manner.

"See for yourself, Mr. Harrison!"

"Perhaps they are in the parlour?"

"Step in, sir," coolly returned Matthews. The man went through the door into the sitting-room, but came back immediately.

"Not there?" said Matthew. The man shook his head. "I don't think you will find them about here," added the bar-keeper.

Mr. Harrison—this was the name by which Matthew had addressed him—stood musing and irresolute for some minutes. He could not be mistaken about the entrance of his sons, and yet they were not there. His manner was much perplexed. At length he took a seat, in a far corner of the bar-room, somewhat beyond the line of observation, evidently with the purpose of waiting to see if those he sought would come in. He had not been there long, before two young men entered, whose appearance at once excited his interest. They went up to the bar and called for liquor. As Matthew set the decanter before them, he leaned over the counter, and said something in a whisper.

"Where?" was instantly ejaculated, in surprise, and both of the young men glanced uneasily about the room. They met the eyes of Mr. Harrison, fixed intently upon them. I do not think, from the way they swallowed their brandy and water, that it was enjoyed very much.

"What the deuce is he doing here?" I heard one of them say, in a low voice.

"After the boys, of course."

"Have they come yet?"

Matthew winked as he answered, "All safe."

"In No. 4!"

"Yes. And the wine and cigars all waiting for you."

"Good."

"You'd better not go through the parlour. Their old man's not at all satisfied. He half suspects they're in the house. Better go off down the street, and come back and enter through the passage."

The young men, acting on this hint, at once retired, the eyes of Harrison following them out.

For nearly an hour Mr. Harrison kept his position, a close observer of all that transpired. I am very much in error, if, before leaving that sink of iniquity, he was not fully satisfied as to the propriety of legislating on the liquor question. Nay, I incline to the opinion, that, if the power of suppression had rested in his hands, there would not have been, in the whole State, at the expiration of an hour, a single dram-selling establishment. The goring of his ox had opened his eyes to the true merits of the question. While he was yet in the bar-room, young Hammond made his appearance. His look was wild and excited. First he called for brandy, and drank with the eagerness of a man long athirst.

"Where is Green?" I heard him inquire, as he set his glass upon the counter.

"Haven't seen any thing of him since supper," was answered by Matthew.

"Is he in his room?"

"I think it probable.'

"Has Judge Lyman been about here to-night?"

"Yes. He spouted here for half an hour against the temperance party, as usual, and then"—Matthew tossed his head toward the door leading to the sitting-room.

Hammond was moving toward this door, when, in glancing around the room, he encountered the fixed gaze of Mr. Harrison—a gaze that instantly checked his progress. Returning to the bar, and leaning over the counter, he said to Matthew,

"What has sent him here?"

Matthew winked knowingly.

"After the boys?" inquired Hammond.

"Yes."

"Where are they?"

"Up-stairs."

"Does he suspect this?"

"I can't tell. If he doesn't think them here now, he is looking for them to come in."

"Do they know he is after them?"

"O yes."

"All safe then?"

"As an iron chest. If you want to see them, just tap at No. 4."

Hammond stood for some minutes leaning on the bar, and then, not once again looking toward that part of the room where Mr. Harrison was seated, passed out through the door leading to the street. Soon afterward Mr. Harrison departed.

Disgusted, as on the night before, with the unceasing flow of vile, obscene, and profane language, I left my place of observation in the bar-room and sought the open air. The sky was unobscured by a single cloud, and the moon, almost at the full, shone abroad with more than common brightness. I had not been sitting long in the porch, when the same lady, whose movements had attracted my attention, came in sight, walking very slowly—the deliberate pace assumed, evidently, for the purpose of better observation. On coming opposite the tavern, she slightly paused, as on the evening before, and then kept on, passing down the street, until she was beyond observation.

"Poor mother!" I was still repeating to myself, when her form again met my eyes. Slowly she advanced, and now came in nearer to the house. The interest excited in my mind was so strong, that I could not repress the desire I felt to address her, and so stepped from the shadow of the porch. She seemed startled, and retreated backward several paces.

"Are you in search of any one?" I inquired, respectfully.

The woman now stood in a position that let the moon shine full upon her face, revealing every feature. She was far past the meridian of life; and there were lines of suffering and sorrow on her fine countenance. I saw that her lips moved, but it was some time before I distinguished the words.

"Have you seen my son to-night? They say he comes here."

The manner in which this was said caused a cold thrill to run over me. I perceived that the woman's mind wandered. I answered—

"No, ma'am; I haven't seen any thing of him."

My tone of voice seemed to inspire her with confidence, for she came up close to me, and bent her face toward mine.

"It's a dreadful place," she whispered, huskily. "And they say he comes here. Poor boy! He isn't what he used to be."

"It is a very bad place," said I. "Come"—and I moved a step or two in the direction from which I had seen her approaching—"come, you'd better go away as quickly as possible."

"But if he's here," she answered, not moving from where she stood, "I might save him, you know."

"I am sure you won't find him, ma'am," I urged. "Perhaps he is home, now."

"Oh, no! no!" And she shook her head mournfully. "He never comes home until long after midnight. I wish I could see inside of the bar-room. I'm sure he must be there."

"If you will tell me his name, I will go in and search for him."

After a moment of hesitation, she answered,

"His name is Willy Hammond."

How the name, uttered so sadly, and yet with such moving tenderness by the mother's lips, caused me to start—almost to tremble.

"If he is in the house, ma'am," said I, firmly, "I will see him for you." And I left her and went into the bar.

"In what room do you think I will find young Hammond?" I asked of the bar-keeper.

He looked at me curiously, but did not answer. The question had come upon him unanticipated.

"In Harvey Green's room?" I pursued.

"I don't know, I am sure. He isn't in the house to my knowledge. I saw him go out about half an hour since."

"Green's room is No.——?"

"Eleven," he answered.

"In the front part of the house?"

"Yes."

I asked no further question, but went to No. 11, and tapped on the door. But no one answered the summons. I listened, but could not distinguish the slightest sound within. Again I knocked; but louder. If my ears did not deceive me, the chink of coin was heard. Still there was neither voice nor movement.

I was disappointed. That the room had inmates, I felt sure. Remembering, now, what I had heard about light being seen in this room through a rent in the curtain, I went down-stairs, and out into the street. A

short distance beyond the house, I saw, dimly, the
woman's form. She had only just passed in her movement to and fro. Glancing up at the window, which I
now knew to be the one in Green's room, light through
the torn curtain was plainly visible. Back into the
house I went, and up to No. 11. This time I knocked
imperatively; and this time made myself heard.

"What's wanted?" came from within. I knew the
voice to be that of Harvey Green.

I only knocked louder. A hurried movement and
the low murmur of voices was heard for some moments;
then the door was unlocked and held partly open by
Green, whose body so filled the narrow aperture that I
could not look into the room. Seeing me, a dark scowl
fell upon his countenance.

"What d'ye want?" he inquired, sharply.

"Is Mr. Hammond here? If so, he is wanted down-
stairs."

"No, he's not," was the quick answer. "What sent
you here for him, hey?"

"The fact that I expected to find him in your room,"
was my firm answer.

Green was about shutting the door in my face, when
some one placed a hand on his shoulder, and said something to him that I could not hear.

"Who wants to see him?" he inquired of me.

Satisfied, now, that Hammond was in the room, I
said, slightly elevating my voice,

" His mother."

The words were an " open sesame" to the room. The door was suddenly jerked open, and with a blanching face, the young man confronted me.

" Who says my mother is down-stairs ?" he demanded.

" I come from her in search of you," said I. " You will find her in the road, walking up and down in front of the tavern."

Almost with a bound he swept by me, and descended the stairway at two or three long strides. As the door swung open, I saw, besides Green and Hammond, the landlord and Judge Lyman. It needed not the loose cards on a table near which the latter were sitting to tell me of their business in that room.

As quickly as seemed decorous, I followed Hammond. On the porch I met him, coming in from the road.

" You have deceived me, sir," said he, sternly—almost menacingly.

" No, sir!" I replied. " What I told you was but too true. Look! There she is now."

The young man sprung around, and stood before the woman, a few paces distant.

" Mother! oh, mother! what *has* brought you here?" he exclaimed, in an under tone, as he caught her arm, and moved away. He spoke—not roughly, nor angrily —but with respect—half reproachfulness—and an unmistakable tenderness.

" Oh, Willy! Willy!" I heard her answer. " Somebody said you came here at night, and I couldn't rest. Oh, dear! They'll murder you! I know they will. Don't, oh!——"

My ears took in the sense no further, though her pleading voice still reached my ears. A few moments, and they were out of sight.

Nearly two hours afterward, as I was ascending to my chamber, a man brushed quickly by me. I glanced after him, and recognised the person of young Hammond. He was going to the room of Harvey Green!

NIGHT THE SEVENTH.

Sowing the Wind.

THE state of affairs in Cedarville, it was plain, from the partial glimpses I had received, was rather desperate. Desperate, I mean, as regarded the various parties brought before my observation. An eating cancer was on the community, and so far as the eye could mark its destructive progress, the ravages were fearful. That its roots were striking deep, and penetrating, concealed from view, in many unsuspected directions, there could be no doubt. What appeared on the surface was but a milder form of the disease, compared with its hidden, more vital, and more dangerous advances.

I could not but feel a strong interest in some of these parties. The case of young Hammond, had from the first, awakened concern; and now a new element was added in the unlooked-for appearance of his mother on the stage, in a state that seemed one of partial derangement. The gentleman at whose office I met Mr. Harrison on the day before—the reader will remember Mr. H. as having come to the "Sickle and Sheaf" in search of his sons—was thoroughly conversant with the affairs of the village, and I called upon him early in the day in order to make some inquiries about Mrs. Hammond. My first question, as to whether he knew the lady, was answered by the remark—

"Oh, yes. She is one of my earliest friends."

The allusion to her did not seem to awaken agreeable states of mind. A slight shade obscured his face, and I noticed that he sighed involuntarily.

"Is Willy her only child?"

"Her only living child. She had four; another son, and two daughters; but she lost all but Willy when they were quite young. And," he added, after a pause— "it would have been better for her, and for Willy too, if he had gone to a better land with them."

"His course of life must be to her a terrible afflic- tion," said I.

"It is destroying her reason," he replied, with em- phasis. "He was her idol. No mother ever loved a son with more self-devotion than Mrs. Hammond loved her beautiful, fine-spirited, intelligent, affectionate boy. To say that she was proud of him, is but a tame expres- sion. Intense love—almost idolatry—was the strong passion of her heart. How tender, how watchful was her love! Except when at school, he was scarcely ever separated from her. In order to keep him by her side, she gave up her thoughts to the suggestion and maturing of plans for keeping his mind active and interested in her society—and her success was perfect. Up to the age of sixteen or seventeen, I do not think he had a desire for other companionship than that of his mother. But this, you know, could not last. The boy's maturing thought must go beyond the home and social circle. The great world, that he was soon to enter, was before him; and through loopholes that opened here and there, he obtained partial glimpses of what was beyond. To step forth into this world, where he was soon to be a busy actor and worker, and to step forth alone, next came in the natural order of progress. How his mother trembled with anxiety, as she saw him leave her side. Of the dangers that would surround his path, she knew too well; and these were magnified by her fears—at least so I often said to her. Alas! how far the sad reality has outrun her most fearful anticipations.

"When Willy was eighteen—he was then reading law—I think I never saw a young man of fairer promise. As I have often heard it remarked of him, he did not appear to have a single fault. But he had a dangerous gift—rare conversational powers, united with great urbanity of manner. Every one who made his acquaintance became charmed with his society; and he soon found himself surrounded by a circle of young men, some of whom were not the best companions he might have chosen. Still, his own pure instincts and honourable principles were his safeguard; and I never have believed that any social allurements would have drawn him away from the right path, if this accursed tavern had not been opened by Slade."

"There was a tavern here before the 'Sickle and Sheaf' was opened," said I.

"Oh, yes. But it was badly kept, and the bar-room visitors were of the lowest class. No respectable young man in Cedarville would have been seen there. It offered no temptations to one moving in Willy's circle. But the opening of the 'Sickle and Sheaf' formed a new era. Judge Hammond—himself not the purest man in the world, I'm afraid—gave his countenance to the establishment, and talked of Simon Slade as an enterprising man who ought to be encouraged. Judge Lyman and other men of position in Cedarville followed his bad example; and the bar-room of the 'Sickle and Sheaf' was at once voted respectable. At all times of the day and evening you could see the flower of our young men going in and out, sitting in front of the bar-room, or talking hand and glove with the landlord, who, from a worthy miller, regarded as well enough in his place, was suddenly elevated into a man of importance, whom the best in the village were delighted to honour.

"In the beginning, Willy went with the tide, and, in an incredibly short period, was acquiring a fondness for drink that startled and alarmed his friends. In going in through Slade's open door, he entered the downward way, and has been moving onward with fleet footsteps ever since. The fiery poison inflamed his mind, at the same time that it dimmed his noble perceptions. Fondness for mere pleasure followed, and this led him into various sensual indulgences, and exciting modes of passing the time. Every one liked him—he was so free, so companionable, and so generous—and almost every one encouraged, rather than repressed, his dangerous proclivities. Even his father, for a time, treated the matter lightly, as only the first flush of young life. 'I commenced sowing my wild oats at quite as early an age,' I have heard him say. 'He'll cool off, and do well enough. Never fear.' But his mother was in a state of painful alarm from the beginning. Her truer instincts, made doubly acute by her yearning love, perceived the imminent danger, and in all possible ways did she seek to lure him from the path in which he was moving at so rapid a pace. Willy was always very much attached to his mother, and her influence over him was strong; but in this case he regarded her fears as chimerical. The way in which he walked was, to him, so pleasant, and the companions of his journey so delightful, that he could not believe in the prophesied evil; and when his mother talked to him in her warning voice, and with a sad countenance, he smiled at her concern, and made light of her fears.

"And so it went on, month after month, and year after year, until the young man's sad declensions were the town talk. In order to throw his mind into a new channel—to awaken, if possible, a new and better interest in life—his father ventured upon the doubtful experiment we spoke of yesterday: that of placing capital in his hands, and making him an equal partner in the business of distilling and cotton-spinning. The disastrous—I might say disgraceful result—you know. The young man squandered his own capital, and heavily embarrassed his father.

"The effect of all this upon Mrs. Hammond has been painful in the extreme. We can only dimly imagine the terrible suffering through which she has passed. Her present aberration was first visible after a long period of sleeplessness, occasioned by distress of mind. During the whole of two weeks, I am told, she did not close her eyes; the most of that time walking the floor of her chamber, and weeping. Powerful anodynes, frequently repeated, at length brought relief. But, when she awoke from a prolonged period of unconsciousness, the brightness of her reason was gone. Since then, she has never been clearly conscious of what was passing around her, and well for her, I have sometimes thought it was, for even obscurity of intellect is a blessing in her case. Ah, me! I always get the heart-ache, when I think of her."

"Did not this event startle the young man from his fatal dream, if I may so call his mad infatuation?" I asked.

"No. He loved his mother, and was deeply afflicted by the calamity; but it seemed as if he could not stop. Some terrible necessity appeared to be impelling him onward. If he formed good resolutions—and I doubt not that he did,—they were blown away like threads of gossamer, the moment he came within the sphere of old associations. His way to the mill was by the 'Sickle and Sheaf;' and it was not easy for him to pass there without being drawn into the bar, either by his own desire for drink or through the invitation of some pleasant companion, who was lounging in front of the tavern."

"There may have been something even more impelling than his love of drink," said I.

"What ?"

I related, briefly, the occurrences of the preceding night.

"I feared—nay, I was certain—that he was in the toils of this man ! And yet your confirmation of the fact startles and confounds me," said he, moving about his office in a disturbed manner. "If my mind has questioned and doubted in regard to young Hammond, it questions and doubts no longer. The word 'mystery' is not now written over the door of his habitation. Great Father ! and is it thus that our young men are led into temptation ? Thus that their ruin is premeditated, secured ? Thus that the fowler is permitted to spread his net in the open day, and the destroyer licensed to work ruin in darkness ? It is awful to contemplate !"

The man was strongly excited.

"Thus it is," he continued ; "and we who see the

whole extent, origin, and downward rushing force of a widely sweeping desolation, lift our voices of warning almost in vain. Men who have every thing at stake—sons to be corrupted, and daughters to become the wives of young men exposed to corrupting influences—stand aloof, questioning and doubting as to the expediency of protecting the innocent from the wolfish designs of bad men, who, to compass their own selfish ends, would destroy them body and soul. We are called fanatics, ultraists, designing, and all that, because we ask our law-makers to stay the fiery ruin. Oh, no! we must not touch the traffic. All the dearest and best interests of society may suffer; but the rum-seller must be protected. He must be allowed to get gain, if the jails and poor-houses are filled, and the graveyards made fat with the bodies of young men stricken down in the flower of their years, and of wives and mothers who have died of broken hearts. Reform, we are told, must commence at home. We must rear temperate children, and then we shall have temperate men. That when there are none to desire liquor, the rum-seller's traffic will cease. And all the while society's true benefactors are engaged in doing this, the weak, the unsuspecting, and the erring must be left an easy prey, even if the work requires for its accomplishment a hundred years. Sir! a human soul destroyed through the rum-seller's infernal agency, is a sacrifice priceless in value. No considerations of worldly gain can, for an instant, be placed in comparison therewith. And yet souls are destroyed by thousands every year; and they will fall by tens of thousands ere society awakens from its fatal indifference, and lays its strong hand of power on the corrupt men who are scattering disease, ruin, and death, broadcast over the land!

"I always get warm on this subject," he added, repressing his enthusiasm. "And who that observes and reflects can help growing excited? The evil is appalling; and the indifference of the community one of the strangest facts of the day."

While he was yet speaking, the elder Mr. Hammond came in. He looked wretched. The redness and humidity of his eyes showed want of sleep, and the relaxed muscles of his face exhaustion from weariness and suffering. He drew the person with whom I had been talking aside, and continued in earnest conversation with him for many minutes—often gesticulating violently. I could see his face, though I heard nothing of what he said. The play of his features was painful to look upon, for every changing muscle showed a new phase of mental suffering.

"Try and see him, will you not?" he said, as he turned, at length, to leave the office.

"I will go there immediately," was answered.

"Bring him home, if possible."

"My very best efforts shall be made."

Judge Hammond bowed, and went out hurriedly.

"Do you know the number of the room occupied by

the man Green ?" asked the gentleman, as soon as his visitor had retired.

"Yes. It is No. 11."

"Willy has not been home since last night. His father, at this late day, suspects Green to be a gambler! The truth flashed upon him only yesterday ; and this, added to his other sources of trouble, is driving him, so he says, almost mad. As a friend, he wishes me to go to the 'Sickle and Sheaf,' and try and find Willy. Have you seen any thing of him this morning ?"

I answered in the negative.

"Nor of Green ?"

"No."

"Was Slade about when you left the tavern ?"

"I saw nothing of him."

"What Judge Hammond fears may be all too true— that, in the present condition of Willy's affairs, which have reached the point of disaster, his tempter means to secure the largest possible share of property yet in his power to pledge or transfer,—to squeeze from his victim the last drop of blood that remains, and then fling him, ruthlessly, from his hands."

"The young man must have been rendered almost desperate, or he would never have returned, as he did, last night. Did you mention this to his father ?"

"No. It would have distressed him the more, without effecting any good. He is wretched enough. But time passes, and none is to be lost now. Will you go with me ?"

I walked to the tavern with him; and we went into the bar together. Two or three men were at the counter, drinking.

"Is Mr. Green about this morning?" was asked by the person who had come in search of young Hammond.

"Haven't seen any thing of him."

"Is he in his room?"

"I don't know."

"Will you ascertain for me?"

"Certainly. Frank,"—and he spoke to the landlord's son, who was lounging on a settee,—"I wish you would see if Mr. Green is in his room."

"Go and see yourself. I'm not your waiter," was growled back, in an ill-natured voice.

"In a moment I'll ascertain for you," said Matthew, politely.

After waiting on some new customers, who were just entering, Matthew went up-stairs to obtain the desired information. As he left the bar-room, Frank got up and went behind the counter, where he mixed himself a glass of liquor, and drank it off, evidently with real enjoyment.

"Rather a dangerous business for one so young as you are," remarked the gentleman with whom I had come, as Frank stepped out of the bar, and passed near where we were standing. The only answer to this was an ill-natured frown, and an expression of face which said, almost as plainly as words, "It's none of your business."

"Not there," said Matthew, now coming in.

"Are you certain?"

"Yes, sir."

But there was a certain involuntary hesitation in the bar-keeper's manner, which led to a suspicion that his answer was not in accordance with the truth. We walked out together, conferring on the subject, and both concluded that his word was not to be relied upon.

"What is to be done?" was asked.

"Go to Green's room," I replied, "and knock at the door. If he is there, he may answer, not suspecting your errand."

"Show me the room.'

I went up with him, and pointed out No. 11. He knocked lightly, but there came no sound from within. He repeated the knock; all was silent. Again and again he knocked, but there came back only a hollow reverberation.

"There's no one there," said he, returning to where I stood, and we walked down-stairs together. On the landing, as we reached the lower passage, we met Mrs. Slade. I had not, during this visit at Cedarville, stood face to face with her before. Oh! what a wreck she presented, with her pale, shrunken countenance, hollow, lustreless eyes, and bent, feeble body. I almost shuddered as I looked at her. What a haunting and sternly rebuking spectre she must have moved, daily, before the eyes of her husband.

"Have you noticed Mr. Green about this morning?" I asked.

"He hasn't come down from his room yet," she replied.

"Are you certain?" said my companion. "I knocked several times at the door just now, but received no answer."

"What do you want with him?" asked Mrs. Slade, fixing her eyes upon us.

"We are in search of Willy Hammond; and it has been suggested that he is with Green."

"Knock twice lightly, and then three times more firmly," said Mrs. Slade; and as she spoke, she glided past us with noiseless tread.

"Shall we go up together?"

I did not object, for, although I had no delegated right of intrusion, my feelings were so much excited in the case, that I went forward, scarcely reflecting on the propriety of so doing.

The signal knock found instant answer. The door was softly opened, and the unshaven face of Simon Slade presented itself.

"Mr. Jacobs!" he said, with surprise in his tones. "Do you wish to see me?"

"No, sir; I wish to see Mr. Green," and with a quick, firm pressure against the door, he pushed it wide open. The same party was there that I had seen on the night before,—Green, young Hammond, Judge Lyman, and

Slade. On the table at which the three former were sitting, were cards, slips of paper, an inkstand and pens, and a pile of bank-notes. On a side table, or, rather, butler's tray, were bottles, decanters, and glasses.

"Judge Lyman! Is it possible?" exclaimed Mr. Jacobs, the name of my companion : " I did not expect to find you here."

Green instantly swept his hands over the table to secure the money and bills it contained ; but, ere he had accomplished his purpose, young Hammond grappled three or four narrow strips of paper, and hastily tore them into shreds.

" You're a cheating scoundrel !" cried Green, fiercely, thrusting his hand into his bosom as if to draw from thence a weapon ; but, the words were scarcely uttered, ere Hammond sprung upon him with the fierceness of a tiger, bearing him down upon the floor. Both hands were already about the gambler's neck, and, ere the bewildered spectators could interfere, and drag him off, Green was purple in the face, and nearly strangled.

" Call me a cheating scoundrel !" said Hammond, foaming at the mouth, as he spoke,—" Me ! whom you have followed like a thirsty bloodhound. Me ! whom you have robbed, and cheated, and debased from the beginning ! Oh ! for a pistol to rid the earth of the blackest-hearted villain that walks its surface. Let me go, gentlemen ! I have nothing left in the world to care for,—there is no consequence I fear. Let me do society one good service before I die!"

And, with one vigorous effort, he swept himself clear of the hands that were pinioning him, and sprung again upon the gambler with the fierce energy of a savage beast. By this time, Green had got his knife free from its sheath, and, as Hammond was closing upon him in his blind rage, plunged it into his side. Quick almost as lightning, the knife was withdrawn, and two more stabs inflicted ere we could seize and disarm the murderer. As we did so, Willy Hammond fell over with a deep groan, the blood flowing from his side.

In the terror and excitement that followed, Green rushed from the room. The doctor, who was instantly summoned, after carefully examining the wound, and the condition of the unhappy young man, gave it as his opinion that he was fatally injured.

Oh! the anguish of the father, who had quickly heard of the dreadful occurrence, when this announcement was made. I never saw such fearful agony in any human countenance. The calmest of all the anxious group was Willy himself. On his father's face his eyes were fixed as if by a kind of fascination.

"Are you in much pain, my poor boy!" sobbed the old man, stooping over him, until his long white hair mingled with the damp locks of the sufferer.

"Not much, father," was the whispered reply. "Don't speak of this to mother, yet. I'm afraid it will kill her."

What could the father answer? Nothing! And he was silent.

"Does she know of it?" A shadow went over his face.

Mr. Hammond shook his head.

Yet, even as he spoke, a wild cry of distress was heard below. Some indiscreet person had borne to the ears of the mother the fearful news about her son, and she had come wildly flying toward the tavern, and was just entering.

'It is my poor mother," said Willy, a flush coming into his pale face. "Who could have told her of this?"

Mr. Hammond started for the door, but ere he had reached it, the distracted mother entered.

"Oh! Willy, my boy! my boy!" she exclaimed, in tones of anguish that made the heart shudder. And she crouched down on the floor, the moment she reached the bed whereon he lay, and pressed her lips—oh, so tenderly and lovingly!—to his.

"Dear mother! Sweet mother! Best of mothers!" He even smiled as he said this; and, into the face that now bent over him, looked up with glances of unutterable fondness.

"Oh, Willy! Willy! Willy! my son, my son!" And again her lips were laid closely to his.

Mr. Hammond now interfered, and endeavoured to remove his wife, fearing for the consequence upon his son.

"Don't, father!" said Willy; "let her remain. I

am not excited nor disturbed. I am glad that she is here, now. It will be best for us both."

" You must not excite him, dear," said Mr. Hammond—" he is very weak."

" I'll not excite him," answered the mother. " I'll not speak a word. There, love"—and she laid her fingers softly upon the lips of her son—" don't speak a single word."

For only a few moments did she sit with the quiet formality of a nurse, who feels how much depends on the repose of her patient. Then she began, weeping, moaning, and wringing her hands.

" Mother!" The feeble voice of Willy stilled, instantly, the tempest of feeling. " Mother, kiss me!"

She bent down and kissed him.

" Are you there, mother?" His eyes moved about, with a straining motion.

" Yes, love, here I am."

" I don't see you, mother. It's getting so dark. Oh, mother! mother!" he shouted suddenly, starting up and throwing himself forward upon her bosom—" save me! save me!"

How quickly did the mother clasp her arms around him—how eagerly did she strain him to her bosom! The doctor, fearing the worst consequences, now came forward, and endeavoured to release the arms of Mrs. Hammond, but she resisted every attempt to do so.

" I will save you, my son," she murmured in the ears

of the young man. "Your mother will protect you. Oh! if you had never left her side, nothing on earth could have done you harm."

"He is dead!" I heard the doctor whisper; and, a thrill of horror went through me. The words reached the ears of Mr. Hammond, and his groan was one of almost mortal agony.

"Who says he is dead?" came sharply from the lips of the mother, as she pressed the form of her child back upon the bed from which he had sprung to her arms, and looked wildly upon his face. One long scream of horror told of her convictions, and she fell, lifeless, across the body of her dead son!

All in the room believed that Mrs. Hammond had only fainted. But the doctor's perplexed, troubled countenance, as he ordered her carried into another apartment, and the ghastliness of her face when it was upturned to the light, suggested to every one what proved to be true. Even to her obscured perceptions, the consciousness that her son was dead came with a terrible vividness—so terrible, that it extinguished her life.

Like fire among dry stubble ran the news of this fearful event through Cedarville. The whole town was wild with excitement. The prominent fact, that Willy Hammond had been murdered by Green, whose real profession was known by many, and now declared to all, was on every tongue; but a hundred different and exaggerated stories as to the cause and the particulars of the event were in circulation. By the time preparations to remove the dead bodies of mother and son from the " Sickle and Sheaf," to the residence of Mr. Hammond, were completed, hundreds of people, men, women, and children, were assembled around the tavern; and many voices were clamorous for Green; while some called out for Judge Lyman, whose name, it thus appeared, had become associated in the minds of the people with the murderous affair. The appearance, in the midst of this excitement, of the two dead bodies, borne forth on settees, did not tend to allay the feverish state of indignation that prevailed. From more than one voice, I heard the words, " Lynch the scoundrel!"

A part of the crowd followed the sad procession, while the greater portion, consisting of men, remained about the tavern. All bodies, no matter for what purpose assembled, quickly find leading spirits who, feeling the great moving impulse, give it voice and direction. It was so in this case. Intense indignation against Green was firing every bosom; and when a man elevated himself a few feet above the agitated mass of humanity, and cried out—

" The murderer must not escape!"

A wild responding shout, terrible in its fierceness, made the air quiver.

" Let ten men be chosen to search the house and premises," said the leading spirit.

"Ay! ay! Choose them! Name them!" was quickly answered.

Ten men were called by name, who instantly stepped in front of the crowd.

"Search everywhere; from garret to cellar; from hayloft to dog-kennel. Everywhere! everywhere!" cried the man.

And instantly the ten men entered the house. For nearly a quarter of an hour, the crowd waited with increasing signs of impatience. These delegates at length appeared, with the announcement that Green was nowhere about the premises. It was received with a groan.

"Let no man in Cedarville do a stroke of work until the murderer is found," now shouted the individual who still occupied his elevated position.

"Agreed! agreed! No work in Cedarville until the murderer is found," rang out fiercely.

"Let all who have horses, saddle and bridle them as quickly as possible, and assemble, mounted, at the Court House."

About fifty men left the crowd hastily.

"Let the crowd part in the centre, up and down the road, starting from a line in front of me."

This order was obeyed.

"Separate again, taking the centre of the road for a line."

Four distinct bodies of men stood now in front of the tavern.

"Now search for the murderer in every nook and corner, for a distance of three miles from this spot; each party keeping to its own section; the road being one dividing line, and a line through the centre of this tavern the other. The horsemen will pursue the wretch to a greater distance."

More than a hundred acquiescing voices responded to this, as the man sprung down from his elevation and mingled with the crowd, which began instantly to move away on its appointed mission.

As the hours went by, one, and another, and another, of the searching party returned to the village, wearied with their efforts, or confident that the murderer had made good his escape. The horsemen, too, began to come in, during the afternoon, and by sundown, the last of them, worn out and disappointed, made their appearance.

For hours after the exciting events of the forenoon, there were but few visitors at the "Sickle and Sheaf." Slade, who did not show himself among the crowd, came down soon after its dispersion. He had shaved and put on clean linen; but still bore many evidences of a night spent without sleep. His eyes were red and heavy and the eyelids swollen; while his skin was relaxed and colourless. As he descended the stairs, I was walking in the passage. He looked shy at me, and merely nodded. Guilt was written plainly on his countenance; and with it was blended anxiety and alarm.

That he might be involved in trouble, he had reason to fear ; for, he was one of the party engaged in gambling in Green's room, as both Mr. Jacobs and I had witnessed.

"This is dreadful business," said he, as we met, face to face, half an hour afterward.   He did not look me steadily in the eyes.

"It is horrible!" I answered.   "To corrupt and ruin a young man, and then murder him!   There are few deeds in the catalogue of crime blacker than this."

"It was done in the heat of passion," said the land-lord, with something of apology in his manner.   "Green never meant to kill him."

"In peaceful intercourse with his fellow men, why did he carry a deadly weapon?   There was murder in his heart, sir."

"That is speaking very strongly."

"Not stronger than facts will warrant," I replied. "That Green is a murderer in heart, it needed not this awful consummation to show.   With a cool, deliberate purpose, he has sought, from the beginning, to destroy young Hammond."

"It is hardly fair," answered Slade, "in the present feverish excitement against Green, to assume such a questionable position.   It may do him a great wrong."

"Did Willy Hammond speak only idle words, when he accused Green of having followed him like a thirsty bloodhound?—of having robbed, and cheated, and de-based him from the beginning?"

" He was terribly excited at the moment."

" Yet," said I, "no ear that heard his words could for an instant doubt that they were truthful utterances, wrung from a maddened heart."

My earnest, positive manner had its effect upon Slade. He knew that what I asserted, the whole history of Green's intercourse with young Hammond would prove; and he had, moreover, the guilty consciousness of being a party to the young man's ruin. His eyes cowered beneath the steady gaze I fixed upon him. I thought of him as one implicated in the murder, and my thought must have been visible in my face.

" One murder will not justify another," said he.

" There is no justification for murder on any plea," was my response.

"And yet, if these infuriated men find Green, they will murder him."

"I hope not. Indignation at a horrible crime has fearfully excited the people. But I think their sense of justice is strong enough to prevent the consequences you apprehend."

"I would not like to be in Green's shoes," said the landlord, with an uneasy movement.

I looked him closely in the face. It was the punishment of the man's crime that seemed so fearful in his eyes; not the crime itself. Alas! how the corrupting traffic had debased him.

My words were so little relished by Slade, that he

found some ready excuse to leave me. I saw but little more of him during the day.

As evening began to fall, the gambler's unsuccessful pursuers, one after another, found their way to the tavern, and by the time night had fairly closed in, the bar-room was crowded with excited and angry men, chafing over their disappointment, and loud in their threats of vengeance. That Green had made good his escape, was now the general belief; and the stronger this conviction became, the more steadily did the current of passion begin to set in a new direction. It had become known to every one, that, besides Green and young Hammond, Judge Lyman and Slade were in the room engaged in playing cards. The merest suggestion as to the complicity of these two men with Green in ruining Hammond, and thus driving him mad, was enough to excite strong feeling against them; and now that the mob had been cheated of its victim, its pent up indignation sought eagerly some new channel.

"Where's Slade?" some one asked, in a loud voice, from the centre of the crowded bar-room. "Why does he keep himself out of sight?"

"Yes; where's the landlord?" half a dozen voices responded.

"Did he go on the hunt?" some one inquired.

"No!" "No!" "No!" ran round the room. "Not he."

"And yet, the murder was committed in his own house, and before his own eyes!"

"Yes, before his own eyes!" repeated one and another, indignantly.

"Where's Slade? Where's the landlord? Has anybody seen him to-night? Matthew, where's Simon Slade?"

From lip to lip passed these interrogations; while the crowd of men became agitated, and swayed to and fro.

"I don't think he's home," answered the bar-keeper, in a hesitating manner, and with visible alarm.

"How long since he was here?"

"I haven't seen him for a couple of hours."

"That's a lie!" was sharply said.

"Who says it's a lie?" Matthew affected to be strongly indignant.

"I do!" And a rough, fierce-looking man confronted him.

"What right have you to say so?" asked Matthew, cooling off considerably.

"Because you lie!" said the man, boldly. "You've seen him within a less time than half an hour, and well you know it. Now, if you wish to keep yourself out of this trouble, answer truly. We are in no mood to deal with liars or equivocators. Where is Simon Slade?"

"I do not know," replied Matthew, firmly.

"Is he in the house?"

"He may be, or he may not be. I am just as igno-rant of his exact whereabouts as you are."

"Will you look for him?"

Matthew stepped to the door, opening from behind the bar, and called the name of Frank.

"What's wanted?" growled the boy.

"Is your father in the house?"

"I don't know, nor don't care," was responded in the same ungracious manner.

"Some one bring him into the bar-room, and we'll see if we can't make him care a little."

The suggestion was no sooner made, than two men glided behind the bar, and passed into the room from which the voice of Frank had issued. A moment after they reappeared, each grasping an arm of the boy, and bearing him like a weak child between them. He looked thoroughly frightened at this unlooked for invasion of his liberty.

"See here, young man." One of the leading spirits of the crowd addressed him, as soon as he was brought in front of the counter. "If you wish to keep out of trouble, answer our questions at once, and to the point. We are in no mood for trifling. Where's your father?"

"Somewhere about the house, I believe," Frank re-plied, in an humbled tone. He was no little scared at the summary manner with which he had been treated.

"How long since you saw him?"

"Not long ago."

" Ten minutes ?"

" No : nearly half an hour."

" Where was he then ?"

" He was going up-stairs."

"Very well, we want him. See him, and tell him so."

Frank went into the house, but came back into the bar-room after an absence of nearly five minutes, and said that he could not find his father anywhere.

"Where is he then ?" was angrily demanded.

"Indeed, gentlemen, I don't know." Frank's anxious look and frightened manner showed that he spoke truly.

"There's something wrong about this—something wrong—wrong," said one of the men. "Why should he be absent now? Why has he taken no steps to secure the man who committed a murder in his own house, and before his own eyes ?"

" I shouldn't wonder if he aided him to escape," said another, making this serious charge with a restlessness and want of evidence that illustrated the reckless and unjust spirit by which a mob is ever governed.

"No doubt of it in the least!" was the quick and positive response. And at once this erroneous conviction seized upon every one. Not a single fact was presented. The simple, bold assertion, that no doubt existed in the mind of one man as to Slade's having aided Green to escape, was sufficient for the unreflecting mob.

"Where is he? Where is he? Let us find him. He knows where Green is, and he shall reveal the secret."

This was enough. The passions of the crowd were at
fever heat again. Two or three men were chosen to
search the house and premises, while others dispersed to
take a wider range. One of the men who volunteered
to go over the house was a person named Lyon, with
whom I had formed some acquaintance, and several
times conversed with on the state of affairs in Cedarville.
He still remained too good a customer at the bar. I
left the bar at the same time that he did, and went up
to my room. We walked side by side, and parted at
my door, I going in, and he continuing on to make his
searches. I felt, of course, anxious and much excited,
as well in consequence of the events of the day, as the
present aspect of things. My head was aching violently,
and in the hope of getting relief, I laid myself down.
I had already lighted a candle, and turned the key in
my door to prevent intrusion. Only for a short time
did I lie, listening to the hum of voices that came with
a hoarse murmur from below, to the sound of feet moving
along the passages, and to the continual opening and
shutting of doors, when something like suppressed
breathing reached my ears. I started up instantly, and
listened; but my quickened pulses were now audible to
my own sense, and obscured what was external.

"It is only imagination," I said to myself. Still, I
sat upright, listening.

Satisfied, at length, that all was mere fancy, I laid
myself back on the pillow, and tried to turn my thoughts

away from the suggested idea that some one was in the room. Scarcely had I succeeded in this, when my heart gave a new impulse, as a sound like a movement fell upon my ears.

"Mere fancy!" I said to myself, as some one went past the door at the moment. "My mind is over excited."

Still I raised my head, supporting it with my hand, and listened, directing my attention inside, and not outside of the room. I was about letting my head fall back upon the pillow, when a slight cough, so distinct as not to be mistaken, caused me to spring to the floor, and look under the bed. The mystery was explained. A pair of eyes glittered in the candlelight. The fugitive, Green, was under my bed. For some moments I stood looking at him, so astonished that I had neither utterance nor decision; while he glared at me with a fierce defiance. I saw that he was clutching a revolver.

"Understand!" he said, in a grating whisper, "that I am not to be taken alive."

I let the blanket, which had concealed him from view, fall from my hand, and then tried to collect my thoughts.

"Escape is impossible," said I, again lifting the temporary curtain by which he was hid. "The whole town is armed, and on the search; and should you fall into the hands of the mob, in its present state of exasperation, your life would not be safe an instant. Remain, then, quiet, where you are, until I can see the sheriff, to whom you had better resign yourself, for there's little chance for you except under his protection."

After a brief parley, he consented that things should take this course, and I went out, locking the room door after me, and started in search of the sheriff. On the information I gave, the sheriff acted promptly. With five officers, fully armed for defence, in case an effort were made to get the prisoner out of their hands, he repaired immediately to the "Sickle and Sheaf." I had given the key of my room into his possession.

The appearance of the sheriff, with his posse, was sufficient to start the suggestion that Green was somewhere concealed in the house; and a suggestion was only needed to cause the fact to be assumed, and unhesitatingly declared. Intelligence went through the reassembling crowd like an electric current, and ere the sheriff could manacle and lead forth his prisoner, the stairway down which he had to come was packed with bodies, and echoing with oaths and maledictions.

"Gentlemen, clear the way!" cried the sheriff, as he appeared with the white and trembling culprit at the head of the stairs. "The murderer is now in the hands of the law, and will meet the sure consequences of his crime."

A shout of execration rent the air; but not a single individual stirred.

"Give way, there! Give way!" And the sheriff

took a step or two forward, but the prisoner held back.

"Oh, the murdering villain! The cursed blackleg! Where's Willy Hammond!" was heard distinctly above the confused mingling of voices.

"Gentlemen! the law must have its course; and no good citizen will oppose the law. It is made for your protection—for mine—and for that of the prisoner."

"Lynch law is good enough for him," shouted a savage voice. "Hand him over to us, sheriff, and we'll save you the trouble of hanging him, and the county the cost of a gallows. We'll do the business right."

Five men, each armed with a revolver, now ranged themselves around the sheriff, and the latter said firmly,

"It is my duty to see this man safely conveyed to prison; and I'm going to do my duty. If there is any more blood shed here, the blame will rest with you." And the body of officers pressed forward, the mob slowly retreating before them.

Green, overwhelmed with terror, held back. I was standing where I could see his face. It was ghastly with mortal fear. Grasping his pinioned arms, the sheriff forced him onward. After contending with the crowd for nearly ten minutes, the officers gained the passage below; but the mob was denser here, and blocking up the door, resolutely maintained their position.

Again and again the sheriff appealed to the good sense and justice of the people.

"The prisoner will have to stand a trial; and the law will execute sure vengeance."

"No, it won't!" was sternly responded.

"Who'll be judge in the case?" was asked.

"Why, Judge Lyman!" was contemptuously answered.

"A blackleg himself!" was shouted by two or three voices.

"Blackleg judge, and blackleg lawyers! Oh, yes! The law will execute sure vengeance! Who was in the room gambling with Green and Hammond?"

"Judge Lyman!" "Judge Lyman!" was answered back.

"It won't do, sheriff! There's no law in the country to reach the case but Lynch law; and that the scoundrel must have.   Give him to us!"

"Never! On, men, with the prisoner!" cried the sheriff resolutely, and the *posse* made a rush toward the door, bearing back the resisting and now infuriated crowd.   Shouts, cries, oaths, and savage imprecations blended in wild discord; in the midst of which my blood was chilled by the sharp crack of a pistol.   Another and another shot followed; and then, as a cry of pain thrilled the air, the fierce storm hushed its fury in an instant.

"Who's shot?   Is he killed?"

There was a breathless eagerness for the answer.

"It's the gambler!" was replied.   "Somebody has shot Green."

A low muttered invective against the victim was heard here and there; but the announcement was not received with a shout of exultation, though there was scarcely a heart that did not feel pleasure at the sacrifice of Harvey Green's life.

It was true as had been declared. Whether the shot were aimed deliberately, or guided by an unseen hand to the heart of the gambler, was never known; nor did the most careful examination, instituted afterward by the county, elicit any information that even directed suspicion toward the individual who became the agent of his death.

At the coroner's inquest, held over the dead body of Harvey Green, Simon Slade was present. Where he had concealed himself while the mob were in search of him, was not known. He looked haggard; and his eyes were anxious and restless. Two murders in his house, occurring in a single day, were quite enough to darken his spirits; and the more so, as his relations with both the victims were not of a character to awaken any thing but self-accusation.

As for the mob, in the death of Green its eager thirst for vengeance was satisfied. Nothing more was said against Slade, as a participator in the ruin and death of young Hammond. The popular feeling was one of pity rather than indignation toward the landlord; for it was seen that he was deeply troubled.

One thing I noticed, and it was that the drinking at

the bar was not suspended for a moment. A large proportion of those who made up the crowd of Green's
angry pursuers, were excited by drink as well as indignation, and I am very sure that, but for the maddening
effects of liquor, the fatal shot would never have been
fired. After the fearful catastrophe, and when every
mind was sobered, or ought to have been sobered, the
crowd returned to the bar-room, where the drinking was
renewed. So rapid were the calls for liquor, that both
Matthew, and Frank, the landlord's son, were kept busy
mixing the various compounds demanded by the thirsty
customers.

From the constant stream of human beings that
flowed toward the "Sickle and Sheaf," after the news
of Green's discovery and death went forth, it seemed as
if every man and boy within a distance of two or three
miles had received intelligence of the event. Few,
very of those who came, but went first into the bar-
room; and nearly all who entered the bar-room called
for liquor. In an hour after the death of Green, the
fact that his dead body was laid out in the room immediately adjoining, seemed utterly to pass from the consciousness of every one in the bar. The calls for liquor
were incessant; and, as the excitement of drink increased, voices grew louder, and oaths more plentiful,
while the sounds of laughter ceased not for an instant.

"They're giving him a regular Irish wake," I heard
remarked, with a brutal laugh.

I turned to the speaker, and to my great surprise, saw that it was Judge Lyman, more under the influence of drink than I remembered to have seen him. He was about the last man I expected to find here. If he knew of the strong indignation expressed toward him a little while before, by some of the very men now excited with liquor, his own free drinking had extinguished fear.

"Yes, curse him!" was the answer. "If they have a particularly hot corner 'away down below,' I hope he's made its acquaintance before this."

"Most likely he's smelled brimstone," chuckled the judge.

"Smelled it! If old Clubfoot hasn't treated him with a brimstone-bath long before this, he hasn't done his duty. If I thought as much, I'd vote for sending his majesty a remonstrance forthwith."

"Ha! ha!" laughed the judge. "You're warm on the subject."

"Ain't I? The blackleg scoundrel! Hell's too good for him."

"H-u-s-h! Don't let your indignation run into profanity," said Judge Lyman, trying to assume a serious air; but the muscles of his face but feebly obeyed his will's feeble effort.

"Profanity! Poh! I don't call that profanity. It's only speaking out in meeting, as they say,—it's only calling black, black—and white, white. You believe in a hell, don't you, judge?"

"I suppose there is one; though I don't know very certain."

"You'd better be certain!" said the other, meaningly.

"Why so?"

"Oh! because if there is one, and you don't cut your cards a little differently, you'll be apt to find it at the end of your journey."

"What do you mean by that?" asked the judge, retreating somewhat into himself, and trying to look dignified.

"Just what I say," was unhesitatingly answered.

"Do you mean to insinuate any thing?" asked the judge, whose brows were beginning to knit themselves.

"Nobody thinks you a saint," replied the man, roughly.

"I never professed to be."

"And it is said,"—the man fixed his gaze almost insultingly upon Judge Lyman's face—"that you'll get about as hot a corner in the lower regions as is to be found there, whenever you make the journey in that direction."

"You are insolent!" exclaimed the judge, his face becoming inflamed.

"Take care what you say, sir!" The man spoke threateningly.

"You'd better take care what _you_ say."

"So I will," replied the other. "But——"

"What's to pay here?" inquired a third party, coming up at the moment, and interrupting the speaker.

"The devil will be to pay," said Judge Lyman, "if somebody don't look out sharp."

"Do you mean that for me, ha?" The man, between whom and himself this slight contention had so quickly sprung up, began stripping back his coat sleeves, like one about to commence boxing.

"I mean it for anybody who presumes to offer me an insult."

The raised voices of the two men now drew toward them the attention of every one in the bar-room.

"The devil! There's Judge Lyman!" I heard some one exclaim, in a tone of surprise.

"Wasn't he in the room with Green when Willy Hammond was murdered?" asked another.

"Yes, he was; and what's more, it is said he had been playing against him all night, he and Green sharing the plunder."

This last remark came distinctly to the ears of Lyman, who started to his feet instantly, exclaiming fiercely—

"Whoever says that is a cursed liar!"

The words were scarcely out of his mouth, before a blow staggered him against the wall, near which he was standing. Another blow felled him, and then his assailant sprang over his prostrate body, kicking him, and stamping upon his face and breast in the most brutal, shocking manner.

"Kill him! He's worse than Green!" somebody cried out, in a voice so full of cruelty and murder that it made my blood curdle. "Remember Willy Hammond!"

The terrible scene that followed, in which were heard a confused mingling of blows, cries, yells, and horrible oaths, continued for several minutes, and ceased only when the words—"Don't, don't strike him any more! He's dead!" were repeated several times. Then the wild strife subsided. As the crowd parted from around the body of Judge Lyman, and gave way, I caught a single glance at his face. It was covered with blood, and every feature seemed to have been literally trampled down, until all was a level surface! Sickened at the sight, I passed hastily from the room into the open air, and caught my breath several times, before respiration again went on freely. As I stood in front of the tavern, the body of Judge Lyman was borne out by three or four men, and carried off in the direction of his dwelling.

"Is he dead?" I inquired of those who had him in charge.

"No," was the answer. "He's not dead, but terribly beaten," and they passed on.

Again the loud voices of men in angry strife arose in the bar-room. I did not return there to learn the cause, or to witness the fiend-like conduct of men, all whose worst passions were stimulated by drink into the wildest fervour. As I was entering my room, the thought flashed through my mind that, as Green was found there, it needed only the bare suggestion that I had aided in his concealment, to direct toward me the insane fury of the drunken mob.

"It is not safe to remain here." I said this to myself, with the emphasis of a strong internal conviction.

Against this, my mind opposed a few feeble arguments; but, the more I thought of the matter, the more clearly did I become satisfied, that to attempt to pass the night in that room was to me a risk it was not prudent to assume.

So I went in search of Mrs. Slade, to ask her to have another room prepared for me. But she was not in the house; and I learned, upon inquiry, that since the murder of young Hammoud, she had been suffering from repeated hysterical and fainting fits, and was now, with her daughter, at the house of a relative, whither she had been carried early in the afternoon.

It was on my lip to request the chambermaid to give me another room; but this I felt to be scarcely prudent, for if the popular indignation should happen to turn toward me, the servant would be the one questioned, most likely, as to where I had removed my quarters.

"It isn't safe to stay in the house," said I, speaking to myself. "Two, perhaps three, murders, have been committed already. The tiger's thirst for blood has been stimulated, and who can tell how quickly he may spring again, or in what direction?"

Even while I said this, there came up from the barroom louder and madder shouts. Then blows were heard, mingled with cries and oaths. A shuddering sense of danger oppressed me, and I went hastily down-stairs, and out into the street. As I gained the passage, I looked into the sitting-room, where the body of Green was laid out. Just then, the bar-room door was burst open by a fighting party, who had been thrown, in their fierce contention, against it. I paused only for a moment or two; and even in that brief period of time, saw blows exchanged over the dead body of the gambler!

"This is no place for me," I said, almost aloud, and hurried from the house, and took my way to the residence of a gentleman who had shown me many kindnesses during my visits at Cedarville. There was needed scarcely a word of representation on my part, to secure the cordial tender of a bed.

What a change! It seemed almost like a passage from Pandemonium to a heavenly region, as I seated myself alone in the quiet chamber a cheerful hospitality had assigned me, and mused on the exciting and terrible incidents of the day. They that sow the wind shall reap the whirlwind. How marked had been the realization of this prophecy, couched in such strong but beautiful imagery!

On the next day I was to leave Cedarville. Early in the morning I repaired to the "Sickle and Sheaf." The storm was over, and all was calm and silent as desolation. Hours before, the tempest had subsided; but the evidences left behind of its ravaging fury were fearful to look upon. Doors, chairs, windows, and tables were broken, and even the strong brass rod that ornamented the bar had been partially wrenched from its fastenings by strong hands, under an impulse of murder, that only lacked a weapon to execute its fiendish purpose. Stains of blood, in drops, marks, and even dried-up pools, were to be seen all over the bar-room and passage floors, and in many places on the porch.

In the sitting-room still lay the body of Green. Here, too, were many signs to indicate a fierce struggle. The looking-glass was smashed to a hundred pieces, and the shivered fragments lay yet untouched upon the floor. A chair, which it was plain had been used as a weapon of assault, had two of its legs broken short off, and was thrown into a corner. And even the bearers, on which the dead man lay, were pushed from their true position, showing that even in its mortal sleep, the body of Green had felt the jarring strife of elements he had himself helped to awaken into mad activity. From his face, the sheet had been drawn aside; but no hand ventured to replace it; and there it lay, in its ghastly paleness, exposed to the light, and covered with restless flies, attracted by the first faint odours of putridity. With gaze averted, I approached the body, and drew the covering decently over it.

No person was in the bar. I went out into the stable yard, where I met the hostler with his head bound up. There was a dark blue circle around one of his eyes, and an ugly-looking red scar on his cheek.

"Where is Mr. Slade?" I inquired.

"In bed, and likely to keep it for a week," was answered.

"How comes that?"

"Naturally enough. There was fighting all around last night, and he had to come in for a share. The fool! If he'd just held his tongue, he might have come out of it with a whole skin. But, when the rum is in, the wit is out, with him. It's cost me a black eye and a broken head; for how could I stand by and see him murdered outright?"

"Is he very badly injured?"

"I rather think he is. One eye is clean gone."

"Oh, shocking!"

"It's shocking enough, and no mistake."

"Lost an eye!"

"Too true, sir. The doctor saw him this morning, and says the eye was fairly gouged out, and broken up. In fact, when we carried him up-stairs for dead last night, his eye was lying upon his cheek. I pushed it back with my own hand!"

"Oh, horrible!" The relation made me sick. "Is he otherwise much injured?"

"The doctor thinks there are some bad hurts inside. Why, they kicked and trampled upon him, as if he had been a wild beast! I never saw such a pack of blood thirsty devils in my life."

"So much for rum," said I.

"Yes, sir; so much for rum," was the emphatic response. "It was the rum, and nothing else. Why, some of the very men who acted the most like tigers and devils, are as harmless persons as you will find in Cedarville when sober. Yes, sir; it was the rum, and nothing else. Rum gave me this broken head and black eye."

"So you had been drinking also?"

"Oh, yes. There's no use in denying that."

"Liquor does you harm."

"Nobody knows that better than I do."

"Why do you drink, then?"

"Oh, just because it comes in the way. Liquor is under my eyes and nose all the time, and it's as natural as breathing to take a little now and then. And when I don't think of it myself, somebody will think of it for me, and say—'Come, Sam, let's take something.' So you see, for a body such as I am, there isn't much help for it."

"But ain't you afraid to go on in this way? Don't you know where it will all end?"

"Just as well as anybody. It will make an end of me—or of all that is good in me. Rum and ruin, you know, sir. They go together like twin brothers."

"Why don't you get out of the way of temptation?" said I.

"It's easy enough to ask that question, sir; but how am I to get out of the way of temptation? Where shall

I go, and not find a bar in my road, and somebody to say—' Come, Sam, let's take a drink?' It can't be done, sir, nohow. I'm a hostler, and don't know how to be any thing else."

" Can't you work on a farm?"

" Yes; I can do something in that way. But, when there are taverns and bar-rooms, as many as three or four in every mile all over the country, how are you to keep clear of them? Figure me out that."

" I think you'd better vote on the Maine Law side at next election," said I.

" Faith, and I did it last time!" replied the man, with a brightening face—" and if I'm spared, I'll go the same ticket next year."

" What do you think of the Law?" I asked.

" Think of it! Bless your heart! if I was a praying man, which I'm sorry to say I ain't—my mother was a pious woman, sir"—his voice fell and slightly trembled—" if I was a praying man, sir, I'd pray, night and morning, and twenty times every day of my life, for God to put it into the hearts of the people to give us that Law. I'd have some hope then. But I haven't much as it is. There's no use in trying to let liquor alone."

" Do many drinking men think as you do?"

" I can count up a dozen or two myself. It isn't the drinking men who are so much opposed to the Maine Law, as your politicians. They throw dust in the people's eyes about it, and make a great many who know nothing at all of the evils of drinking in themselves, believe some bugbear story about trampling on the rights of I don't know who, nor they either. As for rum-seller's rights, I never could see any right they had to get rich by ruining poor devils such as I am. I think, though, that we have some right to be protected against them."

The ringing of a bell here announced the arrival of some traveller, and the hostler left me.

I learned, during the morning, that Matthew the barkeeper, and also the son of Mr. Slade, were both considerably hurt during the affrays in the bar-room, and were confined, temporarily, to their beds. Mrs. Slade still continued in a distressing and dangerous state. Judge Lyman, though shockingly injured, was not thought to be in a critical condition.

A busy day the sheriff had of it, making arrests of various parties engaged in the last night's affairs. Even Slade, unable as he was to lift his head from his pillow, was required to give heavy bail for his appearace at court. Happily, I escaped the inconvenience of being held to appear as a witness, and early in the afternoon had the satisfaction of finding myself rapidly borne away in the stage-coach. It was two years before I entered the pleasant village of Cedarville again.

NIGHT THE EIGHTH.

Reaping the Whirlwind.

I WAS in Washington City during the succeeding month. It was the short or closing session of a regular Congressional term. The implication of Judge Lyman in the affair of Green and young Hammond had brought him into such bad odour in Cedarville, and the whole district from which he had been chosen, that his party deemed it wise to set him aside, and take up a candidate less likely to meet with so strong, and, it might be, successful an opposition. By so doing, they were able to secure the election, once more, against the growing temperance party, which succeeded, however, in getting a Maine Law man into the State legislature. It was, therefore, Judge Lyman's last winter at the Federal Capital.

While seated in the reading-room at Fuller's Hotel, about noon, on the day after my arrival in Washington, I noticed an individual, whose face looked familiar, come in and glance about, as if in search of some one. While yet questioning in my mind who he could be, I heard a man remark to a person with whom he had been conversing—

" There's that vagabond member away from his place in the House, again."

" Who ?" inquired the other.

" Why, Judge Lyman," was answered.

" Oh !" said the other, indifferently ; " it isn't of much consequence. Precious little wisdom does he add to that intelligent body."

" His vote is worth something at least, when important questions are at stake."

" What does he charge for it ?" was coolly inquired.

There was a shrug of the shoulders, and an arching of the eyebrows, but no answer.

" I'm in earnest, though, in the question," said the last speaker.

" Not in saying that Lyman will sell his vote to the highest bidders ?"

" That will depend altogether upon whom the bidders may be. They must be men who have something to lose as well as gain—men, not at all likely to bruit the matter, and in serving whose personal interests no abandonment of party is required. Judge Lyman is always on good terms with the lobby members, and may be found in company with some of them daily. Doubtless, his absence from the House, now, is for the purpose of a special meeting with gentlemen who are ready to pay well for votes in favour of some bill making appropriations of public money for private or corporate benefit."

"You certainly cannot mean all you say to be taken in its broadest sense," was replied to this.

"Yes; in its very broadest. Into just this deep of moral and political degradation has this man fallen, disgracing his constituents, and dishonouring his country."

"His presence at Washington doesn't speak very highly in favour of the community he represents."

"No; still, as things are now, we cannot judge of the moral worth of a community by the men sent from it to Congress. Representatives show merely the strength of parties. The candidate chosen in party primary meetings is not selected because he is the best man they have, and the one fittest to legislate wisely in national affairs; but he who happens to have the strongest personal friends among those who nominate, or who is most likely to poll the highest vote. This is why we find, in Congress, such a large preponderance of tenth-rate men."

"Men, such as you represent Judge Lyman to be, would sell his country like another Arnold."

"Yes; if the bid were high enough."

"Does he gamble?"

"Gambling, I might say, is a part of his profession. Very few nights pass, I am told, without finding him at the gaming table."

I heard no more. At all this, I was not in the least surprised; for my knowledge of the man's antecedents had prepared me for allegations quite as bad as these.

During the week I spent at the Federal Capital, I had

several opportunities of seeing Judge Lyman, in the
House and out of it,—in the House only when the yeas
and nays were called on some important measure, or
a vote taken on a bill granting special privileges. In
the latter case, his vote, as I noticed, was generally cast
on the affirmative side. Several times I saw him staggering on the Avenue, and once brought into the House
for the purpose of voting, in so drunken a state, that he
had to be supported to his seat. And even worse than
this—when his name was called, he was asleep, and had
to be shaken several times before he was sufficiently
aroused to give his vote!

Happily, for the good of his country, it was his last
winter in Washington. At the next session, a better
man took his place.

Two years from the period of my last visit to Cedarville, I found myself approaching that quiet village again.
As the church-spire came in view, and house after house
became visible, here and there, standing out in pleasant
relief against the green background of woods and fields,
all the exciting events which rendered my last visit so
memorable came up fresh in my mind. I was yet thinking of Willy Hammond's dreadful death, and of his
broken-hearted mother, whose life went out with his,
when the stage rolled by their old homestead. Oh,
what a change was here! Neglect, decay, and dilapi-

dation were visible, let the eye fall where it would. The fences were down, here and there; the hedges, once so green and nicely trimmed, had grown rankly in some places, but were stunted and dying in others; all the beautiful walks were weedy and grass-grown, and the box-borders dead; the garden, rainbow-hued in its wealth of choice and beautiful flowers when I first saw it, was lying waste,—a rooting-ground for hogs. A glance at the house showed a broken chimney, the bricks unremoved from the spot where they struck the ground; a moss-grown roof, with a large limb from a lightning-rent tree lying almost balanced over the eaves, and threatening to fall at the touch of the first wind-storm that swept over. Half of the vines that clambered about the portico were dead, and the rest, untrained, twined themselves in wild disorder, or fell grovelling to the earth. One of the pillars of the portico was broken, as were, also, two of the steps that went up to it. The windows of the house were closed, but the door stood open, and, as the stage went past, my eyes rested, for a moment, upon an old man seated in the hall. He was not near enough to the door for me to get a view of his face; but the white flowing hair left me in no doubt as to his identity. It was Judge Hammond.

The "Sickle and Sheaf" was yet the stage-house of Cedarville, and there, a few minutes afterward, I found myself. The hand of change had been here also. The first object that attracted my attention was the sign-post, which, at my earlier arrival, some eight or nine years before, stood up in its new white garment of paint, as straight as a plummet line, bearing proudly aloft the golden sheaf and gleaming sickle. Now, the post, dingy and shattered, and worn from the frequent contact of wheels, and gnawing of restless horses, leaned from its trim perpendicular at an angle of many degrees, as if ashamed of the faded, weather-worn, lying symbol it bore aloft in the sunshine. Around the post was a filthy mud-pool, in which a hog lay grunting out its sense of enjoyment. Two or three old empty whisky barrels lumbered up the dirty porch, on which a coarse, bloated, vulgar-looking man sat leaning against the wall—his chair tipped back on its hind legs—squinting at me from one eye, as I left the stage and came forward toward the house.

"Ah! is this you?" said he, as I came near to him, speaking thickly, and getting up with a heavy motion. I now recognised the altered person of Simon Slade. On looking at him closer, I saw that the eye which I had thought only shut was in fact destroyed. How vividly, now, uprose in imagination the scenes I had witnessed during my last night in his bar-room; the night, when a brutal mob, whom he had inebriated with liquor, came near murdering him.

"Glad to see you once more, my boy! Glad to see you! I—I—I'm not just—you see. How are you? How are you?"

And he shook my hand with a drunken show of cordiality.

I felt shocked and disgusted. Wretched man! down the crumbling sides of the pit he had digged for other feet, he was himself sliding, while not enough strength remained even to struggle with his fate.

I tried for a few minutes to talk with him; but his mind was altogether beclouded, and his questions and answers incoherent; so I left him, and entered the bar-room.

"Can I get accommodations here for a couple of days?" I inquired of a stupid, sleepy-looking man, who was sitting in a chair behind the bar.

"I reckon so," he answered, but did not rise.

I turned, and walked a few paces toward the door, and then walked back again.

"I'd like to get a room," said I.

The man got up slowly, and going to a desk, fumbled about in it for a while. At length he brought out an old, dilapidated blank-book, and throwing it open on the counter, asked me, with an indifferent manner, to write down my name.

"I'll take a pen, if you please."

"Oh, yes!" And he hunted about again in the desk, from which, after a while, he brought forth the blackened stump of a quill, and pushed it toward me across the counter.

"Ink," said I—fixing my eyes upon him with a look of displeasure.

"I don't believe there is any," he muttered. "Frank," and he called the landlord's son, going to the door behind the bar as he did so.

"What d'ye want?" a rough, ill-natured voice answered.

"Where's the ink?"

"Don't know any thing about it."

"You had it last. What did you do with it?"

"Nothing!" was growled back.

"Well, I wish you'd find it."

"Find it yourself, and——" I cannot repeat the profane language he used.

"Never mind," said I. "A pencil will do just as well." And I drew one from my pocket. The attempt to write with this, on the begrimed and greasy page of the register, was only partially successful. It would have puzzled almost any one to make out the name. From the date of the last entry, it appeared that mine was the first arrival, for over a week, of any person desiring a room.

As I finished writing my name, Frank came stalking in, with a cigar in his mouth, and a cloud of smoke around his head. He had grown into a stout man—though his face presented little that was manly, in the true sense of the word. It was disgustingly sensual. On seeing me, a slight flush tinged his cheeks.

"How do you do?" he said, offering me his hand. "Peter,"—he turned to the lazy-looking bar-keeper—

18

"tell Jane to have No. 11 put in order for a gentleman immediately, and tell her to be sure and change the bed-linen."

"Things look rather dull here," I remarked, as the bar-keeper went out to do as he had been directed.

"Rather; it's a dull place, anyhow."

"How is your mother?" I inquired.

A slight, troubled look came into his face, as he answered—

"No better."

"She's sick, then?"

"Yes; she's been sick a good while; and I'm afraid will never be much better." His manner was not altogether cold and indifferent, but there was a want of feeling in his voice.

"Is she at home?"

"No, sir."

As he showed no inclination to say more on the subject, I asked no further questions, and he soon found occasion to leave me.

The bar-room had undergone no material change, so far as its furniture and arrangements were concerned; but a very great change was apparent in the condition of these. The brass rod around the bar, which, at my last visit, was brightly polished, was now a greenish-black, and there came from it an unpleasant odour of verdigris. The walls were fairly coated with dust, smoke, and fly-specks, and the windows let in the light but feebly, through the dirt-obscured glass. The floor was filthy. Behind the bar, on the shelves designed for a display of liquors, was a confused mingling of empty or half-filled decanters, cigar-boxes, lemons and lemon-peel, old newspapers, glasses, a broken pitcher, a hat, a soiled vest, and a pair of blacking brushes, with other incongruous things, not now remembered. The air of the room was loaded with offensive vapours.

Disgusted with every thing about the bar, I went into the sitting-room. Here, there was some order in the arrangement of the dingy furniture; but you might have written your name in dust on the looking-glass and table. The smell of the torpid atmosphere was even worse than that of the bar-room. So I did not linger here, but passed through the hall, and out upon the porch, to get a draught of pure air.

Slade still sat leaning against the wall.

"Fine day this," said he, speaking in a mumbling kind of voice.

"Very fine," I answered.

"Yes, very fine."

"Not doing so well as you were a few years ago," said I.

"No—you see—these—these 'ere blamed temperance people are ruining every thing."

"Ah! Is that so?"

Yes. Cedarville isn't what it was when you first came to the Sickle and Sheaf. I—I—you see. Curse the temperance people! They've ruined every thing, you see. Every thing! Ruined——"

And he muttered, and mouthed his words in such a way, that I could understand but little he said; and, in that little, there was scarcely any coherency. So I left him, with a feeling of pity in my heart for the wreck he had become, and went into the town to call upon one or two gentlemen with whom I had business.

In the course of the afternoon, I learned that Mrs. Slade was in an insane asylum, about five miles from Cedarville. The terrible events of the day on which young Hammond was murdered completed the work of mental ruin, begun at the time her husband abandoned the quiet, honourable calling of a miller, and became a tavern-keeper. Reason could hold its position no longer. When word came to her that Willy and his mother were both dead, she uttered a wild shriek and fell down in a fainting fit. From that period the balance of her mind was destroyed. Long before this, her friends saw that reason wavered. Frank had been her idol. A pure, bright, affectionate boy he was, when she removed with him from their pleasant cottage-home, where all the surrounding influences were good, into a tavern, where an angel could scarcely remain without corruption. From the moment this change was decided on by her husband, a shadow fell upon her heart. She saw, before her husband, her children, and herself, a yawning pit, and felt that, in a very few years, all of them must plunge down into its fearful darkness.

Alas! how quickly began the realization of her worst fears in the corruption of her worshipped boy! And how vain proved all effort and remonstrance, looking to his safety, whether made with himself or his father! From the day the tavern was opened, and Frank drew into his lungs full draughts of the changed atmosphere by which he was now surrounded, the work of moral deterioration commenced. The very smell of the liquor exhilarated him unnaturally; while the subjects of conversation, so new to him, that found discussion in the bar-room, soon came to occupy a prominent place in his imagination, to the exclusion of those humane, childlike, tender, and heavenly thoughts and impressions it had been the mother's care to impart and awaken.

Ah! with what an eager zest does the heart drink in of evil. And how almost hopeless is the case of a boy, surrounded, as Frank was, by the corrupting, debasing associations of a bar-room! Had his father meditated his ruin, he could not have more surely laid his plans for the fearful consummation; and he reaped as he had sown. With a selfish desire to get gain, he embarked in the trade of corruption, ruin, and death, weakly believing that he and his could pass through the fire harmless. How sadly a few years demonstrated his error, we have seen.

Flora, I learned, was with her mother, devoting her

life to her. The dreadful death of Willy Hammond, for whom she had conceived a strong attachment, came near depriving her of reason also. Since the day on which that awful tragedy occurred, she had never even looked upon her old home. She went away with her unconscious mother, and ever since had remained with her—devoting her life to her comfort. Long before this, all her own and mother's influence over her brother had come to an end. It mattered not how she sought to stay his feet, so swiftly moving along the downward way, whether by gentle entreaty, earnest remonstrance, or tears; in either case, wounds for her own heart were the sure consequences, while his steps never lingered a moment. A swift destiny seemed hurrying him on to ruin. The change in her father—once so tender, so cheerful in his tone, so proud of and loving toward his daughter—was another source of deep grief to her pure young spirit. Over him, as well as over her brother, all her power was lost; and he even avoided her, as though her presence were an offence to him. And so, when she went out from her unhappy home, she took with her no desire to return. Even when imagination bore her back to the "Sickle and Sheaf," she felt an intense, heart-sickening repulsion toward the place where she had first felt the poisoned arrows of life; and in the depths of her spirit she prayed that her eyes might never look upon it again. In her almost cloister-like seclusion, she sought to gather the mantle of oblivion about her heart.

Had not her mother's condition made Flora's duty a plain one, the true, unselfish instincts of her heart would have doubtless led her back to the polluted home she had left, there, in a kind of living death, to minister as best she could to the comfort of a debased father and brother. But she was spared that trial—that fruitless sacrifice.

Evening found me once more in the bar-room of the "Sickle and Sheaf." The sleepy, indifferent bar-keeper, was now more in his element—looked brighter, and had quicker motions. Slade, who had partially recovered from the stupefying effects of the heavy draughts of ale with which he washed down his dinner, was also in a better condition, though not inclined to talk. He was sitting at a table, alone, with his eyes wandering about the room. Whether his thoughts were agreeable or disagreeable, it was not easy to determine. Frank was there, the centre of a noisy group of coarse fellows, whose vulgar sayings and profane expletives continually rung through the room. The noisiest, coarsest, and most profane was Frank Slade; yet did not the incessant volume of bad language that flowed from his tongue appear in the least to disturb his father.

Outraged, at length, by this disgusting exhibition, that had not even the excuse of an exciting cause, I was leaving the bar-room, when I heard some one remark to a young man who had just come in—

"What! you here again, Ned? Ain't you afraid your old man will be after you, as usual?"

"No," answered the person addressed, chuckling inwardly, "he's gone to a prayer-meeting."

"You'll at least have the benefit of his prayers," was lightly remarked.

I turned to observe the young man more closely. His face I remembered, though I could not identify him at first. But, when I heard him addressed soon after as Ned Hargrove, I had a vivid recollection of a little incident that occurred some years before, and which then made a strong impression. The reader has hardly forgotten the visit of Mr. Hargrove to the bar-room of the Sickle and Sheaf, and the conversation among some of its inmates, which his withdrawal, in company with his son, then occasioned. The father's watchfulness over his boy, and his efforts to save him from the allurements and temptations of a bar-room, had proved, as now appeared, unavailing. The son was several years older; but it was sadly evident, from the expression of his face, that he had been growing older in evil faster than in years.

The few words that I have mentioned as passing between this young man and another inmate of the barroom, caused me to turn back from the door, through which I was about passing, and take a chair near to where Hargrove had seated himself. As I did so, the eyes of Simon Slade rested on the last-named individual.

"Ned Hargrove!" he said, speaking roughly—"if you want a drink, you'd better get it, and make yourself scarce."

"Don't trouble yourself," retorted the young man, "you'll get your money for the drink in good time."

This irritated the landlord, who swore at Hargrove violently, and said something about not wanting boys about his place who couldn't stir from home without having "daddy or mammy running after them."

"Never fear!" cried out the person who had first addressed Hargrove—"his old man's gone to a prayer-meeting. We shan't have the light of his pious countenance here to-night."

I fixed my eyes upon the young man to see what effect this coarse and irreverent allusion to his father would have. A slight tinge of shame was in his face; but I saw that he had not sufficient moral courage to resent the shameful desecration of a parent's name. How should he, when he was himself the first to desecrate that name?

"If he were forty fathoms deep in the infernal regions," answered Slade, "he'd find out that Ned was was here, and get half an hour's leave of absence to come after him. The fact is, I'm tired of seeing his solemn, sanctimonious face here every night. If the boy hasn't spirit enough to tell him to mind his own business, as I have done more than fifty times, why, let the boy stay away himself."

"Why don't you send him off with a flea in his ear, Ned?" said one of the company, a young man scarcely his own age. "My old man tried that game with me, but he soon found that I could hold the winning cards."

"Just what I'm going to do the very next time he comes after me."

"Oh, yes! So you've said twenty times," remarked Frank Slade, in a sneering, insolent manner.

Edward Hargrove had not the spirit to resent this; he only answered,

"Just let him show himself here to-night, and you will see."

"No, we won't see," sneered Frank.

"Wouldn't it be fun!" was exclaimed. "I hope to be on hand, should it ever come off."

"He's as 'fraid as death of the old chap," laughed a sottish looking man, whose age ought to have inspired him with some respect for the relation between father and son, and doubtless would, had not a long course of drinking and familiarity with debasing associates blunted his moral sense.

"Now for it!" I heard uttered, in a quick, delighted voice. "Now for fun! Spunk up to him, Ned! Never say die!"

I turned toward the door, and there stood the father of Edward Hargrove. How well I remembered the broad, fine forehead, the steady, yet mild eyes, the firm lips, the elevated superior bearing of the man I had

once before seen in that place, and on a like errand.
His form was slightly bent now; his hair was whiter;
his eyes farther back in his head; his face thinner and
marked with deeper lines; and there was in the whole
expression of his face a touching sadness. Yet, superior to the marks of time and suffering, an unflinching
resolution was visible in his countenance, that gave to it
a dignity, and extorted involuntary respect. He stood
still, after advancing a few paces, and then, his searching eyes having discovered his son, he said mildly, yet
firmly, and with such a strength of parental love in his
voice that resistance was scarcely possible.

"Edward! Edward! Come, my son."

"Don't go." The words were spoken in an under
tone, and he who uttered them turned his face away
from Mr. Hargrove, so that the old man could not see
the motion of his lips. A little while before, he had
spoken bravely against the father of Edward; now, he
could not stand up in his presence.

I looked at Edward. He did not move from where
he was sitting, and yet I saw that to resist his father
cost him no light struggle.

"Edward." There was nothing imperative—nothing
stern—nothing commanding in the father's voice; but
its great, its almost irresistible power, lay in its expression of the father's belief that his son would instantly
leave the place. And it was this power that prevailed.
Edward arose, and, with eyes cast upon the floor, was

moving away from his companions, when Frank Slade exclaimed,

"Poor, weak fool!"

It was a lightning flash of indignation, rather than a mere glance from the human eye, that Mr. Hargrove threw instantly upon Frank; while his fine form sprung up erect. He did not speak, but merely transfixed him with a look. Frank curled his lip impotently, as he tried to return the old man's withering glances.

"Now look here!" said Simon Slade, in some wrath, "there's been just about enough of this. I'm getting tired of it. Why don't you keep Ned at home? Nobody wants him here."

"Refuse to sell him liquor," returned Mr. Hargrove.

"It's my trade to sell liquor," answered Slade, boldly.

"I wish you had a more honourable calling," said Hargrove, almost mournfully.

"If you insult my father, I'll strike you down!" exclaimed Frank Slade, starting up and assuming a threatening aspect.

"I respect filial devotion, meet it where I will," calmly replied Mr. Hargrove,—"I only wish it had a better foundation in this case. I only wish the father had merited——"

I will not stain my page with the fearful oath that Frank Slade yelled, rather than uttered, as, with clenched fist, he sprung toward Mr. Hargrove. But ere he had reached the unruffled old man—who stood looking at him as one would look into the eyes of a wild beast, confident that he could not stand the gaze—a firm hand grasped his arm, and a rough voice said—

"Avast there, young man! Touch a hair of that white head, and I'll wring your neck off."

"Lyon!" As Frank uttered the man's name, he raised his fist to strike him. A moment the clenched hand remained poised in the air; then it fell slowly to his side, and he contented himself with an oath and a vile epithet.

"You can swear to your heart's content. It will do nobody any harm but yourself," coolly replied Mr. Lyon, whom I now recognised as the person with whom I had held several conversations during previous visits.

"Thank you, Mr. Lyon," said Mr. Hargrove, "for this manly interference. It is no more than I should have expected from you."

"I never suffer a young man to strike an old man," said Lyon, firmly. "Apart from that, Mr. Hargrove, there are other reasons why your person must be free from violence where I am."

"This is a bad place for you, Lyon," said Mr. Hargrove; "and I've said so to you a good many times." He spoke in rather an under tone. "Why *will* you come here?"

"It's a bad place, I know," replied Lyon, speaking out boldly, "and we all know it. But habit, Mr. Hargrove—habit. That's the cursed thing! If the bar-

rooms were all shut up, there would be another story to
tell. Get us the Maine law, and there will be some
chance for us."

"Why don't you vote the temperance ticket?" asked
Mr. Hargrove.

"Why did I? you'd better ask," said Lyon.

"I thought you voted against us."

"Not I. Ain't quite so blind to my own interests as
that. And, if the truth were known, I should not at all
wonder if every man in this room, except Slade and his
son, voted on your side of the house."

"It's a little strange, then," said Mr. Hargrove, "that
with the drinking men on our side, we failed to secure
the election."

"You must blame that on your moderate men, who
see no danger and go blind with their party," answered
Lyon. "We have looked the evil in the face, and know
its direful quality."

"Come! I would like to talk with you, Mr. Lyon."

Mr. Hargrove, his son, and Mr. Lyon went out together. As they left the room, Frank Slade said—

"What a cursed liar and hypocrite he is!"

"Who?" was asked.

"Why, Lyon," answered Frank, boldly.

"You'd better say that to his face."

"It wouldn't be good for him," remarked one of the
company.

At this Frank started to his feet, stalked about the

room, and put on all the disgusting airs of a drunken braggart. Even his father saw the ridiculous figure he cut, and growled out—

"There, Frank, that'll do. Don't make a miserable fool of yourself!"

At which Frank retorted, with so much of insolence that his father flew into a towering passion, and ordered him to leave the bar-room.

"You can go out yourself if you don't like the company. I'm very well satisfied," answered Frank.

"Leave this room, you impudent young scoundrel!"

"Can't go, my amiable friend," said Frank, with a cool self-possession that maddened his father, who got up hastily, and moved across the bar-room to the place where he was standing.

"Go out, I tell you!" Slade spoke resolutely.

"Would be happy to oblige you," Frank said, in a taunting voice; "but, 'pon my word, it isn't at all convenient."

Half intoxicated as he was, and already nearly blind with passion, Slade lifted his hand to strike his son. And the blow would have fallen had not some one caught his arm, and held him back from the meditated violence. Even the debased visitors of this bar-room could not stand by and see nature outraged in a bloody strife between father and son; for it was plain from the face and quickly assumed attitude of Frank, that if his father had laid his hand upon him, he would have struck him in return.

I could not remain to hear the awful imprecations that father and son, in their impotent rage, called down from heaven upon each other's heads. It was the most shocking exhibition of depraved human nature that I had ever seen. And so I left the bar-room, glad to escape from its stifling atmosphere and revolting scenes.

NIGHT THE NINTH.

A Fearful Consummation.

NEITHER Slade nor his son was present at the breakfast table on the next morning. As for myself, I did
not eat with much appetite. Whether this defect arose
from the state of my mind, or the state of the food
set before me, I did not stop to inquire; but left the
stifling, offensive atmosphere of the dining-room in a
very few moments after entering that usually attractive
place for a hungry man.

A few early drinkers were already in the bar-room—
men with shattered nerves and cadaverous faces, who
could not begin the day's work without the stimulus of
brandy or whisky. They came in, with gliding footsteps, asked for what they wanted in low voices, drank
in silence, and departed. It was a melancholy sight to
look upon.

About nine o'clock the landlord made his appearance.
He, too, came gliding into the bar-room, and his first
act was to seize upon a brandy decanter, pour out nearly
half a pint of the fiery liquid, and drink it off. How
badly his hand shook—so badly that he spilled the
brandy both in pouring it out, and in lifting the glass to

his lips! What a shattered wreck he was! He looked really worse now than he did on the day before, when drink gave an artificial vitality to his system, a tension to his muscles, and light to his countenance. The miller of ten years ago, and the tavern-keeper of to-day! Who could have identified them as one?

Slade was turning from the bar, when a man came in. I noticed an instant change in the landlord's countenance. He looked startled; almost frightened. The man drew a small package from his pocket, and after selecting a paper therefrom, presented it to Slade, who received it with a nervous reluctance, opened, and let his eye fall upon the writing within. I was observing him closely at the time, and saw his countenance flush deeply. In a moment or two it became pale again—paler even than before.

"Very well—all right. I'll attend to it," said the landlord, trying to recover himself, yet swallowing with every sentence.

The man, who was no other than a sheriff's deputy, and who gave him a sober, professional look, then went out with a firm step, and an air of importance. As he passed through the outer door, Slade retired from the bar-room.

"Trouble coming," I heard the bar-keeper remark, speaking partly to himself, and partly with the view, as was evident from his manner, of leading me to question him. But this I did not feel that it was right to do.

"Got the sheriff on him at last," added the bar-keeper.

"What's the matter, Bill?" inquired a man who now came in with a bustling, important air, and leaned familiarly over the bar. "Who was Jenkins after?"

"The old man," replied the bar-keeper, in a voice that showed pleasure rather than regret.

"No!"

"It's a fact." Bill, the bar-keeper, actually smiled.

"What's to pay?" said the man.

"Don't know, and don't care much."

"Did he serve a summons or an execution?"

"Can't tell."

"Judge Lyman's suit went against him."

"Did it?"

"Yes; and I heard Judge Lyman swear, that if he got him on the hip, he'd sell him out, bag and basket. And he's the man to keep his word."

"I never could just make out," said the bar-keeper, "how he ever came to owe Judge Lyman so much. I've never known of any business transactions between them."

"It's been dog eat dog, I rather guess," said the man.

"What do you mean by that?" inquired the bar-keeper.

"You've heard of dogs hunting in pairs?"

"Oh, yes."

" Well, since Harvey Green got his deserts, the business of fleecing our silly young fellows, who happened to have more money than wit or discretion, has been in the hands of Judge Lyman and Slade. They hunted together, Slade holding the game, while the Judge acted as blood-sucker. But that business was interrupted about a year ago; and game got so scarce, that, as I suggested, dog began to eat dog. And here comes the end of the matter, if I'm not mistaken. So mix us a stiff toddy. I want one more good drink at the ' Sickle and Sheaf,' before the colours are struck."

And the man chuckled at his witty effort.

During the day, I learned that affairs stood pretty much as this man had conjectured. Lyman's suits had been on sundry notes, payable on demand; but nobody knew of any property transactions between him and Slade. On the part of Slade, no defence had been made—the suit going by default. The visit of the sheriff's officer was for the purpose of serving an execution.

As I walked through Cedarville on that day, the whole aspect of the place seemed changed. I questioned with myself, often, whether this were really so, or only the effect of imagination. The change was from cheerfulness and thrift, to gloom and neglect. There was, to me, a brooding silence in the air; a pause in the life-movement; a folding of the hands, so to speak, because hope had failed from the heart. The residence of Mr.

Harrison, who, some two years before, had suddenly awakened to a lively sense of the evil of rum-selling, because his own sons were discovered to be in danger, had been one of the most tasteful in Cedarville. I had often stopped to admire the beautiful shrubbery and flowers with which it was surrounded; the walks so clear —the borders so fresh and even—the arbours so cool and inviting. There was not a spot upon which the eye could rest, that did not show the hand of taste. When I now came opposite to this house, I was no longer in doubt as to the actuality of a change. There were no marked evidences of neglect; but the high cultivation and nice regard for the small details were lacking. The walks were cleanly swept; but the box-borders were not so carefully trimmed. The vines and bushes that in former times were cut and tied so evenly, could hardly have felt the keen touch of the pruning-knife for months.

As I paused to note the change, a lady, somewhat beyond the middle age, came from the house. I was struck by the deep gloom that overshadowed her countenance. Ah! said I to myself, as I passed on, how many dear hopes, that once lived in that heart, must have been scattered to the winds. As I conjectured, this was Mrs. Harrison, and I was not unprepared to hear, as I did a few hours afterward, that her two sons had fallen into drinking habits; and, not only this, had been enticed to the gaming table. Unhappy mother!

What a lifetime of wretchedness was compressed for thee into a few short years!

I walked on, noting, here and there, changes even more marked than appeared about the residence of Mr. Harrison. Judge Lyman's beautiful place showed utter neglect; and so did one or two others that, on my first visit to Cedarville, charmed me with their order, neatness, and cultivation. In every instance, I learned, on inquiring, that the owners of these, or some members of their families, were, or had been, visitors at the "Sickle and Sheaf;" and that the ruin, in progress or completed, began after the establishment of that point of attraction in the village.

Something of a morbid curiosity, excited by what I saw, led me on to take a closer view of the residence of Judge Hammond than I had obtained on the day before. The first thing that I noticed, on approaching the old, decaying mansion, were handbills, posted on the gate, the front door, and on one of the windows. A nearer inspection revealed their import. The property had been seized, and was now offered at sheriff's sale!

Ten years before, Judge Hammond was known as the richest man in Cedarville: and now, the homestead he had once so loved to beautify—where all that was dearest to him in life once gathered—worn, disfigured, and in ruins, was about being wrested from him. I paused at the gate, and leaning over it, looked in with saddened feelings upon the dreary waste within. No sign of life

was visible. The door was shut—the windows closed—
not the faintest wreath of smoke was seen above the
blackened chimney-tops. How vividly did imagination
restore the life, and beauty, and happiness, that made
their home there only a few years before,—the mother
and her noble boy, one looking with trembling hope,
the other with joyous confidence, into the future,—
the father, proud of his household treasures, but not
their wise and jealous guardian.

Ah! that his hands should have unbarred the door,
and thrown it wide, for the wolf to enter that precious
fold! I saw them all in their sunny life before me;
yet, even as I looked upon them, their sky began to
darken. I heard the distant mutterings of the storm,
and soon the desolating tempest swept down fearfully
upon them. I shuddered as it passed away, to look
upon the wrecks left scattered around. What a
change!

"And all this," said I, "that one man, tired of being
useful, and eager to get gain, might gather in accursed
gold!"

Pushing open the gate, I entered the yard, and
walked around the dwelling, my footsteps echoing in the
hushed solitude of the deserted place. Hark! was that
a human voice?

I paused to listen.

The sound came, once more, distinctly to my ears. I
looked around, above, everywhere, but perceived no

living sign. For nearly a minute I stood still, listening. Yes: there it was again—a low, moaning voice, as of one in pain or grief. I stepped onward a few paces; and now saw one of the doors standing ajar. As I pushed this door wide open, the moan was repeated. Following the direction from which the sound came, I entered one of the large drawing-rooms. The atmosphere was stifling, and all as dark as if it were midnight. Groping my way to a window, I drew back the bolt and threw open a shutter. Broadly the light fell across the dusty, uncarpeted floor, and on the dingy furniture of the room. As it did so, the moaning voice which had drawn me thither swelled on the air again; and now I saw, lying upon an old sofa, the form of a man. It needed no second glance to tell me that this was Judge Hammond. I put my hand upon him, and uttered his name: but he answered not. I spoke more firmly, and slightly shook him; but only a piteous moan was returned.

"Judge Hammond!" I now called aloud, and somewhat imperatively.

But it availed nothing. The poor old man aroused not from the stupor in which mind and body were enshrouded.

"He is dying!" thought I; and instantly left the house in search of some friends to take charge of him in his last, sad extremity. The first person to whom I made known the fact shrugged his shoulders, and said it was no affair of his, and that I must find somebody whose business it was to attend to him. My next application was met in the same spirit; and no better success attended my reference of the matter to a third party. No one to whom I spoke seemed to have any sympathy for the broken-down old man. Shocked by this indifference, I went to one of the county officers, who, on learning the condition of Judge Hammond, took immediate steps to have him removed to the Alms-house, some miles distant.

"But why to the Alms-house?" I inquired, on learning his purpose. "He has property."

"Every thing has been seized for debt," was the reply.

"Will there be nothing left after his creditors are satisfied?"

"Very few, if any, will be satisfied," he answered. "There will not be enough to pay half the judgments against him."

"And is there no friend to take him in,—no one, of all who moved by his side in the days of prosperity, to give a few hours' shelter, and soothe the last moments of his unhappy life?"

"Why did you make application here?" was the officer's significant question.

I was silent.

"Your earnest appeals for the poor old man met with no words of sympathy?"

"None."

"He has, indeed, fallen low. In the days of his prosperity, he had many friends, so called. Adversity has shaken them all like dead leaves from sapless branches."

"But why? This is not always so."

"Judge Hammond was a selfish, worldly man. People never liked him much. His favouring, so strongly, the tavern of Slade, and his distillery operations, turned from him some of his best friends. The corruption and terrible fate of his son—and the insanity and death of his wife—all were charged upon him in people's minds; and every one seemed to turn from him instinctively after the fearful tragedy was completed. He never held up his head afterward. Neighbours shunned him as they would a criminal. And here has come the end at last. He will be taken to the Poor-house, to die there—a pauper!"

"And all," said I, partly speaking to myself, "because a man, too lazy to work at an honest calling, must needs go to rum-selling."

"The truth, the whole truth, and nothing but the truth," remarked the officer with emphasis, as he turned from me to see that his directions touching the removal of Mr. Hammond to the Poor-house were promptly executed.

In my wanderings about Cedarville during that day, I noticed a small, but very neat cottage, a little way from the centre of the village. There was not around it a great profusion of flowers and shrubbery; but the few vines, flowers, and bushes that grew green and flourishing about the door, and along the clean walks, added to the air of taste and comfort that so peculiarly marked the dwelling.

" Who lives in that pleasant little spot?" I asked of a man whom I had frequently seen in Slade's bar-room. He happened to be passing the house at the same time that I was.

" Joe Morgan," was answered.

" Indeed!" I spoke in some surprise. "And what of Morgan? How is he doing?"

" Very well."

" Doesn't he drink?"

" No. Since the death of his child, he has never taken a drop. That event sobered him, and he has remained sober ever since."

" What is he doing?"

" Working at his old trade."

" That of a miller?"

" Yes. After Judge Hammond broke down, the distillery apparatus and cotton spinning machinery were all sold and removed from Cedarville. The purchaser of what remained, having something of the fear of God, as well as regard for man, in his heart, set himself to the restoration of the old order of things, and in due time the revolving mill-wheel was at its old and better work of grinding corn and wheat for bread. The only two men in Cedarville competent to take charge of the mill were Simon Slade and Joe Morgan. The first could not be had, and the second came in as a matter of course.

"And he remains sober and industrious ?"

"As any man in the village," was the answer.

I saw but little of Slade or his son during the day. But both were in the bar-room at night, and both in a condition sorrowful to look upon. Their presence, together, in the bar-room, half intoxicated as they were, seemed to revive the unhappy temper of the previous evening, as freshly as if the sun had not risen and set upon their anger.

During the early part of the evening, considerable company was present, though not of a very select class. A large proportion were young men. To most of them the fact that Slade had fallen into the sheriff's hands was known; and I gathered from some aside conversation which reached my ears, that Frank's idle, spendthrift habits had hastened the present crisis in his father's affairs. He, too, was in debt to Judge Lyman—on what account, it was not hard to infer.

It was after nine o'clock, and there was not half a dozen persons in the room, when I noticed Frank Slade go behind the bar for the third or fourth time. He was just lifting a decanter of brandy, when his father, who was considerably under the influence of drink, started forward, and laid his hand upon that of his son. Instantly a fierce light gleamed from the eyes of the young man.

"Let go of my hand," he exclaimed.

"No, I won't. Put up that brandy bottle,—you're drunk now."

"Don't meddle with me, old man!" angrily retorted Frank. "I'm not in the mood to bear any thing more from *you*."

"You're drunk as a fool now," returned Slade, who had seized the decanter. "Let go the bottle."

For only an instant did the young man hesitate. Then he drove his half-clenched hand against the breast of his father, who went staggering away several paces from the counter. Recovering himself, and now almost furious, the landlord rushed forward upon his son, his hand raised to strike him.

"Keep off!" cried Frank. "Keep off! If you touch me, I'll strike you down!" At the same time raising the half-filled bottle threateningly.

But his father was in too maddened a state to fear any consequences, and so pressed forward upon his son, striking him in the face the moment he came near enough to do so.

Instantly, the young man, infuriated by drink and evil passions, threw the bottle at his father's head. The dangerous missile fell, crashing upon one of his temples, shivering it into a hundred pieces. A heavy, jarring fall too surely marked the fearful consequences of the blow. When we gathered around the fallen man, and made an effort to lift him from the floor, a thrill of horror went through every heart.   A mortal paleness was already on his marred face, and the death-gurgle in his throat !   In three minutes from the time the blow was struck, his spirit had gone upward to give an account of the deeds done in the body.

"Frank Slade ! you have murdered your father !"

Sternly were these terrible words uttered.   It was some time before the young man seemed to comprehend their meaning.   But the moment he realized the awful truth, he uttered an exclamation of horror.   Almost at the same instant, a pistol-shot came sharply on the ear. But the meditated self-destruction was not accomplished. The aim was not surely taken; and the ball struck harmlessly against the ceiling.

Half an hour afterward, and Frank Slade was a lonely prisoner in the county jail !

Does the reader need a word of comment on this fearful consummation ?   No: and we will offer none.

NIGHT THE TENTH.

The Closing Scene at the "Sickle and Sheaf."

On the day that succeeded the evening of this fearful tragedy, placards were to be seen all over the village, announcing a mass meeting at the " Sickle and Sheaf" that night.

By early twilight, the people commenced assembling. The bar, which had been closed all day, was now thrown open, and lighted; and in this room, where so much of evil had been originated, encouraged, and consummated, a crowd of earnest-looking men were soon gathered. Among them I saw the fine person of Mr. Hargrove. Joe Morgan—or rather Mr. Morgan—was also of the number. The latter I would scarcely have recognised, had not some one near me called him by name. He was well dressed, stood erect, and, though there were many deep lines on his thoughtful countenance, all traces of his former habits were gone. While I was observing him, he arose, and addressing a few words to the assemblage, nominated Mr. Hargrove as chairman of the meeting. To this a unanimous assent was given.

On taking the chair, Mr. Hargrove made a brief address, something to this effect.

"Ten years ago," said he, his voice evincing a slight unsteadiness as he began, but growing firmer as he proceeded, "there was not a happier spot in Bolton county than Cedarville. Now, the marks of ruin are every where. Ten years ago, there was a kind-hearted, industrious miller in Cedarville, liked by every one, and as harmless as a little child. Now, his bloated, disfigured body lies in that room. His death was violent, and by the hand of his own son!"

Mr. Hargrove's words fell slowly, distinctly, and marked by the most forcible emphasis. There was scarcely one present who did not feel a low shudder run along his nerves, as the last words were spoken in a husky whisper.

"Ten years ago," he proceeded, "the miller had a happy wife, and two innocent, glad-hearted children. Now, his wife, bereft of reason, is in a mad-house, and his son the occupant of a felon's cell, charged with the awful crime of parricide!"

Briefly he paused, while his audience stood gazing upon him with half suspended respiration.

"Ten years ago," he went on, "Judge Hammond was accounted the richest man in Cedarville. Yesterday he was carried, a friendless pauper, to the Almshouse; and to-day he is the unmourned occupant of a pauper's grave! Ten years ago, his wife was the proud, hopeful, loving mother of a most promising son. I need not describe what Willy Hammond was. All here knew him well. Ah! what shattered the fine intellect of that noble-minded woman? Why did her heart break? Where is she? Where is Willy Hammond?"

A low, half repressed groan answered the speaker,

"Ten years ago, you, sir," pointing to a sad-looking old man, and calling him by name, "had two sons—generous, promising, manly-hearted boys. What are they now? You need not answer the question. Too well is their history and your sorrow known. Ten years ago, I had a son,—amiable, kind, loving, but weak. Heaven knows how I sought to guard and protect him! But he fell also. The arrows of destruction darkened the very air of our once secure and happy village. And who was safe? Not mine, nor yours!

"Shall I go on? Shall I call up and pass in review before you, one after another, all the wretched victims who have fallen in Cedarville during the last ten years? Time does not permit. It would take hours for the enumeration! No: I will not throw additional darkness into the picture. Heaven knows it is black enough already! But what is the root of this great evil? Where lies the fearful secret? Who understands the disease? A direful pestilence is in the air—it walketh in darkness, and wasteth at noonday. It is slaying the first-born in our houses, and the cry of anguish is swelling on every gale. Is there no remedy?"

"Yes! yes! There is a remedy!" was the spontaneous answer from many voices.

"Be it our task, then, to find and apply it this night," answered the chairman, as he took his seat.

"And there is but one remedy," said Morgan, as Mr. Hargrove sat down. "The accursed traffic must cease among us. You must cut off the fountain, if you would dry up the stream. If you would save the young, the weak, and the innocent—on you God has laid the solemn duty of their protection—you must cover them from the tempter. Evil is strong, wily, fierce, and active in the pursuit of its ends. The young, the weak, and the innocent can no more resist its assaults, than the lamb can resist the wolf. They are helpless, if you abandon them to the powers of evil. Men and brethren! as one who has himself been wellnigh lost—as one who, daily, feels and trembles at the dangers that beset his path—I do conjure you to stay the fiery stream that is bearing every thing good and beautiful among you to destruction. Fathers! for the sake of your young children, be up now and doing. Think of Willy Hammond, Frank Slade, and a dozen more whose names I could repeat, and hesitate no longer! Let us resolve, this night, that from henceforth, the traffic shall cease in Cedarville. Is there not a large majority of citizens in favour of such a measure? And whose rights or interests can be affected by such a restriction? Who, in fact, has any right to sow disease and death in our community? The liberty, under sufferance, to do so, wrongs the individual who uses it, as well as those who become his victims.

Do you want proof of this. Look at Simon Slade, the happy, kind-hearted miller; and at Simon Slade, the tavern-keeper. Was he benefited by the liberty to work harm to his neighbour? No! no! In heaven's name, then, let the traffic cease! To this end, I offer these resolutions :—

" Be it resolved by the inhabitants of Cedarville, That from this day henceforth, no more intoxicating drink shall be sold within the limits of the corporation.

"Resolved, further, That all the liquors in the Sickle and Sheaf be forthwith destroyed, and that a fund be raised to pay the creditors of Simon Slade therefor, should they demand compensation.

" Resolved, That in closing up all other places where liquor is sold, regard shall be had to the right of property which the law secures to every man.

" Resolved, That with the consent of the legal authorities, all the liquor for sale in Cedarville be destroyed; provided the owners thereof be paid its full value out of a fund specially raised for that purpose."

But for the calm, yet resolute opposition of one or two men, these resolutions would have passed by acclamation. A little sober argument showed the excited company that no good end is ever secured by the adoption of wrong means.

There were, in Cedarville, regularly constituted authorities, which alone had the power to determine public measures; or to say what business might or might not be pursued by individuals.   And through these authorities they must act in an orderly way.

There was some little chafing at this view of the case. But good sense and reason prevailed.   Somewhat modified, the resolutions passed, and the more ultra-inclined contented themselves with carrying out the second resolution, to destroy forthwith all the liquor to be found on the premises; which was immediately done.   After which the people dispersed to their homes, each with a lighter heart, and better hopes for the future of their village.

On the next day, as I entered the stage that was to bear me from Cedarville, I saw a man strike his sharp axe into the worn, faded, and leaning post that had, for so many years, borne aloft the Sickle and Sheaf; and just as the driver gave word to his horses, the false emblem which had invited so many to enter the way of destruction, fell crashing to the earth.

THE END.

STEREOTYPED BY L. JOHNSON & CO.
PHILADELPHIA.

THE JOHN HARVARD LIBRARY

*The intent of
Waldron Phoenix Belknap, Jr.,
as expressed in an early will, was for
Harvard College to use the income from a
permanent trust fund he set up, for "editing and
publishing rare, inaccessible, or hitherto unpublished
source material of interest in connection with the
history, literature, art (including minor and useful
art), commerce, customs, and manners or way of
life of the Colonial and Federal Periods of the United
States . . . In all cases the emphasis shall be on the
presentation of the basic material." A later testament
broadened this statement, but Mr. Belknap's interests remained constant until his death.*

*In linking the name of the first benefactor of
Harvard College with the purpose of this later,
generous-minded believer in American culture the
John Harvard Library seeks to emphasize the importance of Mr. Belknap's purpose. The John Harvard
Library of the Belknap Press of Harvard University
Press exists to make books and documents
about the American past more readily
available to scholars and the
general reader.*